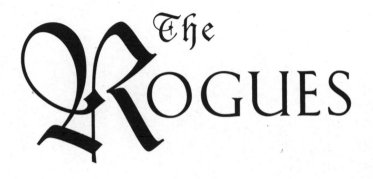

The Rogues

JANE YOLEN
& ROBERT J. HARRIS

PHILOMEL BOOKS

PATRICIA LEE GAUCH, EDITOR

PHILOMEL BOOKS

A division of Penguin Young Readers Group
Published by The Penguin Group
Penguin Group (USA) Inc., 375 Hudson Street, New York, NY 10014, U.S.A.
Penguin Group (Canada), 90 Eglinton Avenue East, Suite 700, Toronto, Ontario,
Canada M4P 2Y3 (a division of Pearson Penguin Canada Inc.).
Penguin Books Ltd., 80 Strand, London WC2R 0RL, England.
Penguin Ireland, 25 St. Stephen's Green, Dublin 2, Ireland (a division of
Penguin Books Ltd).
Penguin Group (Australia), 250 Camberwell Road, Camberwell, Victoria 3124, Australia
(a division of Pearson Australia Group Pty Ltd).
Penguin Books India Pvt Ltd., 11 Community Centre, Panchsheel Park,
New Delhi–110 017, India.
Penguin Group (NZ), 67 Apollo Drive, Mairangi Bay, Auckland 1311,
New Zealand(a division of Pearson New Zealand Ltd.).
Penguin Books (South Africa) (Pty) Ltd., 24 Sturdee Avenue, Rosebank,
Johannesburg 2196, South Africa.
Penguin Books Ltd, Registered Offices: 80 Strand, London WC2R 0RL, England.

Published simultaneously in Canada.   Printed in the United States of America.
The text is set in 12-point Horley Old Style.   Design by Semadar Megged.
Library of Congress Cataloging-in-Publication Data
Yolen, Jane.
The rogues / Jane Yolen & Robert J. Harris.   p. cm.
Summary: After his family is evicted from their Scottish farm, fifteen-year-old Roddy forms
an unlikely friendship with a notorious rogue who helps him outwit a tyrant landlord in order
to find a family treasure and make his way to America.
1. Scotland—History—18th century—Juvenile fiction. [1. Scotland—History—18th
century—Fiction. 2. Adventure and adventurers—Fiction.] I. Harris, Robert J., 1955– II.
Title.   PZ7.Y78Rs 2007   [Fic]—dc22   2006026434
ISBN 978-0-399-23898-7
1 3 5 7 9 10 8 6 4 2
First Impression

For Adam and Betsy,

who love Scotland,

even the difficult parts

—JY

For Carmel and Steve

and Ruth and Robert,

friends in Scotland

—RJH

❧ CONTENTS

I. LAIRD'S PLUNDER

Ye see yon birkie, ca'd a lord,

Wha struts, an' stares an' a' that;

Tho' hundreds worship at his word,

He's but a coof for a' that. . . .

—Robert Burns, "A Man's a Man for a' That"

1 ❧ GHOSTS

I have seen ghosts in a burned-out cottage and the devil on horseback. This is no lie. The first I saw on the day my brother, Lachlan, and I picked our way through the shell of Glendoun. And the devil—well, he followed soon after.

It was a spring day not long ago. We had heard that something awful had happened to some of the villages in the valleys several mountains over from ours. It was said their laird had burned the people off his land and shipped them to the Americas. Such a brutal end to centuries of kinship, the lairds being of the same blood as their tenants, only lots and lots richer. But as Lachlan said, "Can we believe everything we hear?"

I shook my head. "Cousin Ishbel would say, 'Believe only a quarter of what ye hear and half of what ye see.'" And while we didn't always listen to her, she'd never done us any wrong. She'd come to nurse Ma before she died, and then she'd stayed on to cook for us and keep the cottage. "A woman's hand," she called it. "Taming the wild beasts," Da added, meaning us.

Lachlan laughed. "So . . ." He was a year older than me—a year and a day—and he was always the one who got us into trouble, yet I could never help following him.

"So . . . ," I repeated slowly, pushing my hair out of my eyes.

He grinned. "So we go and check and see if all they say about that laird burning folks out is true."

"Don't smile about it," I said. I knew that look. His grin was always the beginning of an adventure. An adventure that usually led us into trouble. "If a laird has burned folks out of their homes, there's nowt to smile at."

Still, Lachlan's grin was irresistible. So, without Da's permission, we rode Rob Roy out of the byre—Lachlan in front and me behind—and headed over the mountain into the next valley. That was where the village of Glendoun stood, fifteen cottages and most of them filled with our distant cousins.

"We'll ask if they've got news, and from there it's an easy ride over the next mountain to see if the rumors are true." Lachlan was still grinning.

It was going to be an adventure indeed.

Cuckoos sang back and forth to one another as we rode along, and white clouds scudded across the sky. It wasn't a day you'd look to bring trouble. Just a late Scottish spring, a bit raw with wind. The prickly yellow gorse was just budding out in great rough bushes on the hillsides. We startled a dozen rabbits from their burrows, and Lachlan cursed that we had brought no snares along.

"Cousin Ishbel would surely love to make a fresh rabbit pie," Lachlan said, meaning he would have loved eating it.

We didn't know what we might hear in Glendoun, nor did we especially care. It was an adventure, an escape from our daily chores, a way to satisfy our curiosity. And if Lachlan could see the lovely Fiona, who was known as "The Beauty of Glendoun," his mood would be lightened, whether she laughed at him or not.

And after, we'd be over the mountain to the next glen.

I found myself grinning like Lachlan.

· · ·

But when we crested the hill that overlooked Glendoun, Lachlan gasped. He said over his shoulder, "My God, Roddy . . ."

I couldn't see past his shoulder, so I jumped off the horse to look myself. And then I gasped as well. Glendoun was a shambles, no longer the pretty huddle of homes we knew so well. The roofs of all the cottages were gone, the thatch burned through, which left the stone walls open to the sky, to wind and rain and buzzards and owls. And half the walls had been pushed down as well. A kind of haze lay over the place, like the remains of smoke.

I turned and looked up at Lachlan. "Oh, Lord," I croaked. "What's happened here?"

But I knew, even without his answer. A natural fire would not have taken all the houses like that. They are stone after all. And even without a roof, a house can be lived in, as long as it isn't winter. Anyone can re-thatch a roof. But it wasn't just the roofs that were gone. The doors of the houses had been pulled off as well, the window frames knocked in. No—it was clear that our laird had made the houses uninhabitable so that the Glendoun folk had to move on.

I felt tears start in my eyes. These weren't strangers who lived far away and over several mountains, but cousins whose names I knew—Big Johnny and Dunc and the beautiful Fiona and the rest. They were but an easy ride from us, their farms in our own laird's holdings. I bit my lip and took several steps closer.

Lachlan rode up to me, pulled me back up behind him, and we rode on down the hillside, growing more and more quiet as we rode along, for we knew that no one would be coming out to greet us.

Lachlan slid off Rob Roy's back and peered through the smashed-in door of the first broken-down croft.

"Look, Roddy," he called, signaling me to him.

I crossed my left leg over and slid down Rob Roy's broad side, letting the reins loose so he could graze where he would.

Sticking my head through the open doorway, I saw an over-turned bowl of porridge and a spilt cup of ale lying close to a wall. There was a baby's cot thrown down on its side, and the mattress of the box bed had been pulled onto the hearth and partially burned. The place was so dead, even the smell of smoke had faded like a dream.

"They must have been . . . ," I began.

Lachlan finished for me, " . . . taken by surprise and chased off like startled birds." His voice was bitter, and I knew he was worrying about Fiona.

Only two weeks earlier, Glendoun had been full of people like Dunc and Big Johnny—working, laughing, drinking whisky, singing songs. We'd come over for a wedding and had danced until dawn, going home without any thought of fear.

But now . . .

"What do ye think happened to them?" I asked. "They didna come to our town for help. We would have taken them in."

Lachlan's shoulders sagged. "I dinna ken. It's as if they've all turned to air and disappeared."

The narrow fields of barley and potatoes on the outskirts of the cottages had been trampled down. I could still see the mark of boots on the new plants. The little peat-water burn trickled halfheartedly down the glen. Not only were there no people here, but there were no cows or chickens or dogs either.

Now we knew for sure that the stories were true. Only now our laird—like others in the Highlands—was clearing out *his* land, sweeping it clean of every living thing to make room for his new

English *friends*. Anyone who stood in his way was to be brushed aside like chaff.

I went back into the first cottage and squinted. For a moment it was as if I could see the family of crofters there: the mother rocking the cradle with her foot as she stirred the stew. The father sitting at the table sipping his whisky. A boy carving a stick. A girl at her small weaving. Then I blinked again and they were gone, like ghosts, in the fading light.

"It makes my skin crawl, Roddy," said Lachlan, coming up behind me. "Ye'd think nobody had ever lived here at all."

I nodded. "Do ye think the laird and his factor will be bringing *them* in soon?"

"By the hundreds," said Lachlan, nodding. "That's what I heard. Thousands even. I don't think I really believed it till now. We'll be the next driven off, ye know. Driven from our hearths and left to starve out in the wilds. Along with the folk of Glendoun."

"Ye're just trying to fleg me, Lachlan." He was always doing that, saying things to give me a scare. For years he'd convinced me that there was a goblin hidden among the rocks by the mill and that if I got too close he would jump out and bite me. Even though I was now old enough to know better, I still gave the mill a wide berth.

"Maybe the laird will stop with Glendoun." I was trying to sound confident. "Maybe that's enough for him."

"Our laird? He's too greedy," Lachlan told me. "Look at what he's done here." He raised his chin to the destruction. "Da says that money's like whisky to our laird. Once he's tasted it, he canna stop at one cup." Lachlan sounded just like Da then, that rough, certain voice.

"We canna just let it happen to us," I said. "Somebody has to tell him no."

"Who?" Lachlan challenged me. "Would ye say nae to his face?" His green eyes got hard as agates. Just like Da's.

I shrugged.

"He's the laird, Roddy," said Lachlan, his voice almost a growl. "The land is his, and we're only his tenants. He can do whatever he pleases with us. Toss us out. Burn us out. Bring in new tenants onto the land. And he'll no turn a hair at the doing of it."

"Not now," I told him. "Da says the English government's put a stop to that. The laird canna just act as judge over the clan, no anymore. He has to pass our troubles over to the courts."

Lachlan began to laugh, his cheeks growing as red as his hair. "What the law says and what really happens here in the Highlands is more a matter of money than justice." That was Da speaking too. What did Lachlan know of money or the law? He was only sixteen, after all, a poor farmer's son. He'd never been farther than the glens.

"Well, *somebody* has to stop him," I said. Then I added almost slyly, "There's always Bonnie Josie."

Lachlan turned a bit dreamy at her name. If it wasn't Fiona he was mooning about, it was Bonnie Josie. "Aye, there's always Josie. If anybody can trip him up, she surely can."

I was about to laugh at the thought when an awful screech made me jump. We whirled around, fists up—and then stared wide-eyed into each other's faces. So—there *were* ghosts haunting this place.

The cry came again, this time more of a squawk.

Lachlan looked about, then his face split in a smile of relief. "Och, it's only a hen!"

Now I saw the bird too, hopping out from behind a bush and pecking the ground. "It must have been left behind."

"Poor wee orphan," said Lachlan. "We should take it home with us. Cousin Ishbel would like that."

I nodded and made a move toward the bird, but it scurried away in a flutter of brown feathers.

"It might take a bit of catching," I said. But when I looked at Lachlan, expecting a joke, I saw he'd lost interest in the hen. Something else had caught his attention. When I listened, I heard it too, echoing off the far side of the hills. Even at a distance, the sound cut harshly through the morning air.

Barking.

"Dogs," said Lachlan, all but spitting out the word.

It was a long series of harsh barks, with a purpose. We both knew there was only one kind of dog that made a noise like that: working dogs.

"So—*they're* here," Lachlan said. "The laird's new tenants. The invaders. To take over the Glendoun hills."

"Aye," I replied, suddenly sure we should be going. The burned-out houses had taken on a deadly air, a warning about our own fate. A tremor ran down my spine, but I wouldn't let my brother see my fear. "Lachlan," I said, as calmly as I could, "should we no be going quickly?"

"Hush!" he answered fiercely, raising a hand. "I want to see this."

So I stood by his side to be a second witness, my fists clenched to keep my hands from shaking.

Soon enough we heard—alongside the barking of dogs—another sound. This second noise started like the drone of pipes swelling up to a march, but as it came closer it broke up into a ragged chorus of bleating voices.

"It's *them!*" I gasped. And that moment, I felt the impulse to take to my heels, like a man spying a rockfall that's about to bury him. I looked to Lachlan. A muscle twitched in his jaw.

So, I turned and stared up at the hilltop, willing it to be still. But then *they* burst over it, like a white tide cascading down toward us, a hundred of them. No, twice that number and more, their black faces like lumps of coal scattered over a field of snow. Four dogs nipped at their heels.

The invaders. The ones the laird had imported to supplant us, his own kin. Hundreds and hundreds of English sheep.

2 &~ THE INVADERS

A pair of shepherds came puffing up to the crest of the hill and paused to peer down into the deep glen. They whistled to the dogs and waved their wooden staffs.

The sheep began spreading out over the valley floor. Some stopped to crop the plants, others to sip at the burn. A few wandered down onto the Glendoun pathways, finding their way into the once carefully tended gardens. One ewe and her lamb even got into a cottage and lay down by the broken door.

I had never seen anything like them before. They were big and plump. With their fluffy wool, some of them looked as large as Highland ponies, not at all like our small, scruffy animals.

"Are ye sure these are sheep?" I asked Lachlan. "They look like a different beast altogether."

"Cheviots, they're called," Lachlan answered, "after the English hills where they're bred."

I wondered how he knew that and asked.

"That's what Da says."

As much as I hated the English sheep taking over our good Scottish land, I couldn't help but be impressed. Their wool was so thick, one of them could have clothed a whole family for a winter. And there was enough mutton on a single ewe to make a feast for a village the size of Glendoun. Fingering my coarse, brown shirt, woven from the untreated wool of our own scrawny breed, I thought

that compared to these plump, snowy animals, ours were little better than rats. But they were *our* rats, not foreign invaders brought
here to swell a greedy laird's purse.

A sudden anger flared up inside me at the thought of how poor
Scottish farming folk were being driven from their land so the laird
could let it out to English sheep farmers at double the rent. I began
to shake with my anger, like a small birch in a high wind. "This is
no place for these fat foreign beasts."

"What are ye talking about?" Lachlan looked at me, his eye-
brows arched up. "Are ye havering, lad?"

I ignored his question and charged at the nearest ewe, whooping
and waving my arms over my head. The animal turned and bolted
off, followed by three others, all bleating in panic. For all their size
they were no braver than the sheep I was used to. Laughing, I turned
and called over to Lachlan, "No havering, big brother. Just spoil-
ing for a fight. Let's chase them back where they came from. Show
them what true Scotsmen can do when they've a mind to it."

He nodded, whooped, and flung up his hands, for once being
led by me. "Ye're right, Roddy," he shouted. "We'll show them the
English have nae welcome here." He soon had a group of sheep racing off in terror, threading their way around the golden gorse.

We charged back and forth across the wee town of Glendoun,
sending the invaders in all directions. All the while I was the loudest of the two of us, for this time the idea had been mine and I was
making the most of it.

Caught up in the rush of it all, I soon forgot why we were doing
it. No longer were we brave Scotsmen fighting off intruders. It
had become a hilarious game of chasing the sheep one way and the
dogs desperately herding them the other. I fell twice, missing the
prickly gorse by little more than a hair the first time and into a deep

puddle the next. But I laughed and got up again to chase the sheep some more. Sometimes laughter is the best way to fight the thing you fear.

The shepherds shouted angrily from the hilltop and shook their fists, but we just made faces back at them. And now the dogs were bounding about, almost as aimless as hares, barking furiously, trying to keep the flock together.

"If they don't . . . like it, they can . . . go back to where they . . . came from," I said, speaking in bursts. I was out of breath from all the running and laughing.

Lachlan nodded in agreement, then stopped short. I looked up to see what had silenced him. A horseman had appeared at the top of the hill and was riding down toward us. There was no mistaking him.

"Willie Rood," said Lachlan, screwing up his face as if the name put a bad taste on his tongue.

William Rood was the new laird's factor, the man who managed the laird's property, collected the rents, and did his dirty work as well. I'd heard he had been a constable down in Glasgow but had lost his job because of his brutality. No one liked him. No one except the laird. But the laird had brought him to the estate to force his will upon the crofting folk. Up until now, that had only meant the brutal collecting of taxes and a beating for anyone late with his rent. Da had missed a beating by a single day and had not stopped talking about it for a full month.

"He's the very devil," said Lachlan, quoting our da.

"Why is he here?" I said, though in my heart I knew.

Lachlan turned and pointed at the broken town behind us. "To check his handiwork, I warrant." Which was my guess as well.

When Rood reached us, he reined in and squinted down his

nose as if taking aim along the barrel of a musket. He was a burly, pig-faced man with squinty eyes and bristly orange hair that stuck out like patches of thistle from under his hat.

"What are ye young ruffians doing?" he demanded. "This land has been leased out. There's no place for yer kind here."

Lachlan put his hands on his hips. "And what kind would that be?"

I wondered at his courage.

"Layabouts, idlers, and thieves," Rood replied harshly. "Get back to yer own farms while ye still can and leave these men to their honest business." He tilted his head toward the shepherds, who were now strolling down the hillside, whistling to their dogs.

"They can do their honest business back in England," Lachlan said.

Ma would have put her hand to her heart hearing him speak so, but she'd never scold. However, Cousin Ishbel would make a tch-ing sound, her tongue against the roof of her mouth. "Nonsense," she'd call it. "Haverings." Da would have had his belt off in a min-ute to get Lachlan to shut up. But it was as if Rood had loosed a devil inside him. "And they can take their fat sheep with them," he added.

Then he leapt at a nearby pair of ewes. They jumped back so suddenly, they made Rood's horse rear up in surprise. He clenched the reins and struggled to stay in the saddle until he calmed his mount.

I did the wrong thing then. I laughed.

Everybody in our glen knew that any hint of mockery was like a wasp's sting to Willie Rood. It goaded him into a rage as ferocious as it was sudden. They say he had whipped old Angus Mac for making a joke at his expense within his hearing, old Angus being twice his age and crippled as well. And he'd backhanded Annie Dayton, who was only a daft serving girl in the laird's house, when she called him a "thick-lipped thief" for stealing a kiss from her. Many's the man in our glen who had a tale to tell about Willie Rood, and every one of them a sour story.

So knowing that, why did I laugh? Fear? Embarrassment? Terror? I don't know. It just ran out of me, like milk from a newly calved cow.

Rood turned the red of a sunset, snatched a cudgel out from under his coat, and before I could make a move to dodge it, lashed out at me. I took the blow square on the side of my head and toppled. Pain filled my skull.

"Roddy!" It was Lachlan's voice, though I barely recognized it through the pain.

I felt a hand under my arm as Lachlan helped me get up. My legs were shaky, and when I opened my eyes, the sunlight stabbed like needles. Lachlan held me protectively, one arm around my shoulders, and shook his fist at Rood.

"There was nae call for that," he protested. "It was only a wee bit of fun. He's only a lad."

All I could see was a blurred version of Rood brandishing the cudgel. "There's plenty left for ye too, lad or no lad, if ye want to test yer luck."

The cudgel hovered in the air above us, so huge to my dazed sight, it seemed to fill the whole sky.

"Hold off there, Willie Rood!" It was a woman's voice but as firm as any man's.

I turned at the sound of it. The movement made me dizzy,

and I would have fallen over if Lachlan hadn't kept a grip on me. Squinting through the painful light, I saw a young woman slowing her horse to a trot and drawing up alongside Rood. I recognized her, though I'd never seen her this close up before. Never talked to her. For when does a crofter's son speak with the gentry? It was Josephine McRoy—Bonnie Josie—the dead laird's daughter, the new laird's niece. The one that Lachlan sometimes dreamed about when he wasn't dreaming on the Beauty of Glendoun.

We called her Bonnie Josie not just because of her pretty face and shining copper hair. We called her that because she had been championing the poor clansmen of Kindarry since she was old enough to pull at her father's sleeve. But her father—who had been a good laird, if sometimes a dab high-handed—was dead this past year. Her uncle ruled these lands now, and he had no soft heart to appeal to. And Willie Rood was his right-hand man.

Josie glared at the factor.

Rood lowered his cudgel and tucked it away under the flap of his coat. "They were trying to steal the sheep," he said, his voice oozing and unctuous, like oil rubbed into leather to soften it.

"That hardly seems likely," said Josie, "not with the shepherds and their dogs so close at hand." Her hands tightened on her horse's reins till the knuckles turned white. That much I could see.

"Well, they *would* steal, given half a chance," Rood insisted stubbornly. "It's in their nature."

"It's in their nature to be boys, no more than that," Josie chided him. "Just as it is in yours to bully those who cannot fight back."

Rood's eyes narrowed and his jaw clenched. With an effort, he summoned up a ghastly imitation of a polite smile. "Ye misjudge me, Miss Josephine," he said. "I'm as kindly as the next man in my own way."

"The next man must be a right heathen then," said Josie tartly. "Go back to your business, Rood, and I'll see that these boys leave your precious sheep in peace." She gestured at the fat Cheviot sheep, which seemed to be making a point of keeping their distance, the dogs and shepherds helping.

Rood wheeled his horse about and looked back over his shoulder. "They're troublemakers, Miss Josephine," he warned. "Ye'd best remember that."

Josie leaned toward him and said, "I can handle trouble from anyone. *You* would best remember that, Willie Rood."

Grunting in response, Rood rode off in the direction of Kindarry House, where the new laird lived. No doubt to report on what he had seen.

"What is your name, young man?" Josie asked Lachlan. Though we recognized her, there was no reason she should know us from a hundred other dirty-faced crofting lads.

"Lachlan Macallan, ma'am, from Dunraw village, on the other side of the mountain." He pointed west, as if Bonnie Josie didn't know her own family's lands—three deep glens and a lot of fine bottom farming. "And this is my brother, Roddy."

"What's left of him anyway," said Josie, leaning down out of the saddle to peer at the bloody mark Rood had left upon me.

The pain was dulling to a throb now, but I still felt sick to my stomach. When I put a finger to the wound, it came away with blood on it.

"Help him climb up here in front of me," Josie instructed Lachlan, reaching down a hand.

"Ma'am?"

"Do I not speak plainly enough? Help your brother up into the saddle. I'm going to take him home with me to see to that wound."

She grabbed the back of my shirt, and with Lachlan taking me by the legs, they wrestled me up so that I was sitting in front of Josie. She curled her arms around me and took hold of the reins.

"Now, Lachlan Macallan, go back and tell your family your brother is in good hands. I'll see him safely home before the day is out."

3 ❧ THE LODGE

Josie kept her horse to a controlled canter, but it made me so dizzy, I swayed forward.

"Hang on to her mane," Josie said. "She won't mind."

I took hold of the horse's hair. My grip was feeble, and it was only then that I realized how weak I was from Rood's blow. The rough grass and heather beneath the horse's hooves seemed to swell and ebb like the sea, and my stomach was heaving with every lurch of our mount.

Overhead a hawk screamed out, but I didn't dare look up.

"Thank ye for helping," I muttered, though it was such an effort just getting the words out, I barely recognized my own voice.

"Hush ye," Josie said in the common speech, like a mother to her bairn. "We'll be at the Lodge soon."

The Lodge. Since her uncle took over Kindarry House on becoming laird, Bonnie Josie and her mother had been moved into the smaller place. I wondered how she felt about that, having grown up in the laird's house. I wondered how Fiona and her brothers felt, having no house to live in at all.

"Are you all right?" Bonnie Josie asked.

I nodded—though I was far from all right—which only made my head hurt more. If I could not glance up, I *could* glance down. The earth seemed even farther away than before, and I became dizzy and started to fall. Josie tightened her arms around me to keep me steady.

So I fixed my eyes on the horse's ears, and though they kept blurring before my gaze, it was better than looking at the ground. We bobbled and bounced along, and I must have dozed off, for when I opened my eyes again, the Lodge came bobbing into view. Yes, it was small compared with the Laird's house, but it was still five times the size of our own cottage, with glass windows and a long walk set off with handsome trees. However, it had a homey look, even inviting, with flower boxes at the windows and a brightly painted front door.

A low hill separated the Lodge from Kindarry House, so close because the Lodge was the old Dower House, something I learned later. The Dower House was where the wife of any dead laird was housed when a new laird came in to rule.

Kindarry was just visible in the distance. Its grey walls and pointed turrets stood in contrast to the Lodge's hominess. But that was because Kindarry House had once been a defense against rival clans and English soldiers. In times of war, the clansmen and their families would have crowded into it, safe from all harm. Now those same walls and turrets were a symbol of the laird's power over his own people. We were kept out of Kindarry because Daniel McRoy squatted there as laird.

Daniel McRoy! I wanted to spit at his name. But the blow seemed to have robbed me of spit as well as my senses. I sighed and looked around.

Some dozen families had set up shelter among the trees and the wooden outbuildings near the Lodge. The folk were all crofters, just like my own family. I wondered if Fiona and her brothers were there but couldn't see well enough to know. Some of the people waved to Josie as we approached the house, but they were just a blur.

"Who are they?" I asked, my voice still hardly above a whisper.

"Some of the Glendoun folk," Josie replied. "The ones who were too sick or too frightened to run any farther after Willie Rood and his men chased them out of their homes. A few of them wanted to go back and see if there was anything they could salvage from the burning. That's why I rode over there today, to check if it was safe."

"Too late," I said hoarsely. "Glendoun's no a place for people anymore."

We halted by a small stable, and a grey-haired attendant hurried forward to hold the reins while Josie slid down from the saddle. She lifted a hand to me, but I didn't take it. It didn't feel right to let a lady do such a thing. Instead, I got off by myself, trying not to cry out when I touched down and the movement jarred my poor head. Once on the ground I found myself swaying.

"Just take it a step at time," Josie cautioned me. "Slowly." She took me by the elbow, and this time I let her help, though I hated being so weak in front of her. Instead, I turned the conversation back to the folk of Glendoun.

"What's going to happen to them?" I whispered.

There was a strain of sadness in Bonnie Josie's voice. "We can give them a place to rest a few weeks, but that's all. We've not the food nor the money ourselves for more."

My mouth must have gaped at that. Imagine—a laird's daughter with not enough food or money. I think at that moment, my anger at Daniel McRoy turned to hate.

"A man needs his own land, or else how is he to live?" I said, thinking of Da, who had worked our small holding, first as a boy with his own father, then as a man.

"By law the land belongs to the laird," said Josie, telling me what I already knew. Her voice was low and earnest. She was still holding me as we walked. "The poor folk that live on it can scarcely grow enough in crops and livestock to feed themselves, let alone afford a high rent. That's why my father never raised the rents. What good would it have done except to beggar every farmer in bad years or steal their earnings in good? Instead, he took the rents out in service to the clan. But Daniel McRoy is not the man my father was, though they were half brothers. The new laird's new friends have promised him rich rewards in exchange for land to graze their sheep on."

"Then what's to become of the Glendoun folk?" I asked, forgetting to concentrate on my walking and almost tripping. "And the others?" Meaning my family and our neighbors. Meaning all of the poor farmers in the glens.

"Some have family in happier places where the sheep haven't come yet. Where the old lairds, like my father, believe in blood before gold. There might be a place for them . . . for a while. Others may trek to the west. There's land to be had on the coast."

I stopped for a moment to catch my breath. I, who could run around several acres of land without heaviness in my chest, was suddenly as feeble as a grandfather. Turning to her to disguise my weakness, I asked, "Is it good land?"

She shook her head. "Not like our land here, Roddy. It's barren and pitted with salt. A man could spend a year trying to get something to grow there and still see nothing for his trouble." Her voice sounded weary, and she brushed a lock of red hair from her eyes. Clearly she'd given this much thought.

"The clan grandfathers fought to keep this land safe," I said, the very words hurting my tongue. "Fought with guns and swords, whenever the lairds asked for their service. And now our folk are to wander and starve?"

"There's always the mines," said Josie thinly. "Hard as that is, there's money to be had there."

I shook my head and started it aching again. "That's a hard turn for them that's lived under the sun all these years. It's like being thrown in a dungeon for committing no crime at all." I was trembling now, more in rage than weakness.

By this time we'd reached the Lodge, and Josie managed to open the door while still supporting me.

"Well, all that's left then is to take a ship to the New World," she said, pushing me through. "That's for those with the courage to try it. Many from Glendoun took that road. I suspect many more will follow."

"The New World," I repeated. The words had a sweet ring to them, as if she were talking about heaven.

"Aye, young Macallan, but it's far away across the ocean," she said, "a world away from Scotland, full of new dangers."

I could hear a note in her voice that told me she wasn't thinking only of the poor crofters, but of where she herself might be driven by her uncle. And for the first time I gave thought to crossing the waters that divided us from the Americas. I knew I had the courage, but did I have the will?

Just then the inside of the Lodge was enough of a new world for me. There must have been nearly a dozen rooms branching off from the wide hallway. It was hard to say why so many were needed. The cottage I lived in may have been only a but and ben—two rooms—but we got along just fine in it: Da, Cousin Ishbel, Lachlan, and me.

Here, though, besides room after room, opening one into the other, was something I had never seen before—little paintings of trees and flowers in round frames hanging on the walls. I had seen a picture only once in my entire life. Cousin Ishbel had been given a wee portrait of a child, small enough to sit in the palm of her hand, with a thin gold frame about it. It had been a gift for bringing a lady's baby into the world. Ishbel kept the picture wrapped in a bit of plaid for safety and had shown it to us only the once. But Bonnie Josie's pictures were much bigger, hanging on the wall for all to see. I wanted to go up close and stare at them, fall into them, but my eyes were too blurry. Besides, Josie was still speaking. I turned to look at her.

"It's no life of ease in the far Americas either," she said. "Or so I hear. The land can be as hard and unforgiving as it is here. But at least there's a chance for freedom there."

"Can a man have land he can't be thrown off?"

"Aye. And there's land there for the taking. Not just for the lairds, but for the farmers too. That's not too big a dream for honest folk, now—is it?"

I had started nodding in agreement when dizziness seized me and my legs gave way. I cursed myself under my breath for showing such weakness, but even my cursing lacked strength. I leaned on the arm of a covered chair, and Josie gradually drew me up again.

"Only a wee bit farther, lad," she said. "I've a place where you can lie down and sleep and no one will disturb you."

We carried on through to the back of the house—room after

room—the air of which was scented with flowers. Josie led me
into a small ben off the kitchen and helped me lie down on a straw
pallet. Here the flower smell was overcome by a richer odor, of
meat cooking and something baking on a griddle. My stomach
growled, but my head did too, as if the idea of food would only
make me dizzier.

"This is supposed to be a pantry," Josie said, "where foodstuffs
are kept, but sometimes we need a place for those folk who can't be
left outside when the nights turn chill."

"It's nice," I whispered, though to tell the truth, my head was
now pounding so hard, I could see little of it. There were shelves
set in the walls dotted with jars and a window high in the wall. The
surprise was that there was glass in it, even in this humble room,
which brought in a great shaft of light. At home we had only slits in
the stone walls and divots of earth to jam in them when we needed
to keep out the wind.

Josie gave my hair a stroke, which set my fingers trembling, the
way Lachlan did whenever he thought of the beautiful Fiona. I had
to make two fists to stop them shaking. I don't think Josie noticed.
She was too busy being my nurse. Then she disappeared for a min-
ute, returning with a basin of water and a linen cloth.

I tried to sit up to look around, but Josie pushed me back down.
Dipping the cloth in the water, she gently dabbed my wounded
scalp. It stung a bit, but I was determined not to show any sign
of the pain. I couldn't have her think I was a softie, flinching at a
wee dab.

The shaft of light from the window poured down over her,
setting up highlights in her hair and casting a sheen of gold over
her cheek. She looked like an angel, which we'd heard about in
the kirk.

"Ye belong in the big house, Miss Josie," I said. "This crampit place is not what ye deserve." Small it hardly was, compared with our croft, but I had seen the laird's mansion many times when the old laird had held the clan games in his far fields. That is, I'd seen Kindarry House from the outside, never from the inside. Kindarry was twenty times the size of the Lodge.

"If this were but a pigsty, I'd still sooner live here than in Kindarry," Josie said, a sudden sharpness in her voice.

For the first time she dabbed my head hard enough to really hurt. I clenched my teeth and didn't make a sound. It was my own fault for bringing up upsetting thoughts. Still, something needed saying, so when the sharpest pain had gone, I said, "Yer uncle Daniel is not an easy man to live with, even if ye dinna share his house."

Josie sighed. "There'll be few enough people around these parts to object to his company before long."

"The old laird would never have let any of this happen," I said, remembering her father, Thomas McRoy. "Folk still gab about the day the English merchants first came to lease his land for their sheep."

"Aye, on condition he threw the people off it first."

"He was too straight a man for that," I whispered, "too straight by far."

I heard her sigh again. "Thanks, young Roddy."

I sat up so we were face-to-face. "I'm nae trying to flatter ye. It's the truth I'm speaking. All the crofters say it."

She smiled at me, still dabbing at my head, though very gently. The streaming light hung about her like a golden haze. "I'd be a liar if I said my father wasn't tempted. There was enough money on offer that he could have spent the rest of his days living like a fine gentleman in a fancy house in Edinburgh. It was the clansmen coming to call that made the difference, that reminded him there are bonds between men stronger than anything money can buy."

Even with the pain, I had to smile back. She made the clansmen calling sound like a wee social visit. But I remembered how word had reached the villages that English merchants were coming to take the land for their sheep. And we'd heard enough tales of what had already been happening in villages in Ross and Sutherland to take alarm at the news. Da had raced from house to house with Lachlan and me hammering on the doors with him. And when we were done with our wee town, we rode out to the far glens with the news. Da had a dram of whisky at every house, and we'd had to carry him home across the horse's back and not a stick of work done for two days after. Didn't we get a lashing of the tongue from Cousin Ishbel then.

"Let's go and see the laird and call for justice," Da had said at door after door.

By the end of the week, a great straggling line of folk—five hundred at least—had come winding their way up the glen with cattle and goats in tow. Some waved torches, others had brought pipes to play, just as if we were off to the games.

"I remember that when we arrived, yer father came to the door, with ye at his side," I said. "Ye got a bigger cheer than he did." That had been the first time I'd seen Bonnie Josie up close, and it was a memory I'd never forgotten.

Josie looked pleased. "Maybe it was the cheering that made the sheep merchants run out the back door and jump onto their horses. They probably thought it was a bloodthirsty mob of Highlanders come to hang them." She put her head back and laughed, and it was a lovely sound, like water in a burn bubbling over the rocks.

"Hanging would have been too good for them," I said, my voice slurring once more. "We gave yer father an even bigger cheer when he promised not to lease out the land."

"Aye, hoisted him onto your shoulders and carried him three times around Kindarry House," said Josie. "I'm not sure he enjoyed that part of it." The memory brought a flush to her cheek, and the tiniest of tears slipped from her eye at the thought of how things stood today. For just weeks after her father had been buried, those same English sheep merchants had been back talking to the new laird, Daniel McRoy. And we could all see how that had turned out.

"Maybe we should have given the new laird a shoulder ride too," I said.

Oh, how she laughed at that. And then, as suddenly as she'd begun, she sobered. "Oh, Roddy, if only it were that simple. But too much has happened. . . ." She looked out past me, past the door. I wondered if she was seeing past the poor folk of Glendoun crowding her garden, all the way to their burned-out houses and trampled fields. The light seemed to have turned off in her face, and I was sad to see it go.

But my head was sore again, as if filled with new-sharpened knives. I had to shut my eyes. Josie's next words faded to a distant buzz, and I slipped off into a troubled sleep.

4 ❧ THE INTRUDER

When I woke up, still in the pantry, Josie had gone and I could tell by the angle of the sun through the window that it was long past noon. I sat up at once, but a shaft of pain in my skull forced me back down with a groan. I touched a finger to my brow and felt a fresh bandage that Josie must have wrapped there.

"Slowly now," I muttered to myself.

I pushed myself up carefully this time, and the pain was not so bad. I looked around the little room. It was bare of furniture except for the pallet I was lying on. However, the shelves on the walls were crowded with jars of flour and pots full of herbs. I thought of our home, with its large black kettle, its one great hanging stew pot and its porridge pot. Yet we made do and hadn't gone hungry yet.

The door was open, and I could see into the kitchen. No one was there, so I hauled myself up and stepped gingerly over to the doorway, careful not to lose my balance.

Taking three paces across the stone floor into the kitchen, I stopped to lean on the big wooden table that was twice the size of our table at home. I sucked in a deep breath to clear my head and caught the scent of food. On the table was a plate laid out with bannocks and cheese along with a pitcher of water. For me? I shook my head. I would not risk taking the food without permission. This was Bonnie Josie's house, after all.

Wondering if I should call out, I stepped toward the kitchen door, the one that led to the hall. Suddenly I heard voices coming from the front of the Lodge. They had the bristle of trouble about them, and that made me worry about Josie. Would she need help? Could I, in my present state, do anything for her? And what if my very presence here was the cause of that trouble? Would I only make it worse? *Perhaps,* I thought, *I should hide,* though I had no idea what room in the Lodge would be safe. When Josie had led me through to the pantry, my head was spinning and my eyes blurred everything. I had no idea which way to go.

That was when I decided that, without knowing more, I could come to no decision. So, I pushed off from the table like a boatman pushing off from shore and set off down the hallway slowly as if swimming a long river. I had to stop to rest once more, this time leaning against the wall. I followed the thread of those voices.

"Getting easier," I told myself. "Just take a few more breaths." I filled my lungs again, and gradually my head did clear.

The voices were clearer too. There were two of them, a man and a woman.

A few more steps took me to another door, which was ajar. I was deep in the shadows, but through the door I could see a small, elegant table with paper on it for writing, as well as two wooden cabinets. On the table sat three tiny painted statues, a shepherd and two dogs. I'd never seen the like before, so fine and delicate they were for so rough a subject. The chairs were of polished wood with pillows to make them soft, the legs of each chair so thin I wondered that anyone could sit without breaking the thing to pieces. Over the windows hung some delicate material decorated with flowers and some gold-colored rope to hold them away from the glass. The room was simple enough for a laird's family, I supposed, but even so there were pieces of furniture I couldn't put a name to and colors of cloth I couldn't begin to describe.

In the midst of this finery a man was talking sternly to a woman seated in a chair. I recognized him at once, for he was our present laird. I had seen him often enough riding up the glen with Willie Rood, surveying his land with satisfaction and his people with disdain, as Da had said more than once. Daniel McRoy. A thin, twisted sort of man he was, who looked like he was made out of sticks and paste instead of flesh and bone, unlike his dead brother, who had been a braw man, fleshed out with his goodness. McRoy wore a long grey coat and had a three-cornered hat tucked under his left arm. With his right, he was drumming on the mantel with his fingers. His lips twitched as he spoke.

"I've warned you before, Elizabeth," he said, giving the woman a hard look, like a minister chiding a sinner. "If you do not clear these vagabonds off the estate, I'll have my men do it for you. Bad enough you have them here at the Lodge, but I hear from my man Rood that Josie has just been out to Glendoun finding more young ruffians to keep her company."

The woman's head was bowed, her fingers twined nervously in her lap. "Oh, how can you speak of them that way, Daniel? These are our clansfolk. We are responsible for their welfare."

Her face was lined and her hair streaked with grey, but there was enough of Josie's kindness in her face for me to be sure she was Lady McRoy, widow of the old laird. When I'd seen her at the clan games, serving wine and whisky to the men, her husband had been alive and she'd been a round-faced happy woman with color in her hair. But—oh—how she had aged. Even I could see that. Everyone knew she'd done poorly since her husband's death. I hardly recognized her now.

Daniel leaned toward her, a long-billed heron poised to snatch a fish out of the water. "In the old days, when a chief needed fighting men at his call, then I'll grant it was worth tending such peasants. But things are different now. The days of war and raiding are over, and a laird must look to the proper cultivation of his lands."

"You make it sound so heartless." The old laird's wife sighed. Her voice was hardly a whisper.

"Improvement is what it's called, Elizabeth," he told her. "I keep telling you this, and one day you will understand and thank me for it. We make the maximum profit from the land, and these peasants are forced to leave behind their shiftless lives and find opportunities to improve themselves elsewhere."

"I've not your way with words, Daniel," she answered wearily. "You must take it up with Josephine when she returns."

The laird let out a laugh that was like a hollow screech. "Talking to your daughter is like talking to the wind. A man might as well save his breath. Do you think I don't know it's her doing that you've a camp outside your door filled with the idle and the useless?"

Josie's mother clenched her hands together and looked up. "When people come to us for help, we cannot turn them away. They are of our blood."

Hurrah, Madam! I thought.

"Not my blood, Elizabeth. It runs too thin in those peasants to be counted anymore."

"Daniel! How can you say such a thing?" The old woman sounded shocked. "Oh, if only my Thomas were here."

"Your Thomas is gone and his flesh off the bones," the laird said, almost with satisfaction. "He was too soft for the times."

She began to weep.

Almost as if realizing he'd gone too far, the laird slowly went down on one knee before her so she could not avoid his gaze, his hat still under his arm. "That is why you should give this up," he said, his voice oily with false concern. "When Thomas left you this part of the estate for your own, I know he did not intend it to be a burden to you and your daughter."

It made my skin crawl to hear him, and perhaps it did hers too, for she shrugged hopelessly, as if she had run out of arguments.

"That is why you should take the money I have offered for the Lodge, for Josephine's sake if not your own. I have explained this all to you before." The honey in his voice was too sweet for eating. "With it you could go live comfortably with your relatives in Lochaber and no longer have a care for what happens in these pitiful glens."

"For Josephine's sake, you say?" The widow seemed to take some strength from the thought of her daughter's future and leaned forward toward him.

He put a hand on hers. "Elizabeth, my dear, when you die—and may the day be far off—the Lodge reverts to me by right. There will be nothing left for Josephine but whatever pennies you two have managed to save. Unless, of course, we can marry her well. Though with her . . . odd views . . . you have to admit, that may take some doing. So take that money now, I beg you." He was almost convincing, except for that smug look on his face and the oiliness of his voice.

Suddenly I could stand to hear no more. I wanted to burst into the room, place myself at the widow's side like a loyal clansman, and defy Daniel McRoy to his face. I wanted to tell him there were good men aplenty who would take Bonnie Josie to wife, house or no house, views or no views. But in my weakened condition I would hardly make much of a fight on her behalf. Besides, my presence had obviously already caused trouble for Josie and her mother, and I was smart enough to realize bursting in would not help.

I was thinking that I should simply leave by the back door, as silently as I had come, when I heard footsteps emerging from the kitchen. I turned in time to see a skulking figure slip down the hall away from where I stood and go into one of the back rooms.

A warning prickle stabbed at the nape of my neck. Keeping one hand close to the wall to steady myself, I tiptoed back up the hall. The intruder had closed the door behind him, but I could hear him moving inside. Some instinct told me that this was part of the laird's plot against Josie and her mother and that I could not ignore it.

I took a grip on the handle and gently eased the door open. Beyond was a bedchamber. To my right was a bed, larger and softer than anything I could ever have dreamed of. Set into the wall opposite was a stout wooden cabinet and above it a hanging silver platter of some kind.

Willie Rood was standing by the cabinet with a metal bar in his hand. He was pressing one end of the bar into the crack between the cabinet door and the wall, trying to force the lock. It was clear to me he was on an errand from the laird while his master kept the widow occupied at the front of the house. Sheer rage made me forget my injury and my fatigue.

"What are ye about, Willie Rood?" I exclaimed.

Rood spun about, a guilty look on his round, piggy face. When he spotted me, his eyes narrowed and his lip curled. "Am I never to be rid of you, you whelp?" He raised the metal bar, making ready to strike me.

I had been in a few fights in my time, too many to just stand there and let myself be hit. Not again. I flew at him, ramming my shoulder into his belly. He bashed into the wall and slumped down into a sitting position.

"Damn ye!" he cried, flailing out at me with the bar.

I dodged, and whether it was the desire for revenge on him or the urge to protect Bonnie Josie's home that drove me on, I forgot my reeling head, my weak legs, and fought back with a fury. I lunged again, locking my arms around his neck and shoving him right down onto the floor.

He tried to push me off and we rolled over, bumping up against the bed. He made to raise the bar, but I struck first, punching him right in the eye, and he dropped the iron rod in his agony. Then, throwing himself back, he kicked hard at my ribs. But I dodged him and jumped onto the bed, my fists raised.

"I'm ready this time," I told him. "Ye'll not catch me by surprise again."

Staggering, Rood clambered to his feet, clutching his bruised eye. "I'll beat ye to a jelly!" he thundered. But he had dropped his weapon and had to stand there looking around for it before he dared take me on.

"What is the meaning of this?" asked a quavering voice from the doorway.

I turned and saw Lady Elizabeth standing there with her knuckles pressed to pale lips.

Taking advantage of the distraction, Rood made a clumsy grab for me, but I jumped off the other side of the bed, landing close to the widow. My legs started to give way, and I grabbed onto the windowsill.

The lady took a fearful step back. "You're the boy Josie brought home," she said.

"You might as well have loosed a wild beast in your midst," Rood declared hoarsely.

The laird appeared at the widow's shoulder. "Rood?" he inquired. "Have ye come here on business?"

There was a false note to his question. Surely the widow could tell as clearly as I that the factor was here on the laird's orders, carrying out his bidding.

"I did," Rood answered, struggling to compose himself. He straightened his coat, but his flushed face and heavy breath marked him as the guiltiest man I'd ever seen. "As ye asked, sir, to meet ye here. On . . . business."

"He came here to rob ye, ma'am," I cried. "And I caught him at it."

The laird fixed his eye on me, a look that was like the sharp point of a dirk. "And who might *you* be?" he asked. His voice indicated that what I might be was some kind of midge, an insect to be squashed between his fingers or under the flat of his hand whenever he liked.

5 ❧ UNCLE AND NIECE

Before I could answer, urgent footfalls came racing up the hallway.

"Uncle Daniel!" an angry voice exclaimed. "I told you the last time you called on us—you are not welcome here. Father would not have treated his tenants the way you do. I speak for him who can no longer speak at all."

The laird turned to face the door with a cold smile on his face. "You spoke only in the heat of the moment, Josephine, so I do not hold you to it."

"You should," Josie told him as she peered into the bedroom.

"I am only looking after your best interests," the laird said. "Consorting with riffraff hardly befits you."

"And speaking of riffraff, Uncle, who is this?" She came in and pointed to Rood. "You both must have slithered in under the jamb like a pair of snakes."

"Now, Josephine, don't be speaking to your own kin in such a disrespectful fashion," the laird said. It was clear even to me that he was trying to make his voice mild, to show the widow he was a reasonable man, but it sounded as hard as a standing stone. "I'm your father's own brother, after all. And your laird."

"His half brother," Josie reminded him as she stepped into the room. "And only half the man as well."

McRoy turned to Josie's mother and put up his hands as if to say, "Can ye not see how outrageous she is?" It was a gesture I'd seen Ishbel make too often to my father to miss.

But Bonnie Josie ignored his protest. "You lived off my father's good heart and good name for far too long, Uncle, and now you run roughshod over his widow and daughter and expect gratitude? For shame, sir. For shame."

"Miss Josephine," Rood interrupted, "it's a good thing I came along when I did. I found this whelp trying to rob you."

"Liar!" I couldn't get the word out fast enough.

Josie seemed to notice me for the first time. Putting her hands on her hips, she looked at me askance. "I am absent no more than an hour, and all manner of capers break out behind my back. What have you to say for yourself, Roddy Macallan?"

"It was him!" I said, pointing at Rood. "He was trying to force open that cabinet in the wall."

"The position was quite the reverse." Rood's voice was a low growl, and a fresh flush rushed to his cheeks. "He was looking for money, I'll wager. Had an iron bar with him. The boy's a common thief. I've warned you before about these people, Miss Josephine."

"I doubt any common thief would go to such trouble," said Josie. "To come into the dowager's house in broad daylight? And the boy certainly had no iron bar with him when I brought him here a few hours ago. Faith, he could scarcely stand up from the beating you gave him, Willie Rood. And even I would be hard put to find an iron pry bar around the house." She glared at Rood. "But *someone* certainly came here with the pry in hand, and I think I can guess who that might be. Especially since this room and that safe is just where an uncommon thief might hope to find the deeds to this property."

I stood there stunned. Clearly I had happened upon terrible acts without meaning to. What were these *deeds* Bonnie Josie spoke of? And why would Rood—or the laird—need to steal them? None of it made sense to me. I opened my mouth, then closed it again. As Cousin Ishbel liked to say, "An open mouth gathers flies. A closed mouth gathers secrets."

Rood's nostrils flared. "Miss Josephine—you would take the word of this unwashed field mouse over mine?"

The widow's hand fluttered about like a moth seeking a flame, but Josie answered calmly, "This field mouse is a guest in this house." She smiled slightly before adding, "Unlike you, whom I do not recall inviting."

"I'll see him up before a judge," said Rood. "I swear I will. We can let the law decide. And then we'll have the right of it." But I noticed his right hand was trembling as he spoke.

"You'll have a hard time pressing charges against the boy when neither my mother nor I will have any part of it," Josie warned.

Her mother nodded slightly.

Waving a hand in the air, as if to quiet everyone, the laird said, "This is a very vexing puzzle indeed, but so far as I can see, no great harm has been done to either party."

Rood glowered his disagreement, but a hard look from the laird kept him silent. "Mister Rood, I am sure you have pressing business elsewhere on the estate." His tone made it clear that this was an order.

Still furious, Rood stepped out of the room and stomped away toward the back door.

"There," said the laird. "Now, let us retire to the parlor and discuss our business like gentlefolk."

He turned and led them back to the front parlor, where he had been talking just minutes before with the widow. And though I doubted he meant to include me in "gentlefolk," I was not about to leave Bonnie Josie and her mother alone with the man. He was dangerous. And—I feared—he meant them no good. But I went no farther than the parlor door, where I stood slightly in shadow.

Josie saw her mother seated once again on one of the cushioned chairs, then stood beside her, a hand on the widow's shoulder for comfort. Next to the chair was a shining wooden table with the thinnest legs I'd ever seen. A tray with a dainty cup and saucer and a teapot, of some white china, sat atop it.

"Get rid of this boy," the laird said, waving at me as if once again shooing away a fly. He had remained standing and now folded his arms over his chest. Often Da stood the very same way when he was about to hand down punishments for Lachlan and me.

"He'll stay until I am satisfied he took no permanent harm at the hands of your henchman." Josie's face looked set in stone.

"Rood's methods are simple, but his heart is in the right place," said the laird. "It is you who are behaving unwisely, young lady, and guiding your poor mother to do the same."

I bit my lip to keep from shouting out at him.

The laird ignored me and continued, "Surely you must see that all those people who have been legally evicted from the estate cannot be allowed to remain encamped around the Lodge. It gives them false hope. It keeps them from finding work and starting their lives anew." Once again, his voice was gentle, but the intent beneath it was pure steel.

There was a flash of anger in Josie's eyes, and she answered him back steel for steel. "They needn't have had to start anew without your bully boys burning them out. At least with them camped here, it will be known throughout the Highlands that there's one corner of McRoy land where the old clan loyalties are not forgotten."

The widow leaned back in her chair, as if shrinking from a pair of snarling dogs.

Raising his hands, the laird said, "You are upset, Josephine. I can see that. And your thinking is confused, as if you were one of them, a peasant, and not the daughter of a laird. It's what comes of having all these idle rascals on your doorstep, living off your goodwill. I'm done with all that."

"Have done with kindness?" said Josie, with a shake of her head. "Have done with family and honor and loyalty? I cannot live that way, Uncle. I *will* not live that way."

I would have lifted my cap to her then, had I been wearing one.

"It is like hearing your father again." The laird gave her the sort of smile given a bairn when it says something amusing. "He could have been a rich man if not for his sentimentality about the clan."

The widow raised her hand and wiped a tear from the corner of her eye. She spoke low, as if she understood the argument but would not shout it out. "Thomas was rich enough, Daniel, just not in the way you mean. His treasure was the love of his people."

The laird snorted and turned away from her to stare out of the window. It was an amazing window with a view over a great lawn of grass. All that grass and nothing pastured on it but squatters. I was amazed.

"For hundreds of years," McRoy said, "that ignorant rabble has followed the laird just like sheep, so we might as well have sheep in their place and do without the inconvenience of the rabble's dirt and noise. This is a mercantile world we live in, my dear. It's time these Highland folk learned that."

I could stand it no longer. Stepping forward from the doorway, I said, "Ye talk about people like they are animals and animals like they are people!" And then I shut my mouth again, my teeth hard against my bottom lip. I could not believe the sound of my own voice. And speaking out that way to the laird. *The laird!* It was as if the spirit of the clan had seized me and spoken through me.

"Bravo!" declared Josie. "I could not have said it better."

The laird turned back and stared at me, rubbing his fingers on his sleeve as if wiping away a stain. "If you keep mixing with this sort, Josephine, you will become one of them in the end. I had higher hopes for you than that."

"You had *hopes* for me?" Her face began to turn a sunrise color, and she put her hand again on her mother's shoulder, as if steadying herself.

"You are my niece. Of course I wish the best for you. Your dear mother cannot care for you much longer. It is long past time you made yourself a good match."

"What? To one of your sheep farmers?"

The laird tapped his chin with a long forefinger. "You know that Mr. Rood plans to farm a part of the estate himself?"

Josie looked appalled. "You cannot *seriously* think I would consider marrying that man!"

"Seriously indeed," said the laird. "Rood is an up-and-coming man, and while not of your station, my dear, he stands close to me. Marriage to my niece would raise him up. I count on him enormously. I suggest you take this proposal as seriously as I do. Life here could get very uncomfortable if I put my mind to it, and your dear mother is in such precarious health."

I clenched my fists and stood aside. *What would Lachlan do?*

I wondered. And then I knew. I opened my mouth to tell the laird what I thought of him, but Josie darted me a warning glance. It was a clear signal to keep quiet. Or as Cousin Ishbel would say, "Keep yer breath to cool yer porridge."

"I think you'd best go now, Uncle," Bonnie Josie said, "before your tongue carries you any further along that path. This house is still ours by law. We do not have to listen to such . . . such threats while we still have possession of it."

The laird made a small bow in the widow's direction and headed for the door. Pausing for a moment, he turned. "Think hard on what I have said, Josephine. Times are changing, and if you are not part of the change, you will be crushed by it as it rolls over you."

When he was gone, Josie swung a fist in the air and let out an exasperated noise between her teeth. "I'd like to challenge that man to a duel and shoot him through the heart!"

"It would be too small a target," I said. Surely Cousin Ishbel wouldn't mind my saying that.

Josie laughed uproariously, like a man, not a young woman, and her face got as flame red as her hair. "I suppose it would."

"I'll fight him if ye ask me," I said, swelled up with my courage and her laughter.

Josie stopped laughing and looked at me. "I think you've fought enough battles for one day, young Roddy. Are you steady on your feet now?"

"I am indeed," I told her, lifting my feet one after another to show her, though I wasn't entirely sure. "Da always says that a good fight works wonders for any Highlander. 'Stirs the blood and stirs the stumps,' he says."

She smiled at that.

"But," I continued, "if it be none of my business, I will nae ask again. What was Rood up to anyway? Why did he come to rob ye? And in daylight. And with the laird's permission?"

"It's no secret," Bonnie Josie said. "With your bruises you have won the right to ask." She looked over at her mother, who nodded in agreement. "Under the normal law of inheritance," Josie explained, "if a laird dies without a son, the estate passes to his brother."

I interrupted her. "I know that much!"

"What you may *not* know," she said, putting up a hand, "is that my father did not trust his half brother—and rightly so, it seems—so he had a separate deed drawn up for the Lodge. He signed it over to Mother before he died."

"So what could yer uncle do about that?" I asked, though I thought I could guess.

"Well, if the deed to the house were to go missing . . ." Her eyes had become slits and her mouth pursed as if she'd eaten something sour. "Why, then he could argue in court that the normal rules of inheritance should apply. That way, the Lodge would belong to him along with the rest of the estate. And trust me, Roddy, he's got many a tame lawyer who'll do his bidding and many a friendly judge to see his will carried out."

So, I had guessed right. "He meant to throw you off your land." I drew in a deep breath. "Just as he has thrown out the rest of his clansfolk."

"Oh, what if he had found the deed!" exclaimed the widow, a hand fluttering over her mouth.

"Do not worry, Mother, the Lord provides. Did we not have our own wee terrier on guard?" Josie laughed again, but there was little mirth in it this time.

Wee terrier! I liked that. Though I'd rather she thought me a larger dog. Especially if it would help guard them. I grinned.

"But now that Uncle has made clear his intentions, I will make sure he cannot get his hands on that deed. I will put it beyond the reach of Rood or any other intruder." Josie turned away from both of us and looked out the window, where the late afternoon sun was trying to break through the mist.

Regaining her composure, the widow stood up. "Let us brew a pot of tea for this young warrior," she said. "Then we had best pack him off home before it gets dark."

Tea. I had heard of the drink. But it was much too dear for any crofter's pot. And then I thought: what a day I'd had! I'd been a warrior and I'd been wounded; I'd been a terrier inside a great house. And now I was to taste a cup of tea. I could hardly wait to tell Lachlan.

"Good thought, Mother," Josie said. "A pot of tea will be just the thing. You find young Mairi to put the kettle on, and I will find a new hiding place for our much sought-after deed."

6 ❧ HOME

I reached home in the gloaming, the twilight time when the sun dies like an ember behind the hills. Ahead of me on the rocky path I could see our stone cottage. As I got closer still, I could smell the bitter peat fire smoke drifting through the hole in the turf roof. Suddenly the place seemed rough and poor and hardly room enough for one, though four of us lived there. How quickly a person's life can change. How quickly his dreams get bigger.

I wondered if we could ever hope to have a house with high brick walls, glass windows, and a lofty chimney like the Lodge. A house with painted pictures of birds and fruit and shepherd maids hanging on white walls. A house with a separate kitchen and pantry, not just a hearth in the main room where mutton cooking spattered its grease on the wall.

Stopping on the path, I shook my head to clear it of such stupid dreams. Even if the cottage and the land about were ours to sell and not the laird's property, it could never raise enough money for a fine home like the Lodge. Not if we sold all our furniture and pots and pans and Ishbel's horse in the bargain.

Yet as I tried to count up our meager possessions, I thought suddenly of the Blessing, the secret gift my mother had passed down to us from my grandfather Duncan MacDonald. Mother always said that her family had been given the treasure by Bonnie Prince Charlie himself and it was worth a fortune. We were to keep it safe until the

Bonnie Prince returned and a Stuart king sat once more on the throne of Scotland. But the Bonnie Prince had died a long time ago in a foreign land, no matter that the old songs said Charlie would come back again. That much I knew. Da had told Mother, and it was hard not to overhear him when they argued. So if the prince was dead, there was no reason to keep the Blessing now when by selling it, we could get ourselves a better life. And maybe help Bonnie Josie as well.

Above me an owl went on silent wings to a nearby tree, becoming a shadow on a branch. I shivered as if the owl were an omen. And maybe it was. After all, the secret of where the Blessing lay hidden had died with Mother. How could we sell what we couldn't find? Maybe the owl meant her death and the death of my dream.

All right, it was just a dream. But after what Josie and I had talked of in the Lodge, perhaps it was a dream worth having.

I tried to recall everything I'd heard about the Blessing. Da had sighed when Lachlan and I had asked him some months past where it might be.

"Yer mother was havering," he said. "Dying women speak of heaven as though it's but a step away. Dinna fash yerselves about it." Da still found any mention of Ma painful. He kept her memory like a burr under his shirt.

As for Ishbel, she wouldn't stand for any talk of the thing either. "That was a harmless fancy of yer mother's," she told us sharply, "a happy dream of princes she used to cheer herself with when things were hard. If it had been real, she would have shown it ye, whatever it is. Or we would have found it after . . ."

I didn't agree. I believed Ma had hidden the Blessing to keep it safe. In the house or outside the house—that was the question that had no answer. When the fever took her, she died so quickly, she couldn't pass on the secret of where the Blessing lay.

We'd gone through the house after she was buried and after the townsfolk came for the wake. A wild wake it was too. There was much drinking and storytelling and the women in tears. Cousin Ishbel made us clean up after, going through every cupboard and drawer and writing down what was there. Nothing that looked like a Blessing was in our accounting.

But I was sure it was here somewhere, like the Bible story of the pearl hidden in a field. It was as real to me as my heart beating in my breast; indeed, it was suddenly the very heart of all my hopes for the future.

As I entered the darkness of the cottage, Ishbel was bent over the hearth, stirring a bubbling pot of stew over the smoky peat fire. The croft had not the clean, flowery scent of the Lodge. I could smell musky peat, earthy neeps and potatoes, but little else. No one had snared a hare, then. And clearly Lachlan had not caught any of the Glendoun chickens.

"He's back," Lachlan announced, looking up from his perch on the stool. "See, I told ye he'd be fine."

Ishbel looked up sharply from the stew and fixed her eyes on me. The flames sent shots of gold through her bushy red hair. "Fine? It looks as if his head's been cracked like an egg." She pointed the spoon at me accusingly. "If trouble comes to us because of your daft capers, we'll know where the blame lies." Ishbel had a way of turning our brave adventures into a child's foolish games.

No sooner had she spoken than my head began to ache again, though it had been free of pain all along the road. I touched my forehead and sighed.

Rising from his own stool, Da placed a hand on my arm. "Are ye really all right, son? We were worried, in spite of what Lachlan said. I was ready to ride down to the Lodge to fetch ye back." It was rare to hear him so concerned.

"I'm fine," I assured him. "It hardly even hurts anymore." The truth, though, was that I was suddenly exhausted, and my skull had begun throbbing like the inside of a drum. Rood's first blow with the cudgel had been strong, but then I'd been shaken again when we'd wrestled at the Lodge. Clearly I was not as well as I thought.

Placing the wooden spoon carefully on the pot's edge, Ishbel marched briskly toward me and grabbed me by the arms and Da sat down again at the table. "Come over here, closer to the fire, so I can have a better look at ye." She maneuvered me roughly into position, then took hold of the bandage and pulled it up to expose the bloody weal. The wound stung so much I gave a grunt of pain.

"Bear up like a man," Ishbel said. "I dinna have to be gentle with ye, seeing as I'm not yer ma." She was always saying things like that. I had only recently begun to understand that these remarks were aimed at Da, not me.

"I've had rougher handling than this," I said, "and this day too." Then I ground my teeth against the pain, wondering how much I could safely tell them.

"Have ye not enough to do that ye can find time for this nonsense?" she demanded. "I might have to drag ye down to the burn and pitch ye in to wash away the blood and dirt." Then she squinted at the injury. "That's a bad knock," she said at last, "but it's been well tended."

"It was Josie that did it," I said, "Bonnie Josie."

"That's Miss Josephine to ye, lad," said my father. "Keep a respectful tongue in yer head."

Just then the fire popped a coal onto the hearth as if it too were scolding me.

Ishbel turned and shook a finger at Lachlan because she knew who always led me on. "Best *ye* don't get into such scrapes too," she said. "We've enough to cope with without making an enemy of Willie Rood."

"He's already every man's enemy," I said. "Though the laird seems to like him too well."

My father slammed his hand down on the table, which made his cup of whisky jump. "That's as may be, but ye need to mind yer place, lad. There's sheep in Glendoun now, so Lachlan tells me, and we must leave them alone."

"We were just playing a game," I said. My voice rose in a whine. "It's not like we were thieving. It was Rood who made a great fuss over things. And Rood who tossed out the Glendoun folk. Burning them out. Because the laird told him to."

Da glowered at me and took another sip of his whisky.

I leaned toward him and said, "Da—they were all burned out of their cottages. There's hardly a wall standing."

He looked down at his whisky. "So Lachlan says. But that's Glendoun, and this is Dunraw."

"And will they say that of us down in the valley when we're burned out?" I said.

"Nae one is purposing to burn us out," Ishbel said. She took Da's empty glass from his unresisting hand.

"What about the Lodge?" Lachlan asked, keen to change the subject. "What was it like? Did they give ye venison and cakes and—"

Ishbel cut him off with a clout across the head. "All ye think about is yer belly, Lachlan Macallan," she said. "I've a perfectly fine vegetable stew coming to the boil here."

"Aye, I'm sure it will be good," Lachlan, answered, lowering his head. "If ye like a thin meal."

"Is thin my fault, then? Where were the bonnie hares ye could have snared on yon hillside?" Ishbel asked. "Or a bird or two?"

"I'm not hungry," I said, lying. "I've already had bannocks with fresh butter. And tea."

"*Tea* is it?" said Ishbel. Hands on hips, she asked, "And what did *that* taste like?"

I shrugged. "Like nothing much," I replied. "Ye make it by boiling up bits of grass in a pot of water."

"Sounds bad for the liver!" She turned and gave the stew another stir. "The laird might have lived longer and his wife not be so peely-wally if they'd never touched the stuff."

Da made a sound somewhere between a sigh and a laugh. I couldn't tell if he found her amusing or annoying.

Suddenly I felt as if a great hand was pushing on the top of my head. Going over to the table, I sat down heavily on my own stool, saying, "Things are getting worse for the widow McRoy, Da. The laird tried to talk her into giving up her property. Then I caught Rood with a pry bar in Josie's bedchamber and . . ."

"Enough!" said my father with a decisive chop of his hand. "That's the laird's family and nae business of ours. If ye've been eavesdropping, Roddy Macallan, ye should have the decency not to repeat what ye hear. Not even to yer own family."

"But this is *important*," I protested. "If the laird can push out his own close kin, what won't he do to us, his clansmen? If we don't stand up for Bonnie Josie, who will stand up for us when Rood's men come to torch our home?"

"They'll have to fight their own cause," said Ishbel. "It's not for the likes of us to stand between the laird and his family." She turned again to stir the stew. The hearth flung out several more nuggets of fire. But the croft seemed darker with each bit of flame.

"The widow McRoy said we should be loyal to each other, as clansmen and their chiefs were in the old days," I told her.

Da gave a snort. "Even in the old days, the chief's business was his own," he said. "Ye've nae call to speak of it or meddle in his affairs."

"As yer father says," Ishbel added, looking meaningfully at me over her shoulder, "what's in the family stays in the family, and it's nae business of an outsider. That goes for our family as well as the laird's." She held up the dipper. "Come now, lads, bring your bowls and eat up this stew. I've been long enough cooking it. It shouldna go to waste."

Standing, we carried our wooden bowls to the stew pot, and she dished the watery stuff out for us. The smell nearly overcame me, but I managed to get back without spilling a drop. Then we all sat down at the table on our little stools and ate in silence. Even me, though moments earlier I had declared myself not hungry at all.

After supper Da had a second whisky. Lachlan and I talked quietly about the sheep, while Ishbel cleaned off the table and dipped the dishes into a bucket of water. When she was done washing, I took the water bucket outside and sloshed it over the hillside while Lachlan banked the hearth fire. Then we lay down for the night.

Da and Lachlan and I slept in the little room, Ishbel at the end of the kitchen. She had a sackcloth curtain to give herself some privacy, not being strictly a member of the family. The thin, shabby curtain was not at all like the fine carved doors at the Lodge. And as I lay restless on the bed I shared with Lachlan, I realized how uncomfortable the flattened heather mattress was.

Taking a deep breath, I let the familiar smell of the cottage wash over me: peat fire, cooked stew, unwashed bodies, and the lingering stink of all the animals we brought inside during the winter. Of course, it wasn't just a concern for the beasts' health that made us shelter them. Having them indoors meant more warmth for us as well. But as I lay there, I recalled the crisp smell of the bannocks and clean aroma of the tea at the Lodge.

How poor we are, I thought. Then I closed my eyes, but as I had already napped during the day, I couldn't fall asleep.

As soon as Da started snoring, Lachlan turned over on the mattress and poked me in the ribs, whispering, "Come on then, Roddy, tell me all about it."

"About what?"

He poked me again, harder. "Ye know fine and well what. About the widow and Bonnie Josie, about the laird and Rood."

"Are ye sure Da is asleep?" He'd already warned me once about telling tales, and I couldn't stand a belting, not the way I was feeling.

"I'm absolutely sure. Just listen to him snore."

Needing no more prodding, I told Lachlan all. I couldn't see his face in the dark, but I could imagine his expressions of surprise at each stage of the tale. He even gasped when I described my fight with Rood.

"Willie Rood is likely to kill ye if ye go a third round with him," he warned.

"I'm not afraid of him," I said. But deep down I knew that was a lie. Only a sudden rage had driven me to attack him. Lying in the dark and thinking more clearly, I knew Rood was bigger, stronger, and infinitely more vicious than I. Lachlan was right. One good blow from his cudgel might do for me the next time. "If there *is* a next time."

Lachlan stirred beside me, rose up on his elbow. "Of course there will be a next time."

I nodded, even though he couldn't see me do it.

"And if you are telling me true . . ."

I sat up indignantly. "Of course I am telling you true!"

"Then the laird is worse than even Da imagines. He's ready to throw his own niece and sister-in-law out, so why should he not send the English sheep into *our* glen?"

As usual, Lachlan was right. I knew that. And I also knew that if Bonnie Josie needed my help again, I would brave any danger: Rood's cudgel's, the laird's anger, or even worse. Though what could be worse, I could not imagine. Except, perhaps, in a bad night's dream.

II. TENANTS' ANGER

What though on hamely fare we dine,

Wear hoddin grey, and a' that;

Gie fools their silks, and knaves their wine;

A man's a man for a' that! . . .

—Robert Burns, "A Man's a Man for a' That"

7 &~ THE ROGUE

Over the next few days life carried on as normal. I tried to forget about what had happened at the Lodge, tried to keep myself to myself so that I didn't find trouble. But I knew trouble was coming, as certain as hail in winter. Lachlan had the right of it. The laird was sure to send his English sheep over our hill. But just when that was to happen, we didn't know. So we tried to work as though nothing was wrong. Or as Ishbel promised, "God will provide." Though she didn't say if He would provide arms and ammunition or a fast escape route.

Lachlan and I were in the byre milking the cows when the first word of the new trouble came. Outside there was a gale blowing, so we didn't hear anyone approaching because of the wuthering of the wind.

Suddenly the door blew open and in stomped Hamish Kinnell, puffing and waving his arms furiously. A lanky lad with a gap in his front teeth, Hamish made a whistling noise when he was excited. Sometimes, just for fun, Lachlan tried to goad him on just to hear that whistle.

"Have ye heard?" Hamish asked, the words singing through the gap. I was busy milking Thistle while Lachlan stroked her nose to keep her steady. We both looked over at him, waiting for his news, which was not long in coming. "Tam MacBride's cows have been arrested!"

It wasn't what either of us was expecting, and I almost fell off
the stool laughing. I succeeded in squirting milk all over my breeks.
"Cows arrested? Yer mad!"

Thistle mooed and twitched her head, as if alarmed by Hamish's
words or my wild cackling.

"Don't be daft!" said Lachlan, gripping Thistle by a horn to
steady her.

"It's true!" Hamish insisted. "Tam's cows strayed into the
middle of the Glendoun sheep pastures. The shepherds rounded
them up, and Rood's had the animals arrested. They're penned up
in a field at the back of Kindarry House. Rood calls it the im . . .
impound."

"Why don't they just give the cows back to Tam and have him
promise to take better care?" I asked. "The old laird would have."

"Because now it's a crime to let yer cattle stray onto sheep land,"
said Hamish. His whistling had stopped because he'd realized he
knew something we didn't. Grinning, he added, "That's called *trespassing*. Like in the Lord's Prayer. Tam can only get them back if he
pays a five-pound fine."

I stood up so fast with the surprise of it, the milk stool turned
over. *"Five pounds!"*

Lachlan added, "It might as well be a hundred."

"The laird and Rood dinna care about the money," I said. "It's
sma' pickings for them. They just want to make life hard for us
so it will be easier to drive us away." I grabbed up the stool and
milking bucket.

"How can ye be sure?" asked Hamish, wide-eyed.

"I was just down at the Lodge last week," I said casually, "and
Bonnie Josie herself told me." Well, it wasn't *exactly* what she told
me, but who was to know? I walked toward the open door, shoulders

squared, certain that Hamish's mouth would be agape. I could hear Lachlan starting to tell him the story, knowing that in my brother's version, my role would grow and grow. Lachlan always made things bigger than they were. Not a liar, but a storyteller.

"He *spoke* with Bonnie Josie . . . ?" Hamish's whistle followed me out.

Over the next week, strange things kept happening. Many more animals from our village strayed into the pastures of the laird and his friends and were quickly impounded by the factor's men. Cattle, goats—and even some of our own straggly sheep—all must have decided to go calling on their plump cousins like poor relations begging on the doorstep. Why they should suddenly take to wandering was a puzzle we didn't understand at first. After all, it was a long way to go to Glendoun, and plenty of grass on our side of the mountain for their grazing.

Finally two of our own milk cows ended up in the impound. They were missing one morning when we went into the byre to milk them, and when we found Da out in the neep field, he was fuming. He led us back to the cottage and said not a word till we were inside, the door carefully shut behind us.

"And where do ye think those cows had got to?" he asked. His voice was low but angry. He didn't wait for a reply. "To Glendoun. Frolicking amongst the laird's new sheep!"

Lachlan and I swore to Da that it hadn't been our fault. "We kept them far away from Glendoun," I said as we stood before him, heads bowed. Behind us, Cousin Ishbel clanged about her pots, cleaning them vigorously, though they'd been cleaned once already.

Lachlan added, "The cows were clear on the other side of Ben

Dorrach with us yesterday and then we brought them home and locked them in the byre. Just as we do every night." He dared to look up at Da. Catching the movement from the corner of my eye, I did likewise.

Da's face was almost crimson with anger, an awful sign. "Ye've been over-fond of visiting that cursed glen," he accused. "How do I know ye didna sneak over there again with our animals trailing after ye? Cows are no much smarter than sheep and will follow the hand that feeds them anywhere." His hand was on his belt as he spoke.

"God is our witness, Da!" Lachlan pleaded. "We've kept well away since that run-in with Rood. I wouldna let Roddy chance another blow. His head is soft enough as it is." If he was hoping to make Da laugh, he was sorely mistaken.

Da glared at him for a long moment, then said, in that slow way he sometimes has before anger takes him entirely, "Would ye no?"

I waited for the trap to snap.

Then Da bent closer to where Lachlan stood. "Then how is it that one of the factor's own men found me in the field this very morning to serve a fine on me for trespass?"

Neither Lachlan nor I said a word. Answering back would earn us each a clap on the head, and we knew it.

"What are we to do?" asked Ishbel, coming to our rescue by speaking herself. "We've nothing to pay with."

"*Nobody* has," I said, knowing it was safe now to say something. "And the laird knows it full well. But why is he doing this slowly, trying to bleed us of money, instead of just sending in the sheep?"

Da's hand was raised slightly, but he didn't strike me. Instead, jaw set grimly, he scratched his beard. "That, lad, is a good question and one I have to consider."

Cousin Ishbel offered, "Perhaps there are no more sheep?"

Lachlan said, "Perhaps he's afraid of the men of this village because we are now forewarned."

"Perhaps Bonnie Josie has served him notice . . . ," I added.

Da shook his head and held up his hand. "A wee lass will not stop such a man, and there are *always* more sheep. Lachlan is right, though. McRoy knows how the men of this village have organized before to stop a laird, and he's hoping we will go quietly and without a fight."

This made sense to us all, and we said so.

"The men of the village are meeting this afternoon in the kirk. The minister's awa' to Glasgow or he'd likely forbid it. We'll decide there how best to go about getting our animals back."

"Have we no enough troubles wi'out raising Minister McGillivray's hackles?" Ishbel asked, waving a pot at him. "He's a prickly creature at the best of times, except to the laird."

"Och, he's the laird's wee lapdog," scoffed Lachlan, repeating what he'd heard from others. "He'd rather serve McRoy than God, for the pay's better."

"When McGillivray's away, God has the kirk to Himself." Da took out a cup and poured himself a draught of water from the barrel before answering. "I don't think He'll scorn to open His kirk door in a good cause. Didna Christ say that the poor will inherit the earth?"

"*Meek*," Cousin Ishbel said. "The meek will inherit the earth, and ye are hardly that, Murdo Macallan."

"Can we go too?" Lachlan asked, eager as a dog after sheep.

Da's face got grim again, but Ishbel put a hand on his arm. "This concerns us all, Murdo, and they're at that age now when they should listen to the men at counsel." She gazed up at him under half lids and, astonishingly, he softened.

"Aye, perhaps," he said. Then he turned his back on us all, but Ishbel nodded at us and put a finger to her lips before setting the pot back down on the hearth.

We knew enough to be silent. A promise, of sorts, had been given.

The kirk sat off on the side of the road, a small grey stone building. The women of the village had done careful plantings of wildflowers by the door, the only bit of real color about the church. I had heard that the papists have colored windows in their chapels and cathedrals, as well as paintings of the Gospels on the inside walls. But we didn't hold with such customs. I am not sure why.

By the time we arrived, the kirk was full. Not only were the village men crowded into the hard wooden pews, but many of their women came as well. The few children accompanying them fidgeted at the back, kicking the seats and giggling. There were also folk from villages farther down the glen who had had animals impounded. Some I recognized, but most were strangers. There must have been a hundred people in all.

The sun slanted through the windows, setting a pattern of light on the middle pews so there was no need for the lamps to be lit. Standing in front of the pulpit, Tam MacBride was telling everybody how he'd gone to Kindarry House to make his appeal, his hands relating the story a second time as he talked.

"I said to the laird I couldna pay the fine and the rent as well." His short black beard seemed to bristle angrily with each word.

There was a low murmur of respect. Going to face the laird is never an easy task. At least not *this* laird.

"Aye, Tam, nor can any of us," somebody put in, "no the way he's raised the rents twice this past year alone."

" 'Fine,' says he," Tam continued, as if no one had interrupted. His right forefinger punched the air. " 'Ye can have yer cattle or ye can have yer land. Ye take yer pick.' "

Another low murmur went through the huddled men.

"It was the same for me," called out Colin Kinnell. He was Hamish's father and even lankier and bonier than his son. "He said if I couldna keep my animals under control, I'd only myself to blame."

"Blame?" one of the outlanders shouted. And the others echoed him. "Blame?"

Da stood up, his voice a low grumble. "So it's cattle with nae land to graze on or land with nae means of livelihood." He looked around. "That's a hard choice."

"That's nae choice at all," cried the outlander.

But no one had yet thought to ask how all our animals had strayed into the path of the laird's sheep.

There was an angry uproar among the men, which Da waved to silence. "Look," he said, "we know Daniel McRoy is no the man the old laird was. Not half. But he is still our chief, the head of our family. And like any father, he might say things he doesna hold to at second thought."

I knew how true that was, how Da had sometimes refused us something when he was in a sour mood, then thought better of it later in the day after Ma had sweetened him. *Or now, Ishbel,* I thought. But who would soften this laird's stance? Bonnie Josie had tried, and it only seemed to have strengthened his resolve to rid himself of his tenants.

"What are ye saying, Murdo Macallan?" Colin asked, standing and turning toward Da. "That we should wait around for the laird to change his mind?"

Da shook his head. "Nae, Colin. I'm saying we should send representatives to the laird to *remind* him of his responsibilities. We need to change his mind for him." The way he said the word *remind* made a ripple of laughter go around the room.

"Bell the cat," Colin said, and we all laughed because everyone knew *that* story.

Then Da turned and spoke to the rest of the men, his voice filling the kirk as much as the minister's ever did. "Need I remind all of you that the blood of our ancient chieftains still runs in the laird's veins, however thinly."

"Thin indeed," called out someone.

"Thin as watered whisky," another voice added.

There was a large current of laughter now, but Da held up his hand again. "Thin his blood may be, but there's still a bond between us that canna be broken. The laird holds the land, but we're the ones that tend it for him. He canna just take our livelihood away."

"Aye!" The single word was repeated all around the kirk like an echo beating off the whitewashed walls.

But, I thought, *he already has. Just ask the folk of Glendoun.* Still, I didn't dare say it aloud. I was only a lad, after all. And lads, like women, are supposed to keep silent.

"Remember," Da said, "remember how the old laird sent the sheep merchants packing when he saw his people at the door. Perhaps this laird will rise to his heritage."

There was some grumbling, and someone shouted out, "We'll see a trout rise in winter before that happens!"

But stocky Sandy Philipson piped up, "Ye're right, Murdo. There's still a bond between a chief and his people."

What bond, I wondered, *if he would even try and put his own niece out in the cold?*

"Aye, presenting our grievances is better than doing nothing," agreed Tam.

"It's worse than doing nothing," declared a new voice. "It's falling to yer knees and begging. Nae like men but like weak old women."

All heads turned, and there was a murmur of surprise as a tall, unshaven man in a wide-brimmed black hat stepped out of the shadows of the back of the kirk. He wore a long blue coat strapped around the middle with a leather belt and high military boots. There was a musket tucked under his right arm and a cluster of whisky jugs tied together with twine that hung from his left shoulder. He carried himself with an air of casual defiance that made him stand out against the grey inner walls of the kirk.

"I hadn't thought to see ye here, Dunbar," said Da.

Now I knew who he was: Alan Dunbar, the whisky runner. The English king had long ago banned the Highlanders from keeping weapons, but Dunbar had got his gun fighting as a soldier in the king's pay.

I nudged Lachlan, and he turned to give me back a big-eyed stare.

"The Rogue o' the Hills," he whispered.

I nodded. We'd heard his name before, but neither of us had ever met him. I stared as he walked forward, his boots a slow drum-beat on the kirk floor. There was something big about him, bigger than any of the other men. And he'd dared to say aloud what I had only whispered to myself.

He spoke in time to each step, his voice echoing in the silent kirk. "When men get to blethering, there's a thirst sure to follow." He grinned and rattled the jugs under his left arm. "And a thirsty man is a ready market for my whisky."

"You've the devil's own nerve," said Tam, "to come peddling your lawless brew here in God's own house."

"I force nae man to buy," Dunbar responded innocently, "and any man who does is free to go to the excise man and pay the duty on his jar."

"Which is more than ye'll ever do," said Da.

Dunbar was at the front of the kirk now, with his back to the communion table, and he stood still, slowly looking over the congregation. Then, as if preaching, he said in his strong voice, "The day the government does me a favor, that's when they can have my payment."

A few of the men laughed out loud.

"Ye all know my story."

I leaned forward. I couldn't take my eyes off him.

" I took the king's shilling when only a lad and went off across the sea to fight the French and see off that wee corporal, Napoleon," he said, as if telling a tale over a glass of whisky by the fire. "Five years of that, of blood running like mountain streams. And when I came home, was there a parcel of land waiting for me as promised?"

We were all silent, waiting. Even those who already knew his story.

Dunbar smiled, but there was no comfort in it. He shook his head. "Nae, there was nothing. *Nothing!* My family had been thrown off their farm to make way for sheep. *For sheep!* With no roof over their heads and no money in their purse, my ma and da died in the hills that very winter, hand in hand in a snowdrift."

"That was in Glengarry territory, not here," said Da. "Here they'd have been taken in. No left to starve in the snow."

I thought: *And did we take in the lovely Fiona and her brothers?*

Dunbar started to spit, thought better of it, and swiped his sleeve across his mouth. "It's the same all over, Macallan. My story's no so original. In Sutherland, Glengarry, or here, no one has a care the poor crofters are being turned out of their homes to make way for flocks of fat English sheep. Instead of being their protectors, their lairds have become their worst enemies. I'll never again put my fate in anybody's hands but my own. And if it's men ye are, no puling, whining old women, ye'll do the same."

I could hear the children sneaking down the right side of the kirk to squeeze in next to their mothers, as if shrinking from a dark shadow that was closing in on us all.

"That's a fine course for them that wants a bandit's life," said Tam, raising his voice, "but we're all honest farmers here."

Tam is right, I thought. *Maybe I'm rushing to judgment.*

Dunbar laughed scornfully. "Aye, like my father. An honest farmer and dead in the winter hills. Dinna be a fool, man. Ye'll go on being honest while Daniel McRoy and Willie Rood go on robbing ye blind."

"What they've done may be hard, but it's within the law," said Da.

"Aye, so I hear," said Dunbar, "a law that punishes goats and cows for their transgressions." He laughed, and it was a short, sharp sound. "Do none of ye *honest farmers* see what's going on here?"

"Speak plain, Dunbar!" shouted a voice.

The sun suddenly disappeared behind a cloud and the whole kirk grew dark. No one moved to light a lantern, for all were hot blood and anger.

"I'm saying there's all kinds of thievery," Dunbar said, "and all kinds of thieves, some more honest than others." He leaned forward toward the men in the pews. "Do ye think Rood and his men are above rounding up a few cows in the night while ye sleep? Did ye know that they drive yer beasts into the pastures themselves?" There was a sudden silence in the pews. "Or just take them straight to Kindarry to be impounded and say they were found on the hills?"

Suddenly everyone was talking at once, but low, like the sound I imagined the ocean would make, grumbling in its low bed. And I was swimming in that tide, swimming toward the Rogue. *Of course. Now it all made sense. Why hadn't I seen it?*

Da took a deep, loud breath and said sternly, "Those are serious charges, Dunbar, and nae man here would dare lay them against his laird without proof."

From the angry mutters that had followed Dunbar's words, I wasn't so sure that Da was right.

Dunbar shook his musket at Da. "*His laird?* His laird? Yer talking like it was a hundred years ago, Macallan," he said, "when ye went to the laird for justice. This laird's got nae interest in justice now. It's yer money and yer land he wants, not yer loyalty. He's got sheep for loyalty as long as there's grass, and for all he cares, every man and woman here can be drowned in the sea. Dinna ye see it, man, the old ways are being destroyed while ye cower in the kirk and hope the minister willna mind ye meeting here."

A new silence descended, and this time the air hung heavy with dark thoughts. Even the children were still.

Finally Dunbar grinned and lifted up his cluster of whisky jugs. "Now, is anybody thirsty enough to buy?"

One man tried to step forward, but his wife pulled him back. "No in the kirk, ye daftie," she whispered, but loud enough so everyone could hear, "or God will strike ye dead."

"It's all right, Fergus," Dunbar told him with a wink. "I'll see ye get yer supply at the usual place." He looked around at the other men. "And the rest of ye as well, if yer too shy to buy here."

"Yer a fine one to talk to us about the laird, Dunbar," said Da. "It's clear yer only here to line yer own pocket. Well, we'll deal with our problems without yer advice or yer whisky."

With a shrug, the Rogue hefted his musket and his whisky. He winked at Ishbel and me, saying loud enough for everyone to hear, "If ye willna act like men, ye may as well drink like sots." Then he turned on his heel and headed back up the aisle and out the door at a jaunty pace. He left the door wide open, and many eyes followed him—mine especially—and a few voices grumbled at his departure.

A child cried out, "I'm hungry, Ma."

As if that were some kind of signal, the women gathered their children and funneled out the open door.

Tam went to light the lamp near the pulpit, and its feeble light sent shadows racing about the front of the kirk.

"Now the entertainment's gone, we need to pick a deputation," said Da, calling everybody's attention back to the matter at hand. "Nae more than a dozen men. We mustna be taken for a mob or that will make matters worse." There was a small rumble of approval, and he added, "We'll put it to the laird that he must reconsider what he's done, for the good of the clan and his own immortal soul."

"Nae!" cried a voice. "The Rogue is right! This laird will never listen. Nor will he ever change."

Da stared hard at the congregation through the fading light, anger and disbelief warring in his face. "Was that *ye* speaking, Roddy?"

I bit my lip and stood, but I couldn't take back what I'd just said. The Rogue had been right. He'd shown us the way. "Aye, Da, it was me." I said my piece and would stand by it, even if Da whipped me with his belt, for I'd only spoken the truth, and well he knew it.

There was a sudden silence in the kirk as if God himself had decreed that all the men be mute. I started to tremble. *What had I begun?* I wondered. *What had I begun?*

Da's scowl was thundery as the sky outside. Shadows made his face dark. "Curb that tongue, laddie. Only grown men are allowed to speak in kirk."

"Maybe we should hear the lad out," said Tam, "since we're talking here, no praying." Then, without waiting for Da to agree, he leaned forward and said to me, "What do ye mean, Roddy, that Alan Dunbar is right about the laird?"

Whatever spirit had made me bold enough just a moment before began to waver like a dying candle, but I recalled my encounter at the Lodge, and that stoked my anger. Though the kirk was chilly, I was afire with the memory.

"I've been to the Lodge," I said, my voice soft, though all leaned toward me to listen. "I've heard the laird speak about us as if we were dumb beasts. 'Ignorant rabble,' he called us. He said, 'We might as well have sheep in their place and do without the inconvenience of the rabble's dirt and noise.'" I took a deep breath and went on. "And I've seen Bonnie Josie defy him to his face, and she only a lass."

Da folded his arms over his chest. His face was awful to behold, dark and with a deep crease between his eyes. "Well, now ye've made a start of it, son, go on with it."

I took a deep breath and thought about Bonnie Josie and her mother and how they'd called me a terrier. Then I put my teeth into the thought, shook my head with it, and began again, this time louder.

"As little as he cares for us, the laird cares less for his own kin. I saw that with my own eyes, heard it with these two ears." I took another deep breath, my heart hammering so fast beneath my breastbone, I was sure everyone could see it. "He wants to take from Bonnie Josie and her mother the little the old laird left them, because they've given refuge to the Glendoun folk."

There was a rustling all around me as the men reacted to this.

"That's as may be," said Colin, "but what can we do about it?"

Suddenly my hammering heart went quiet, my voice grew firmer. "If ye've given up already, what have ye come here for?" I felt a growing strength, as if the Rogue had left a part of his courage behind for me.

"Tell them," Lachlan whispered. Then louder, he said, "Roddy, tell them about the sheep."

I wasn't sure what he wanted me to say, but I began anyway, looking at the men one at a time as I spoke, every one of them but Da. "My brother, Lachlan, and I were in the glen when the Cheviot sheep arrived. I admit when I first saw them pouring over the hillside, I was afraid. But then, when they were all about us, I could see they were just dumb animals. And so we started to chase them off."

"Aye, and ye took a knock from Willie Rood for yer trouble," said Colin.

I glanced at Da, but he had fallen silent. I couldn't tell if he approved of my words or if he was leaving me to make a fool of myself and face my punishment later.

"The point is . . . ," I said, "that everybody is acting like those sheep are something to be scared of, like they canna be stopped any more than a flood or a storm. At Culloden our grandfathers charged the English cannon. Bravely right into the fire. We've heard that tale over and over. My da told me of their courage many times. Are we all too soft now to shake our fists at some English sheep when our grandas took on the English cannon?"

"At Culloden they all died," somebody called out.

"Aye, but like men," Tam said, loudly and with feeling.

"This is nae battle," Da objected at last. "It's farming and business. There's nowt to charge."

"If we let the sheep in here as they are in Glendoun," I told him, "it willna be long before there's no place for any of us on Kindarry land. There'll be nothing but sheep and a laird growing fat on the profit he takes from them." I bit my lower lip, then charged ahead. "Lachlan and I chased the sheep as a game. But if we all worked together, we could drive them back to their English homes."

"Drive them all the way back to England?" asked Colin. "We could never make it that far. And what would become of our farms while we were gone?"

"No all the way to England," I said carefully. "Just to Kindarry House. If the laird loves the sheep so much, let him take care of them himself and give us our cattle back."

There was some laughter at this foolish talk, but I heard a voice say, "There's some point to this laddie's words." I tried to see who it was, but the kirk was too dark for that.

"He's said what many a man here was feerd to," added another from out of the dark congregation.

"Do ye want to go up against the law?" Colin asked, wagging a bony finger. "Do ye want to end up a fugitive like Alan Dunbar?"

"The laird's bent on making us that, if we let him," I answered. "Isn't it better to make a fight of it?"

"Aye," Lachlan piped up, holding up a fist, "let's make a fight of it."

Tam turned to Da. "Roddy's yer boy, Murdo. What do ye say? Is he daft?"

"He's daft most of the time," said Da, and the men laughed. "But . . ." He hesitated and I felt my heart pause too. "But maybe no today. As I now see it, we would still only be bringing our grievances before the laird, which is our right. But we'd be bringing the cause of our grievances there as well. We willna be fighting the laird, but asking his aid. And offering our own."

"Bringing our grievances . . ." The phrase went around the men.

"Aye," said Tam, "it *could* work." He rubbed his hand against his nose.

I let out the breath I hadn't known I was holding. The kirk seemed suddenly filled with light, and I realized that the clouds had moved away from the sun. A few more voices called out their approval, and those few calls quickly became a roar.

Lachlan leaned close to me and whispered, "For yer sake I hope this turns out well."

"Ye agreed with me!" I rounded on him.

"Aye, but just to stir things up," he answered with a crooked smirk. "Mind ye, I never thought yer idea would work."

I jammed my elbow into his ribs, and he doubled half over, but that didn't wipe the grin from his face.

We strode home proudly, like soldiers returning from a great victory, not something a Highlander knows a lot about. We laughed and joked along the way. Even Da seemed excited about what we had decided, as if it had been his own idea.

The last of the afternoon sun was once again disappearing behind dark clouds. That did nothing to dampen our spirits. But as we drew closer to our cottage, our confident steps faltered. When we could smell the peat fire, we stopped, as if signaled to halt.

Da began to chew on his mustache. I knew what he was thinking. Ma had always cheered us on in our endeavors, but Ishbel was different. What would she make of this turn of events?

We held back until we looked foolish, all three of us standing nervously in front of the door, and Lachlan said, "Da?" And Da grunted, squared his shoulders, and pushed through into the cottage.

Ishbel was bent over the cook pot with her back turned toward us, the light of the peat fire blazing a halo around her. "So yer home at last," she said without looking around.

"Aye, home and hungry too," said Da, staring at the table that wasn't yet set for dinner.

We boys didn't say a word but simply sat down quickly on our stools.

"There's fresh water in the bucket," Ishbel said.

After a pause, Da added, "Best see to it, boys."

We went to the bucket and took turns washing our faces and hands. When we sat down again, we wiped our palms dry on our jerkins. I smiled at Ishbel's back.

Lifting four wooden bowls down from the shelf, she ladled stew into them, turned and held them out to us one at a time, along with wooden spoons. We stood, grabbed the bowls, then sat again, spooning the vegetables into our mouths with hardly a pause for breath, as if that could keep us from talking.

Ishbel took a slow spoonful from her own bowl and asked, "So, what was the end of yer meeting?"

Lachlan and I kept shoveling the food in and let Da answer her.

"If ye were so curious, ye should have come along," he said. "Some women were there."

"With their husbands, I would guess," Ishbel retorted sharply. "I'm an outsider here. There'd be no place for me."

Da shrugged. "There was a lot of talk," he said slowly. "That's all."

"There's always a lot of talk," said Ishbel, shrugging back at him. "But is anything to be done?"

Da took another mouthful of stew and chewed it thoughtfully. He chewed so thoroughly, he must have made mush. At last he said, "We're sending a deputation."

"To the laird?" She held up her spoon.

"Of course to the laird, woman," said Da.

"To do what?" She leaned forward.

"To ask him politely to release the cattle."

Ishbel huffed derisively. "And why should he listen? It's a poor pipe that blows only wind."

"Because we'll be taking all the sheep with us!" Lachlan piped up loudly.

Da glared at him, but it was too late.

"The sheep?" Ishbel repeated. "Ye mean the sheep from Glendoun?"

Da nodded mutely.

"And whose cracked notion was that?" She stood and went over to stir the fire, which made shadows dance around the table.

We all three stared down into our bowls, but I could see Lachlan's eyes flicking toward me. My belly began to twist into a tight knot. If Ishbel knew I was behind it, if she thought I was getting the family into trouble, I'd be living on thistles and silence for a week.

Ishbel's question hung over us like a sharpened ax dangling from a thread as she returned to the table and sat down again.

Finally Da said, "It was Alan Dunbar who stirred things up."

I let out a silent breath.

Cocking an eyebrow, Ishbel asked, "And what was that rogue doing at a meeting of decent folk?"

"He came to sell whisky," said Lachlan brightly. Then he fell silent.

"By the sound of it, ye must all have drunk yer fill."

"No one bought a drop of his brew," said Da.

"Then why have ye taken up this mad scheme?"

Into the new silence that greeted her question, I finally threw an answer. "His words affected us strongly. Better than any brew."

"*His words!*" Ishbel repeated mockingly. "And is Alan Dunbar a minister that ye should listen so closely to him? He poaches off the laird's land and worse besides."

"He's bold," said Lachlan, "and takes his lead from nae man. I heard he once stole a whole herd of a neighboring laird's cattle all by himself, took them all the way to Edinburgh. He sold them at the market before the sheriff's men could catch him."

I could see from Ishbel's stern expression that was the wrong thing to say, and I decided to leap to Dunbar's defense. "I heard he killed twenty Frenchmen at the Battle of Waterloo," I said quickly, "and took a gold coin from the emperor Napoleon himself!"

"Aye, it's easy to believe he was killing and thieving even then," said Ishbel, changing my words.

"It's all rumors, Ishbel," Da said quietly, looking steadily at her. "And nobody should be condemned because of rumor."

Ishbel fell silent, and her brow wrinkled. Next her eyes filled with tears, and she stood up again, going over to stir what was left of the stew with a shaking hand.

Da meant the rumors that had spread through the village about him and Ishbel, of course, rumors that they lived as man and wife without being married in the kirk. Lachlan and I knew they slept apart and sometimes didn't even speak to each other for days. We knew that any soft words between them were so rare as to be small miracles. So if *those* rumors weren't true, maybe the things said about Alan Dunbar weren't true either. At least I thought that was what Da meant. But I hoped Dunbar really did have Napoleon's coin. I would dearly love to see it.

Ishbel turned back, her eyes shining with unshed tears. "I canna see that ye'll get justice from theft."

"It's nae theft," said Da. "We're taking the sheep direct to the laird's house. And asking him to remember what bonds are between a laird and his kin."

"And if ye're caught before ye arrive there? Nae matter what ye mean to do, it's the likeness of what yer doing ye'll be hanged for."

Da looked down and said to his bowl, "What would ye have us do, Ishbel?"

"I understand now, even if ye dinna, that times are changing," she said slowly. "This poor country life is doomed. When there's a flood coming, ye have to move to higher ground. It's that or be drowned."

Da looked up and said quietly, "Ye want me to leave this land my family has lived on for generations?"

She nodded, gazing straight into his eyes. "Yes, Murdo. Leave their graves behind before ye join them."

I held my breath, and I could hear Lachlan doing the same. The fire in the hearth too seemed to stop burning for the moment.

"Ye speak easily of abandoning graves when ye have nane to leave," Da said.

Ishbel stood and stacked the empty bowls together with a loud clatter. "Yer wife was my cousin, and dinna ye forget it. I have graves here as well. But there's places we can go while we've still got a choice and not lying in our own dirt."

I suddenly remembered what Josie had said to me. "Do ye mean going to the New World?" I burst out.

"Nae such nonsense," said Ishbel. "I mean the cities—Glasgow, Aberdeen. There's work to be had for those with willing hands."

Lachlan snorted. He knew what Da's answer would be before it was spoken. As did I.

"Locked up behind brick walls, laboring all day out of sight of the sun, and all for another man's profit?" Da's tone would have withered an oak tree.

"And what profit do ye expect to find here?" Ishbel demanded sharply.

He glared at her. "There's profit in the old ways, of a man plowing the fields that his father and grandfather plowed before him. Of putting my hand on the trunk of a great tree that I planted as a boy. Of knowing that my sons will visit my grave after I am gone."

"It's nae longer yer choice, Murdo," she said in a sudden quiet voice. "The laird's mind is set."

"We'll see tomorrow," Da answered grimly. "We'll take the bloody sheep to the poxy laird and find out how set his mind really is. But we'll do it gently." He slammed the flat of his hand down on the table. "And that is that." Da turned and walked out of the cottage, leaving Lachlan and me to face Ishbel alone.

But she turned her shining eyes to the hearth and said simply, "Go after him. I'll no be having him going to the laird's in the morning hung over from angry drinking."

So we went.

9 🙠 THE RAID

Da didn't get drunk, nor did we follow him far, only to the kirkyard, where we heard him talking to Ma in her grave. A small cross marked the spot, still looking fresh amid so many moss-covered stones, with the kirk looming black against the darkening sky. Da went down on one knee, a hand touching his brow.

We stood back and didn't eavesdrop. There are times when a man's sons have to leave him alone. Besides, we each had our own times talking to Ma. Mine mostly took place in the morning once or twice a month, after my chores. Usually after Da had had at my backside with his belt.

When we went back to the cottage, we spoke no more about what had been said. I think we all longed for the morning and action.

The morning was overcast, three layers of clouds crowding the sky and all of them threatening rain. My stomach churned as if a battle were being fought there. I had grown up on the tales of clan cattle raids and border skirmishes, battles against the redcoats and the bloody great wars. It was never the victory that mattered, only a man's courage, we were told, mostly because though we Scots managed to win a few battles, we rarely won the wars.

Yet as we marched out the door, sticks in hand, I wondered: Had any of my ancestors felt the way I did at this moment? Had their bellies turned like butter in a churn as they went on their way to the fight?

Lachlan seemed to be taking everything in his stride as we followed Da down to the crossroads. Crows followed us as we went, crossing and recrossing overhead and commenting on everything below.

I said to Lachlan, "Bad sign," pointing up at the black birds, but Lachlan only laughed.

"Cheer up, Roddy!" he said, slapping me on the back. "This is going to be a rare lark."

"Lark, not crow?" I said through parched lips. "And if it all goes wrong, I'll be the one taking the blame."

"Oh, dinna carry on so," he told me cheerily, waving his stick. "The notion was already hanging in the air. Like an apple on a tree ready for the picking. Only it was you that plucked it."

Thinking of apples tart off the tree set my stomach roiling again. Which made me think about the meager breakfast I'd managed. Those few spoonfuls of porridge weighed me down as if I'd eaten a sack of neeps. I set my lips together and looked away.

At the crossroads, with a small raw wind rising and a sky threatening rain, we met up with the men and boys of our village.

"A good day for battle," Colin called out, holding his stick in the air. He was wearing a blue bonnet on his head, the kind our grandfathers had worn when they marched behind the prince to fight the English. It made his bony face seemed skull-like in the dawn's half-light. "A great day for battle."

"Aye," Da said. "Grey."

Colin laughed as if Da had made a joke, and his son, Hamish, laughed with him, but I knew better. Da never joked. Especially about important things.

"All here, then?" Da asked.

"Every man and boy," Tam McBride called out, waving a hand over the crowd.

I looked at the faces I knew so well—two dozen or more—and saw grim determination written across every one. Not a smile among them. The wind blew everyone's hair about and almost snatched Colin's bonnet off. He clamped his hand on top of it and smiled, but there was little mirth in it.

"Then let's go, lads!" Da called.

We marched on up the road three and four abreast, more men rushing to join us as we went. Now a thin sun, like an old copper coin, was peering through the grey clouds. By the time it was shining full on us, I'd begun to sweat with it despite the continuing wind.

Soon we'd gathered nearly half a hundred more men and boys from the neighboring towns. That surprised me. I suppose a call had gone out, as in the old days when the men were roused to battle, but I hadn't heard word of it. Yet still I felt wary. I wondered if they felt as nervous as I, for they were a grim-looking lot.

To lighten the mood, Tam started singing. "A beggar man came o'er yon lea. . . ." His black beard waggled with each word, and the others quickly took up the song.

Lachlan bellowed out the chorus—"Lassie to my tow roo ray!"—in such a tuneless voice, I couldn't help but laugh. When I finally joined in, my stomach felt fine again. There were fifteen or so verses in the song, which took us well over a mile. We followed it with rousing versions of "Johnny Cope" and a round of "Maggie Lawder" as well, and so we passed over the hills.

As we neared Glendoun—a solid wave of men—we were spied by a solitary shepherd. He almost dropped his staff as he turned and ran down into the valley. Probably going to warn his companions.

Da raised a hand to bring us to a halt. "Once we march over that hill," he said, pointing to the spot where the shepherd had disappeared, "there'll be nae turning back. That's where we'll be rounding up the sheep. It's illegal to touch the laird's sheep, as ye all know well enough, even if our excuse is that we are bringing them to him. So, if there's any who want to leave, do it now. After that, we are all in it together, for curse or cure."

There was a gruff murmur of agreement and a slow nodding of heads. No one made a move to go back. We were Highlanders, after all. Cattle and sheep raids were in our blood.

"Good, then," Da said. Then he and Tam McBride ordered us to spread out in a long line just an arm's length apart. It made us look like an army lined up for a charge. Though some army we were, with nae sword nor musket in sight.

Then up the slope we went, keeping our line, all chatter quieted, all songs fled.

I nodded at Lachlan, at Hamish, at the other boys I knew, but didn't whisper any encouragement. It felt like the moment before battle, and I was now cold as ice but hot too.

When we overtopped the hill, we saw the sheep spread out below us, drifting about in small knots, like eddies in a snowy sea. If we were a hundred, they were a thousand, but we'd come to make them work for us, not against us, to turn the tide of their coming. One or two turned their black faces up to have a look at us, but the rest kept cropping the grass.

The shepherds who retreated to the far side of the glen clung tightly to their staffs, as though their flimsy shafts of wood lent them some authority. A bearded fellow, short and stocky, raised his staff at us as if firing a musket, then Colin laughed and pointed at him, and he lowered it again. We were far too many for them to fight, and they did the right thing by keeping away from us. No need to suffer a broken head for another man's property. Besides, they could identify us later to the sheriff and his men.

Down we went, our line curving in to keep the flocks contained, driving them together into one bleating band. As we closed in, the sheep swayed this way and that, like water sloshing in a tub. For all their size and richness of fleece, they were no cleverer than our own animals and just as easy to drive. A great heaving sea of sheep.

The sheepdogs looked puzzled, keeping their distance and growling deep in their throats. Still, without encouragement from their masters, without a whistle and a shout to guide them, they didn't dare move. They were too well trained to go out on their own.

Lachlan and I were standing by Da when one of the shepherds shouted at us. I could hardly hear his voice above the bleating sheep.

"This is no more than stealing!" His voice was raw and flat, an English voice, not a Scot's.

Da faced the man squarely and shouted back, "We're taking them to our laird's house," he said. "How can that be stealing?"

The shepherd's large jaw gaped open. He hardly knew what to answer. Taking several giant steps forward, he waved his fist at Da and called out, "You'd best keep those beasts safe. Any one of them is worth more than the whole gang of you!"

I gave a sharp snort of laughter. Imagine saying that a sheep was worth more than a man. "We'll keep them safe," I answered him, "safer than ye'll be if ye follow us."

Lachlan laughed, but Da frowned at me. "Dinna let yer tongue keep running away," he warned. "There's nae sense in stirring up more trouble than there's need for."

He was right, of course. I must have still had the Rogue's spirit in me. Or that terrier.

"Aye, ye dinna know what ill will might come back to haunt ye later," added Tam. As he spoke, a sudden wind whistled down the valley, spooking the sheep. They ran about in frantic circles, their black faces all alike, blank and white-eyed, bleating in chorus. I should have taken it as a warning.

But in my heart I couldn't regret my words. Already this felt like a victory: the English shepherds who were trying to take the land from us had been reduced to a cowering band of helpless watchers.

The sheep milled about like bugs under a tipped-over rock, running about without reason. But sheep are like that. Any little thing can spook them. Some men are like that too, I have come to learn.

Then the wind left as quickly as it had arrived, and we rounded up the sheep once again, driving them northward, leaving the shepherds behind us to snarl and sputter in frustration, more like dogs than the dogs themselves. There were additional flocks farther up the glen and we gathered them up as well, too many for counting. We were an army now, marching against the laird, who thought less of us than the sheep we were driving to his yard.

10 ⅋ A DEAL

ventually the Lodge came into view on our left, and I thought about all I had seen inside it—the pictures and the soft cushions on chairs, the rooms opening up one after another. I was suddenly struck with how rich it all seemed.

The Glendoun folk who had taken refuge there waved at us from the yard and cried out cheers. We called back to let them know what we were about, and some of the men joined us in our herding. Lachlan looked about for Laughing Johnny or Big Dunc and especially for the beautiful Fiona, but none of them were there.

Coming out the front door, Bonnie Josie peered curiously at us. I might have heard her laugh, but I wasn't sure. It was hard to hear anything over the bleating sheep, upset at having left their grazing land, and the cheers of the Glendoun folk.

I wanted to go up and talk to Josie, but Da would surely have disapproved, reminding me that I needed to behave like a man who was about serious business, not a boy playing a game.

Then the widow appeared at her daughter's shoulder, shook her head and retired indoors, as if afraid of an approaching storm. And perhaps she was right to do so. For we were gathering like bad weather over the mountains and bringing it down on the laird's head. Bleating bad weather and a storm of white sheep.

• • •

As we neared Kindarry, some of the laird's men stepped into
our path and made a feeble effort to block our way. But the sheep
surged around them, as sheep will, and as the men tried to struggle
toward us, they looked like swimmers floundering in a fast river.
Eventually they gave up, shaking their fists and falling back, till
they were driven right to the door of the laird's grand house.

The house itself, with its high tower and steep grey walls and
many open windows, looked astonished by this invasion, a gentleman set upon by a gang of raggedy beggars.

I could see servants at the lower windows pointing their fingers.
One young maid—perhaps she was Annie Dayton, who'd given
Rood such a hard time—held her hand over her mouth, as if trying
to muffle her laughter.

In an upstairs window, a pair of shutters was suddenly thrown
open and a pale face peeped out. He must have thought it had
snowed in the night, for the grounds about Kindarry House were
now covered with white sheep.

"Look!" Lachlan cried, pointing. "It's the laird."

We greeted him with a raucous cheer. But Da cut us short with
a reminder. "We are doing this politely, lads. Honey, no vinegar."

All at once, Willie Rood appeared around the side of the house,
his face flushed, cudgel in hand. His beady eyes swiveled from side
to side and he stepped warily, as if all these sheep might really be
wolves in disguise.

"What's this?" he spluttered. "Thievery?"

There was a sound like thunder, and it took me a moment before I realized it was our laughter echoing off the hills.

Da stepped forward. "Only honest men would come and stand

before ye like this. Bringing the sheep back is no stealing." His voice raised well above the bleating sheep.

That's when the laird called down at last. "The world is corrupted indeed if you are what pass for honest men." He glared at us. "Get rid of them, Rood."

Rood looked from us to his master, then back again, his feet shuffling as if he didn't rightly know how to proceed. We were too many for him. At heart, I guessed, he was a coward. He shook his cudgel. Suddenly a large ewe barged into him and he was knocked off balance.

It was so funny, I began to laugh, and Lachlan after me. The laughter spread throughout our men.

Rood began to tremble with anger. He hated to be made mock of. "Return to yer villages!" he commanded, though there was little conviction in his voice. "Leave the bloody sheep in the pen over there." He pointed to a large enclosure across the road and some hundred yards from the house. "We'll settle this business at a later date."

"We'll settle it now," Da said firmly.

Tam MacBride took a step forward and raised his hand toward the laird in the window. "We offer ye a choice between sheep and men," he shouted up to the laird. His black beard waggled fiercely, and he did all but shake his fist at the window, which had not been our plan at all. Soft talk and cozening was what we were to do. We were to be polite. But it was clear matters had gone too far, and Tam no longer remembered the plan. "If ye have any care left for the men of your clan, who supported the McRoys for as long as they held the land, give us back our animals that ye have penned up. Give us back our livelihood."

In answer, the sheep began to baa again and stamp their feet restlessly.

"This is an outrage!" the laird spluttered. "I'll not be spoken to like that in my own home. Be off or I'll call out the militia and have you all dragged off to gaol at Fort William."

"The sheep too?" someone called out, to a chorus of chuckles.

The laird narrowed his eyes. Then he leaned out the window, and his voice dropped threateningly. "You'll not laugh when there's a musket in your face and you stand before the gallows!"

That shut us up, though not the sheep.

After a long moment, Da spoke up again, his voice sweeter than Tam's. "We've no come here to do harm. All we ask for is what is just."

"The law will decide that, Macallan," spat Willie Rood, waving his cudgel again. For all his loud talk, though, he kept his distance.

"Well," said a light, cheerful voice, "it's a long while since the Kindarry men came to pay their respects to their laird like this."

I turned and saw Josie on her horse. She'd set out so quickly, she was without a saddle and sitting a-straddle. Her beaming face was in sharp contrast to the menacing mood hanging over us. As she moved toward us, the sheep opened up a path for her.

"Respect is the last thing on their minds," her uncle shouted at her from his window.

Josie's horse moved a step backward as if the laird's loud voice startled him, but she kept her seat, even though one ram leapt up and knocked into another. Calmly, Josie answered, "If I understand rightly, Uncle, these sheep have been brought here as a service."

Rood rounded on her sharply, hardly disguising his malice. "What are ye talking about?"

This time the horse moved forward, crowding into Rood, who

was forced to step aside, right against a huge black-faced ewe. There was a ripple of laughter from all of us at that. His cheeks and nose turned a bright red.

"Well," said Josie innocently, "it's my understanding that the sheep wandered from their pastures and strayed onto the farmland of these people, causing great damage to their crops."

I looked at Lachlan, who looked at Da, who turned and stared, astonished, at Josie. Josie winked at him.

"Nobody's said that," said the laird.

"Not yet," said Josie, turning back and smiling at him. "You didn't give them time, Uncle. But there's enough men here that, if they all swore to it, you'd be hard put to deny them."

The laird quirked an eyebrow. "Oh, *would* I?"

"Especially," she said, waving her hand at all of us, "as the good people of your clan have done you the great kindness of bringing the lost sheep here to you."

"You'll not spite me with a lie," called down the laird.

This time Josie's horse stood its ground and the sheep stopped moving about as well.

"It's no lie if enough people swear it's true." Josie turned again on the horse's back and looked at us. At me.

"That's right," I called out. "I'll swear to it. Why, the sheep were all over our fields, rooting up the potatoes and chewing the barley. Is that no right, Da?"

Da hesitated. He never liked to tell a lie. He thought it against God's express word. "I suppose it might be said," he murmured, just loud enough to be heard.

"It's a scandal!" old Fergus cried out. "Those beasts running wild all over. If the shepherds canna control them, the woolly invaders should be driven off."

"Aye, there's nae place for them in our gardens," Colin added.

More voices rose, a hubbub of agreement. The sheep answered back. For a moment it looked as if chaos would overcome us.

Then Josie raised her hand for silence. It was as if she'd cut off the noise with a knife. Only the horse made a sound, a soft blubbing with its lips. And a couple of lambs bleated plaintively.

"I'm sure nobody here wants to drag this business before a magistrate," she said. "Isn't that right, Uncle?"

"This is an outrage!" the laird fumed. "You've stirred up twice the trouble there was before you came, young lady."

"Not at all," Josie answered him mildly. "I've come to bring harmony. After all, Uncle, what do you want but to see these sheep safely grazing while you collect your profit from their owners? And what do these good people here want other than to work their land in peace?"

He growled so loudly at that, we could all hear him. Then he shouted down, "It's not their land; it's *mine*."

"Common law says that when they have given service to their laird when asked, it is their land as long as they farm it, Uncle." Behind her, we all stirred but kept silent. Even the sheep.

"And what is your point?"

She smiled sweetly up at him. "Oh, Uncle, I am so glad you asked. My point is simple. Take the sheep and give these people back their cattle. Then no one is the loser."

The laird's eyes flitted from Josie to the clansmen to the sheep and back to Josie again. Clearly, he was weighing up where his advantage lay, whether he should hold a strong line against us and possibly start a riot that could ruin his house and grounds. Or he could give way now and bide his time. He probably guessed we had enough of the spirit of our forefathers that we could easily turn this into a fight. Indeed, I could hear the murmurs urging such a thing all around me. Colin was once again saying something about a good day for a battle, and even Da was agreeing. There was no doubt that the numbers were on our side. The murmurs grew louder till I was sure they could be heard up at the laird's window. The skin on the hindquarters of Josie's horse seemed to ripple as if the horse knew what might happen too.

At last an oily smile spread across the laird's pasty face. "There's no call for all this rancor," he said. "At root we've all the same interests at heart, whatever harsh words might have been spoken."

"So," said Josie, "do you agree, Uncle, to a fair exchange to end this trouble?"

"I've never sought trouble," he answered smoothly. "All I want is to ensure the future of the estate."

"Then release these people's livestock," said Josie, "and let's all part as friends."

"Friends," he echoed with a thin, humorless smile. A smile that I distrusted. "Yes, a man can never have too many friends. Especially at home. Mister Rood, release those beasts."

Willie Rood's face looked like a pigskin pumped full of blood and ready to burst. It was easy to guess his thoughts. He wanted to lash out and hurt somebody, but his cowardly nature held him back, as well as the laird's orders. So he ground his teeth as fiercely as if chewing on a bone. Then he walked over the road to the enclosure where our animals were penned and opened the gate.

Our cow Nettle was the first out, followed by a motley assortment of skinny cattle, straggly Highland sheep, and bony goats, none of them as well fed or cared for as the black-faced sheep we'd brought back to the laird. We walked over to meet them, grinning broadly, as if greeting long lost relations.

"Keep those animals clear of the garden!" Rood bellowed.

For a moment I didn't know if he meant us or the livestock. Then I saw one of the Cheviots butt open the gate of the laird's rose arbor. A servant hurried to shoo it away and it backed off, bleating indignantly.

"See that these sheep are returned to Glendoun," the laird commanded his men. Then he turned a thin smile down on Josie. "I guarantee you they will not stray again."

His word held more than a hint of menace, and it was as if a cloud passed over Josie's face. But she quickly shook it off and beamed back at the laird. If I was to guess, I think she was delighted to have beaten her uncle. But I also think she wanted to encourage us Highland folk, who had also caught the threatening edge of his words. Then she hauled on her horse's mane to make it back up.

"Come, lads!" Da called over the sound of the animals. "Let's take our beasts home."

Lachlan and I went to either side of Nettle, a hand each on her flanks. I gave her an encouraging pat and Lachlan clicked his tongue against the roof of his mouth to get her moving. Nothing could spoil the triumph of the moment. Not Rood's stormy face nor the laird's bitter commands.

As we herded our animals down the road, Tam broke into "The Hielandmen Cam Doon the Hill," and we joined him in uproarious chorus. The sun was already lying easily on the top of the mountains, streaking the sky with oranges and reds. Laughter filled the air, of men content with themselves and what they had achieved.

"Aye, we showed him," Lachlan said to me. "Him and his dirty man, Rood."

"Aye, we did," I said, laughing. I turned to look back at the rooftop of Kindarry House slipping out of sight. I was not such a child to think there would be no consequences of the day. But it was a win for now, no doubt.

Da called to the others as we drove our animals along. "Well done, lads. He knows now we mean business." His voice sounded light and happy.

Still, I guessed the insult would rankle in the laird's dark heart. Sooner or later he would strike back. Rood too would not soon forgive our mockery. But would it be at Josie they would hurl their anger or at us clansfolk? I could not take the measure of it, so I put it out of mind as we walked the way home.

11 ❧ FEAST

That night, in a meadow on the south side of the village, we celebrated as our clansmen did after a battle, whether in victory or merely survival. It being late spring, the nights were long and grey-white instead of black. Cushie doos called from the low branches, a soft cooing. A small wind, soft and warm, promised that summer would come soon.

Da, along with some of the other men, had slaughtered a cow that was mostly past milking age, and it was roasting merrily over a bonfire. The meat was passed around with slices of crusty bread to dab in the gravy, and every villager got a share. Lachlan and I ate up hungrily. I decided battle is hard work, even if it is only a battle of words. Besides, it had been some time since I had had beef, and the gravy dripped down my chin. I wiped it off with a finger and sucked that finger dry.

Angus McDonnell played his fiddle, and his son was on the small pipes. And if they were not entirely in tune, we were used to them. They made such a racket, the night birds were silent.

"Going up against the laird was worth it for this," Lachlan said, grinning and wiping the grease from his mouth with the back of his hand. Then he gestured to the feast, which took in the music and everything else.

"When did we last eat this well?" I asked through a mouthful of bread.

Lachlan shrugged. Running a crust of the bread around the edge of his wooden bowl, he soaked up the last few drops of gravy. "Maybe we'll do it more often from now on." He popped the bread into his mouth. Lachlan is not a quiet eater. But then, neither am I. "As long as the laird leaves us in peace," he added.

Yet I could not believe that would happen. The laird and Rood were a pair that would pick a scab until it bled.

All around us everyone else seemed just as cheery. And loud. Who could blame them? The meat was rich, the ale was flowing freely. And after years of scraping a bare living off borrowed land, as well as dodging trouble from the laird and the magistrates, we'd finally grabbed hold of our own fates. I think it was that as much as the ale that made everyone so merry.

I watched as the singing and dancing progressed. Even Da and Ishbel had joined in the reels, careless as bairns. Ishbel had a look on her face I rarely had seen. She was smiling dreamily and danc-ing like a lassie with the wind at her heels. Not me. I have two left feet and always make a fool of myself at dances, so I rarely kick up my heels.

Just then Angus and his wife began a jig so wild, they ended up bashing their heads together and falling to the ground on their backsides. The whole village started laughing, a great rumbling sound that echoed off the hills. First Angus and then his wife joined in the laugh, even as they rubbed their aching skulls.

At that, Ishbel turned aside, the smiling look gone. She came over to where I was standing. Glancing at the platters of meat, she began to tut over the waste. "All this food could have lasted a week or more, given a bit of care." She said it loudly, not worrying about who might hear her.

"Leave off yer thrift for a night, woman," Da said, though he was grinning. "Drink some ale and we'll join another reel." He'd clearly already had far too much ale himself. He wiped his mouth with his sleeve, then offered Ishbel his own cup, but she was done with the feast and the dance and pushed the cup away.

"When ye wake up in the morning, Murdo, it will still be the same world ye're living in," she said. "Nothing has been changed by this wee battle with the laird. Better no to face dawn with a pounding head."

Startled, I looked over at Ishbel. In the firelight her face was drawn but handsome except for her mouth, which was always turned down, as if she constantly ate something bitter. But it suddenly came to me, like a holy vision: I agreed with her. *Ishbel was right.* We'd won a battle, but not the war. For folk like us life would always be a struggle, and at every turn defeat might be waiting for us. Defeat, eviction, or burned from our houses. The end of all our hopes.

I turned to tell Lachlan about my insight, but he was already away, off to steal a dance from Agnes Kinnell. I saw him chasing after her as she ran off giggling behind the cottages.

It was then I noticed the Rogue, Dunbar, lurking beyond the firelight. Half a dozen whisky kegs were slung over his shoulder, and he was turning a tidy profit from the men's thirst. Yet he looked neither shamed by his work nor proud of it. Just a man doing a job, cool enough at his shadow work, as whisky and coins kept changing hands.

It occurred to me that it was not Lachlan I should be telling my vision to, but him. Of all the men in the glen right now, he was the one who would understand what I meant. Still, though my head and heart were ready, my feet seemed unable to move. It was as if I'd been bound fast to the ground. Not witchcraft, but a sudden shyness, a fear of seeming silly or stupid or, at fifteen, way too young.

The music of the fiddle and pipes was loud all around me, but I seemed in the still center of it. And then Dunbar looked up and over, catching sight of me just standing there, staring at him. He nodded. Like a spell breaking, that nod gave me the nerve to go over and speak to him.

By the time I reached him, he was hunched over, lighting his pipe by the side of a gorse bush. The first puff of smoke caught me right in the face, making me cough, which brought a smile to his lean, weathered face.

"Ye're Murdo Macallan's boy, aren't ye?" he asked, rising up to his full height.

I nodded, still too choked to answer.

"I hear ye were the first to speak up after I left. There's some here that are calling ye 'the Wee Rogue.' "

"I hadna heard that," I managed to whisper.

"Seeing ye here, quiet as a rabbit, it's hard to believe."

I flushed at that and stammered out, "It's—it's good there's something to celebrate at last. A battle won." I was about to go on about the war, but he interrupted me, his face darkening.

"Aye, it's good to celebrate while ye can. But dinna think yon pasty laird will sit still for yer celebrations."

I nodded, for it was what I had already begun to think.

"Nae, in a battle it's only the last charge that counts. This is just the first skirmish."

"Aye, but I'm ready to face the next one."

His face took on an amused look, a different kind of smile lurking about his thin mouth. "Are ye, now."

"Ye'll stand with us, Dunbar, won't ye?" My voice cracked on the last two words.

"Me?" He shook his head vigorously. "I stand with nae man."

"But ye're one of us," I protested.

"I've done my share of fighting, laddie—for King George and the Duke of Wellington. My family is dead. I'm no in the market for another."

I stared at him, suddenly furious and stunned that I had so misjudged him, having all but given him my hand in friendship. The words tumbled out before I could call them back. "Yer a mean-hearted man, Alan Dunbar," I said, "to turn yer back on yer own kind."

He smiled slowly and blew some more smoke my way, but the wind had shifted entirely and the white smoke covered his own face, like a highwayman's mask.

Just then Ishbel caught sight of me talking to Dunbar, and she marched over with her right hand up, ready to scold. But whether it was me or the Rogue she meant her wagging finger for, I didn't know.

"It's bad enough," she began, looking at us both, "that you bring shame to most of the men in this village, Alan Dunbar. But if I catch you around my boys again . . ." She stopped, drew a deep breath, and was about to finish her sentence when the Rogue laughed and put up his hands as if warding off a wild animal.

"Peace, peace," he said. "He's a good boy, Mistress Macallan, and not likely to be made rotten by one like me."

We turned from him and were a half-dozen steps away before I realized that neither she nor I had corrected the Rogue for calling her Mistress Macallan, as if she were married to Da. And that she'd called me one of her own boys. In fact, neither of us mentioned these things again, then or later, even though we walked all the way home together along the darkening lanes.

12 ❧ CHURCH

Next morning was Sunday, and all the villagers set out again for the kirk, which stood on a hill at the opposite end of the glen from Kindarry House. The old laird had let our minister have the Lodge, like a member of the family. But when the laird and the minister died within months of each other, there had been a huge change.

Now at the back of the kirk was a tidy little manse the new laird had built for Mr. McGillivray, the new minister, the same way he built a kennel for his pack of dogs. As Da liked to say, McGillivray acted just like one of the laird's dogs too. Obedient, subservient, wagging his hind end whenever the laird said, "Come by."

Over and over in kirk, I heard Mr. McGillivray tell us to be meek and obedient, like little lambs, and always to remember where our duty lay. In other words, he was telling us to obey the laird in all things, God and the laird being of one mind, evidently. Until this morning, I hadn't given that sermon much thought. A boy may have to go to the kirk every Sunday, but it doesn't mean he has to listen very hard. But now I found myself thinking about the minister and what he would have said had he caught us planning our sheepherding trick in his kirk.

"What do ye think the minister is going to say today?" I whispered to Lachlan as we followed Da and Ishbel. Above us the sky threatened rain.

"Maybe he's no back yet," Lachlan whispered back.

It was clear I wasn't the only one worrying. We all trooped silently into kirk that morning, hoping that one of the elders would take the pulpit instead. But no—there the minister was, sitting by the communion table with his long, drooping face, glowering at all of us as we entered. He straightened the folds of his long black robe and drew himself up like a judge.

I remembered Da once said of Mr. McGillivray that he was better fed, better dressed, and better housed than any of us, though he never looked the happier for it.

Ishbel had answered him, saying, "That man dotes on misery like it was his own wee bairn. He holds it to his breast, then presses it onto all his neighbors."

Our family slid into a middle pew, trying our best not to draw attention to ourselves. Da went first and after him Ishbel, then Lachlan, then me. When I glanced at Mr. McGillivray, he was scowling as usual, as if heaven held a special place for sour folk.

It seemed to me he always kept his darkest face for my family, and whenever the sermon turned to "sins of the flesh," his voice would grow sharper as he looked our way, his eyes boring into Ishbel's till she was forced to look down at her feet. It was the only time I felt sorry for her. Once I even reached over and took her hand in mine, and she shook it off with such ferocity, I never tried that again.

Da had explained to the minister more than once that he and Ishbel did not live as man and wife, and so there was no sin involved. She had just come to take care of her deceased cousin's sons, as a family duty, and that was the end of it. But Mr. McGillivray obviously thought otherwise, and he never tired of reminding us of it. Which made Lachlan and me wonder somewhat too.

I remembered one Sunday afternoon, after the service, when we were home for our Sunday meal, Ishbel had said to Da, "Would it no be easier if we just got married? I'm sick of those looks Mr. McGillivray gives me in kirk. And he's no the only one." Her voice sparked, but her eyes were puffy as if she was ready to weep.

"Other people's looks are a poor reason for marrying," Da had answered her. "And even if they weren't, who's to say I'd want to marry ye?"

There was a sharp intake of breath from Ishbel, but she didn't answer back immediately.

Lachlan and I kept our heads down as they talked, but we didn't stop listening.

Then Ishbel said softly, "And why shouldn't ye want to marry me?" She turned and stamped about the kitchen, touching things as if making them tidy when in fact they needed nothing of the sort. First the pot hanging over the fire, then clooties slung over a rack to dry. "Am I no bonnie enough?"

"I've seen bonnier and less bonnie too."

Lachlan snorted at that but with his hand before his face, so they couldn't hear.

Ishbel whipped around, hands on her hips. "Is there anything a good wife should do that I can't?"

"If I think on it long enough, something will come to mind," Da said, looking into his bowl.

Ishbel huffed and served up our dinner with a great clattering of plates and cups. After that neither one of them brought up the question of marriage for a good long while.

So there we were in the kirk, with the dour-faced Mr. McGillivray glaring at us and scowling at Ishbel. Abruptly he rose and announced that we would sing one of the psalms: "The Lord Is My Shepherd," which everybody sang even more slowly than usual, as if to put off the awful moment of the sermon.

As the droning singing finally tailed off, Mr. McGillivray climbed into the pulpit like a hangman mounting the gallows. I shrank back against the pew as he went up. Casting a stern eye over the congregation, as if each and every one of us was marked for death, Mr. McGillivray began.

"There are some here today as are feeling mightily pleased with themselves."

I glanced at Lachlan, and he was nodding. Of course he was pleased. I was pleased. We all were pleased.

"Well," snapped Mr. McGillivray, "the pleasures of a wicked man are poison to the soul, and his pride is a trap waiting to swallow him whole."

I slunk down even farther in my seat, as did Lachlan. Farther down the pew, Da seemed to shrink in size. There couldn't have been a bigger contrast to the night before, when we had been excited and happy and full of fun. When we had been a large family, a clan.

The minister continued on, speaking with grim relish, telling us that we were no good, an unhappy, doomed lot. He shook his right fist and leaned over the pulpit, hissing at us, "Ye'll be the last in line when the blessed troop into paradise."

I felt first cold, then hot. I could hardly sit still.

"In fact," McGillivray rumbled from his perch, "ye sinners of the glen are much more likely to be headed the opposite way from paradise." He twisted his head so sharply to the left I was afraid his neck might snap. "The other way," he repeated. "And in hell there's no dancing and drinking. Instead your feet will burn on red-hot coals, and blazing pitch will be your liquor."

We darted guilty glances at one another, all wondering the same thing: Who had told on us? One of our own? Or Willie Rood? Or perhaps Mr. McGillivray, all unseen, had himself found a way to spy on our feast?

"What an ungrateful, wicked flock ye are," he roared, shaking his fist down at us.

When Mr. McGillivray referred to us as a flock, I knew he really meant it. To him we were sheep to be kept on the straight and narrow path. We were to be guided into a well-guarded pen from which we could never escape till we were fleeced and eaten for mutton. He had told us that over and over in other sermons. I expect he believed we would listen to him. But now? Now we had broken out, run wild over the hills, chewed the clover of our master's garden. Mr. McGillivray was not pleased. I didn't know whether to look up and act awed or start to laugh. Or both.

I looked up.

Slowly Mr. McGillivray opened the great Bible on the lectern in front of him. It looked big enough to contain all the sins of the world. Taking a moment to clear his throat, a noise like the distant rumble of an approaching storm, he turned a page. Shook his head. Turned another and stabbed his finger down as if spearing it.

"Got it!" Lachlan said. "That's one Bible verse that willna get away." He whispered it, then put his head down in his hands, but I heard every word. The problem was not to laugh out loud.

"A reading from the Letter of St. Paul to the Romans," Mr. McGillivray announced, pausing briefly to make sure he had our full attention.

Ishbel hissed at Lachlan and dug her elbow into his ribs. "Lift yer head up, ye daft laddie."

Lachlan sat up and looked straight ahead, as did I.

"Let every soul be subject unto the higher powers," Mr. McGillivray pronounced in his groan of a voice. "For there is no power but of God: the powers that be are ordained of God. Whosoever therefore resisteth the power, resisteth the ordinance of God: and they that resist shall receive to themselves damnation. For rulers are not a terror to good works, but to evil." He closed the book with a booming clap and a righteous smack of his lips, as if the words had left a sweet taste in his mouth.

"There's many here should take note of the Lord's word," he said, "for they have raised up their heads in sin and pride when they should have been bowed in humility and obedience." Now he stared down at us, scanning row after row. "Those of ye who stole the laird's sheep—and ye know who ye are—risk damnation now and forever."

I could sense Da tensing, and when I glanced sideways at him, I was shocked to see Ishbel putting her hand on his. And shocked further to see a mischievous smile pasted across Lachlan's face, as if annoying the minister had been the whole point of yesterday's adventure.

Mr. McGillivray's voice droned on. " 'Render therefore to all their dues,' says the Lord. 'Tribute to whom tribute is due; custom to whom custom; fear to whom fear; honor to whom honor.' " He went on, quoting scripture, relating all of it to our recent sins, and the longer he talked, the harder the pew grew beneath me. Soon I was wriggling about like a fish stranded on the deck of a boat.

"Keep still!" Ishbel leaned over and hissed at me.

"But he's talking havers. It was nae like that at all. It was—"

"Shhh! Or it's nae supper for ye tonight."

"In Ephesians," Mr. McGillivray continued with his drone, "St. Paul tells us that servants must be obedient to them that are their masters according to the flesh, with fear and trembling, in singleness of heart, as unto Christ."

By this time, some of the congregation were shuffling their feet in protest. It was as much as they dared. But Da could stand no more. He stood up slowly as if he didn't want anybody to notice. "Come away," he told us quietly. "We're off home."

Lachlan and I rose up with him, and they both got past Ishbel with no trouble. But as I struggled by, she grabbed me by the sleeve and yanked me back down till I was all but sitting in her lap.

"And what's amiss with ye, Murdo Macallan?" Mr. McGillivray demanded sharply to Da's back as he walked down the aisle. "Are ye taken ill?"

Da turned around, though he kept his eyes downcast and his voice low. "I canna bear to listen to any more of this gabble," he answered.

"Aye, because it rankles whatever conscience ye have left," shouted the minister.

"Nae, Minister, because it stokes up a rage in my heart that is out of place in a kirk," Da said, daring to look back at Mr. McGillivray. I could see the rage in his eyes. "We are no lambs to be led to the laird's slaughter. We are men and should be treated as such."

"Then ye can add wrath to yer sins," Mr. McGillivray told him. "And thanklessness. Stiff-neckedness and ingratitude." His head started shaking again on his scrawny neck. No stiff neck for him. "The count now is high, Macallan. Hell is closer than you know."

I pulled myself free of Ishbel's grasp and stood up. My tongue was suddenly like a dog off its leash. "And didna Jesus lose his tem-

per with the moneylenders and drive them out of the temple with a
whip, Minister?" I asked loudly. "Where was the sin in that?"

The minister's eyes blazed with outrage, but before he could
speak, a voice behind me said, "Not a sin, young Macallan, but look
at what happened to Jesus because of it."

All heads turned to see Willie Rood framed in the doorway.
With all that was going on, no one had heard the door open or seen
him come in, and there was an audible gasp that ran around the
church. His piggy face leered at us, and he rubbed the back of his
hand across his nose.

Mr. McGillivray drew himself up to as great a height as he could
muster and puffed out his thin chest. "Laird's man or no, I'll not
tolerate any blasphemy in this church, Mr. Rood," he said.

Rood smiled as he doffed his head in apology. "I was just drawing a lesson for your flock."

"What are you doing here, Willie Rood?" Hamish demanded.
"A kirk's a queer place to find you, even on a Sunday."

"Usually my business takes me elsewhere," said Rood, "but
happily today it brings me right here into your midst."

"This is a place of worship, not business," said the minister,
flushing.

"Today they coincide," said Rood. He pulled a document out of
his pocket and held it aloft so everybody could see. "This is a notice
of eviction," he said. "All of you are to be out of Dunraw and off the
laird's land by noon tomorrow to make way for the new tenants."

"Tenants?" Da roared. "What tenants?"

Willie Rood's eyes laughed. He opened his mouth and said,
"Baaaaaaaa . . ."

13 ☙ BURNING

I fell into sleep that night as if hit on the head with a cudgel, and I dreamed the entire time. Nightmares, I think, though I remembered none but the last of them, for when I awoke, it was to a worse nightmare than any I had dreamed.

In that final dream, I heard a pounding on the roof of the cottage, a deep, soft sound like bales of hay being dropped from the clouds. I sat up on my pallet and looked around. Lachlan and Da hadn't stirred, and I could hear Ishbel's sleepy breathing from behind the rough blanket that separated her from us.

I got up and in my nightshirt walked out the door to see that the ground was covered in hilly folds of light, fluffy snow. More snow was coming down, falling as quick as water, and soon it was up to my knees. I tried to take a step, but my legs were as weighed down as if I were standing knee-deep in mud. Twisting about, I looked back at the cottage, which was completely enveloped in the snow and looked like a huge, white haystack. Da, Lachlan, and Ishbel would be trapped inside and freeze to death while they slept. I could feel my heart stutter in my chest. They had to be warned.

I tried to call out to them, but my voice was frozen and the words fell out of my mouth in chunks of ice. Now the snow was up past my shoulders. I tried to struggle free, but it was no use. The white tide rose up over my head, and as it did so, the snow turned a deadly black. I coughed and spluttered, trying to suck in breath, but it was like drowning. So I shoved my arms through the drifts, trying to swim, but the darkness grew thicker, and my belly and lungs were turning to ice. I wondered as I died if I would wake up in hell.

Then I felt someone grab me, pull me up toward the light. I woke up, gasping, with Ishbel's hand on my shoulder, shaking me awake.

"Up ye get!" she was saying. "There's work to be done."

I wondered groggily how I could be expected to work when I was dead. Then I smelled porridge cooking over the fire and realized I was alive and at home. Lachlan was already hauling on his breeks so that he could grab the first bowl of porridge, the one that would have the creamiest helping, fresh from the top of the pot.

There was a thin trickle of daylight slipping through the window. As I shook off the dream, the awful reality of this day forced itself upon me, like the glint of a sharpened sword at our throats. We were being evicted. I wondered if I'd dreamed that too.

"Where's Da?" I asked, getting to my feet and struggling into my own shirt and breeks.

"He's already eaten and gone out to gather the cattle," Ishbel answered as she ladled out porridge into two bowls. "We're to be off the land today."

"But we can't just pack up and go just like that," I said, my voice rising as if I were angry with Ishbel and not the laird. "Go just on Rood's say-so. Surely Da wouldna . . ."

"For once yer da is being sensible," Ishbel said, her voice tight as she kept a rein on her anger. She turned from me, bringing the porridge pot back to the fire. "The laird has the law on his side, as rich men always have." Her shoulders went up in a shrug.

"And he has the soldiers too," Lachlan added.

Ishbel turned, looked at me, her voice softening. "Sit and eat, Roddy. I won't have us going on empty stomachs. Yer ma wouldna have liked that."

"Going where?" Lachlan asked, his mouth now full of porridge, hungrily spooning it down as if it might be his last hot meal, as it very well might be.

Ishbel shrugged but didn't answer. I suddenly realized she knew no more than we did. So I sat down on the bench at the table, and Ishbel plunked a bowl of steaming porridge in front of me. I added salt and a spot of milk and waited for the porridge to cool. Unlike Lachlan, who ate his burning hot, I liked mine almost cold.

"There's no foretelling what will happen," said Ishbel, "but we need to be ready for whatever comes." She brushed a strand of red hair back from her high forehead and sighed. "Yer da and some of the other men were talking last night after the two of ye were in bed. Something about holding on here while they make an appeal to the magistrate."

"An appeal to the magistrate could take weeks," said Lachlan through a mouthful of porridge. "And there's no saying it will come to anything."

Ishbel nodded. "Yer da knows that, which is why we're to be packed anyway. Some magistrates go by the law and some by their friendships with the laird. We have to be prepared for either."

"But Ishbel . . . ," I began, sick to my stomach that Da should give in so easily. I pushed the bowl away from me.

"Eat up, Roddy," Lachlan urged me. "Ye'll need yer strength for the road ahead."

I was stunned to hear *him* accept defeat, Lachlan, who'd always been the one to thumb his nose at authority. Talking about the road ahead when we should have been planning how to fight. I shook my spoon at him. "Ye'll not quit so easy over this, will ye? Remember how we chased the sheep, how we marched on Kindarry?"

He bent his head low over the bowl, scraping up the last spoonful of porridge. "That was a lark, a boys' game, Roddy. Battling the law's something else. A poor man has nae chance there."

I still hadn't eaten a drop, and now I slammed my spoon down angrily on the table. "If the law's only for the rich, then why should we not all be outlaws? Like the Rogue?"

"Wheesht and eat yer breakfast," said Ishbel, pushing the bowl back at me. "There is nae sense in arguing. At least no before ye've eaten."

But Lachlan had the bit between his teeth now and carried on doggedly. "A man knows when to quit the field, Roddy. When the war is lost. Believe me, ye'll not want to be left behind."

I spooned up some porridge. It was still hotter than I liked, but I ate it anyway, in one quick swallow. It burned going down, and I swear it set my heart on fire too, so I set the spoon aside. "I never reckoned ye for such a fairdie, brother!"

Lachlan pushed away his empty bowl and glowered at me. "A fairdie, am I?" He pointed his finger at me. "Look what's happened to ye already. Don't ye think Willie Rood would be glad of another crack at yer stubborn skull?"

"There's still Bonnie Josie to stand against him," I said. Somehow even saying her name seemed to give me courage. "She'll take our side for sure."

"Have ye no heard?" said Ishbel. "Nae—how could ye? The widow's took sick. Josie's only care now is to tend her mother night and day and bring her as much comfort as she can."

My mouth dropped open. I forced it shut with my right hand.

"All the more reason for us to stay," I muttered. "We shouldna leave her to the laird's mercy, nor to Rood's."

"Worry what mercy they'll have on us," said Ishbel sharply. "We've no kinship nor title to guard us. Your Bonnie Josie will do just fine. The rich always do. Now eat up before I force that good porridge down yer throat, for I'll not have it thrown away."

I gave Lachlan a last glower, and he gave back as good. Then standing, he went over to the basin to splash off his face. I ate up the porridge, my anger having made me hungry. Yet even when I'd finished, there was still a pain gnawing at my stomach. *We can't just run off and leave our homes to the laird's fat sheep,* I thought. *Surely Da won't stand for that.*

Lachlan snatched up his bonnet and opened the door, but Ishbel called him up sharply. "Where do ye think you're going, Lachlan Macallan?"

"I'm going to help Da," he answered.

"He's no need of yer help. Yer to stay here and help me pack our belongings."

"Och, taking care of the house is woman's work," said Lachlan, stepping outside. "Roddy will stay and help ye."

"You're not leaving me to that!" I called. Dodging around Ishbel, I dashed out after him. I was surprised to find he'd come to a stop right outside the cottage. He was frowning and sniffing at the air.

"What's fashin' ye?" I asked.

"Can't ye smell it?"

I sniffed and knew at once. There was a bitter tang to it, the wind blowing it north to the other end of the glen. We hadn't a chance of smelling it till we were outside of the cottage's thick walls, but here the reek was unmistakable. I leaned out and saw a plume of smoke rising against the sky and below it a flicker of flame where the Kinnells' cottage stood.

"A fire?" I said. "But what would anybody be burning this time of morn?"

"Look!" Lachlan exclaimed, pointing.

There was a small group of figures hurrying toward us.

"It's Hamish Kinnell and his family!" I said as they drew closer. They were our closest neighbors.

"God help us!" I heard Ishbel gasp. Only then did I realize she was standing behind us, staring in horror.

The Kinnells gave us no greeting but made to hurry past, their faces pale and their eyes wide, as if a mad hound was snapping at their heels.

"Hamish," Lachlan cried out, for they were best of friends. He reached out a hand to them.

But Hamish, his parents, and his grandfather had only a few belongings slung over their shoulders, though the aging grandfather was really as much baggage as they could manage.

"What's happened?" Ishbel asked.

Hamish's mother was too distressed to speak, his father too burdened with the grandfather, so Hamish spoke for them all. They went on down the road for a moment without him. He spoke quickly, his words galloping into one another.

"The laird's men came at dawn with Rood at their head and rousted us out of bed by flinging a torch into the house. You'd best run while you have the chance. If we go back, they said they'll throw *us* in the fire. Not that there's anything left to go back to." He nodded at Lachlan, a swift farewell, and was gone after his family.

"I thought we had till noon at least," Ishbel called after him, but none of the Kinnells answered back. They were too set on escaping the men who had set torches to their home.

And now we could see those very men. They were striding down the glen toward us with flaming torches and cudgels in their hands. Marching with dogged determination, they looked as if they were in no hurry to be done with their foul work.

"Right—grab what you can!" Ishbel ordered us.

"But what about Da?" Lachlan objected. "We have to warn him."

"He'll know what's happening soon enough. All he has to do is look up at the sky," Ishbel said. She pointed, and when I looked up, the morning sky was already dark with smoke as if the laird had turned day into night. "He'll find his own way to us," she added. "Now hurry!"

She pushed me inside and started making bundles of clothes. I gathered up my own few things, but inside, I was dying to make a stand. That was when I heard Lachlan's voice and rushed outside after Ishbel to see what was going on.

Lachlan had found a stick and was waving it over his head, threatening the laird's men, who were nearly at our house. "Awa'!" he shouted at them as if herding sheep. "Awa'!"

They didn't look a bit frightened. In fact, one of them, a broad-shouldered man with a red beard, even laughed.

"Out of the way, boy!" he ordered. "We've got written leave from the laird to clear this glen of all trespassers."

Ishbel snatched the stick out of Lachlan's hand and tossed it to the ground. "Dinna mind the boy. He's weak in the head." And when Lachlan tried to protest, she hissed at him like an adder before turning back to the laird's men. "Besides, we're nae trespassers." She smiled at them. "This is our home till noontime. We're allowed that at least. Willie Rood's paper said so."

"Yer to be off Kindarry land by noon," the red-bearded man corrected her. The sternness in his face showed that her smile had not moved him a bit. "That's what Willie Rood says, what the paper says. And he's off to tell the laird of our progress. So, ye best stop gabbing and make a start, woman, or be caught trespassing."

Ishbel pushed Lachlan and me away from the men. "Don't give them cause for more trouble than can be avoided," she instructed us. Then she darted back into the cottage to salvage what she could.

As she did so, I tugged Lachlan's sleeve and pointed toward the hillside. Da was charging down toward us, waving his crook, his shirt flapping as he ran. He had seen the smoke in the glen and guessed what was afoot.

"Awa' there!" he yelled. "Awa' from my property!"

As if fate was bringing them together, at the same time Willie Rood came riding up on his horse, back from reporting to the laird, his podgy face wrapped in a smirk.

Da planted himself between Rood and the cottage. "Ye've no right to treat us like this, like tinkers tramping across the land instead of lifelong tenants."

"The law says we do," Rood answered him. He waved his rough-looking crew forward, Red Beard as well as two men with great knife scars on their faces and two more who looked enough alike to be brothers, with the same missing teeth and blue eyes. "We've wasted enough time here."

One of the scarred men started toward the house, thrusting his torch ahead of him.

"Nae, no while I breathe!" Da declared. He passed by Rood with an angry sweep of his crook, making the horse rear up, then grabbed the man with the torch by the arms. They began to struggle and Da, with his righteous anger, seemed to be getting the better of it. Before anyone else could move, Rood had his horse once more under control and spurred it forward, driving it right into Da and knocking both him and his opponent to the ground.

The other four men closed in on the house. The red-bearded man picked up the fallen torch and with it lit the torches of the others.

Lachlan and I tried to stop them, running at them kicking and punching. But they were huge men and too strong for us, simply shoving us aside. Lachlan landed on his arm and I on my bum. As we scrambled to our feet, we could only watch helplessly as Red Beard flung his torch through the window and another man flung his torch through the open doorway.

There was a loud whoosh as the torches landed and began gobbling up anything around them.

"Ishbel!" I cried, suddenly remembering she was inside.

She rushed out with a scream, a bundle under her arm. The fire had caught her skirt as she escaped, and I dived forward, beating out the flame with the palms of my hands.

As soon as she saw Da lying on the ground, Ishbel dropped her bundle and threw herself down beside him. "Murdo!" she cried. "What's happened to ye?"

Rood's scarred man had climbed unsteadily to his feet and was staggering away back up the hill. From the look on his face, he had no more fondness for the factor now than we did.

"Rood rode him down with his horse," said Lachlan, glowering at Rood with clenched fists.

"And it will go even worse with the rest of you if you don't shift yourselves off the laird's property," Rood said with a sneer.

He turned to his men. "Fire the outbuildings too. We'll leave no shelter."

"Can we no gather our animals?" asked Lachlan, his voice suddenly breaking as if he had just realized what was happening.

"They will just slow you down," said Rood. His voice sounded as if he meant this as a helpful comment, but his mouth spoiled that with a smirk. "Trust me, you want to be on your way quickly."

The other scarred man was already leading Rob Roy away.

"Not our horse," I cried.

Rood smirked even more. "Yon beast'll settle yer last month's rent, for all he's only ribs and skin."

I turned and gazed in horror at the fire consuming the inside of the house. The thatch of the roof suddenly ignited, crackling and cackling as if it was enjoying itself. I peered through the open door and could see the wooden beams feeding the hungry flames. It was only a small cottage, cramped, not elegant as Bonnie Josie's house. But it was all we had.

Ishbel picked up her bundle under one arm and with the other helped Da to his feet. He looked dazed and lost, and when he tried to walk, his left leg started to give way under him. Ishbel gave him her shoulder for support, and they started to trudge westward, along the path that the Kinnells had so recently taken.

"Come along, boys," she said. "There's nothing left for us here."

"That's sense," said Rood, "and from a woman too. Ye young villains had best heed her."

My whole body trembled with rage. *What more could happen to me,* I thought, *if I leapt up and dragged Rood off his horse, my fingers closing on his throat?* But I knew better. It would be mad to start a fight now with Da in such a state and all those huge men itching for a fight.

Picking up the few belongings that lay scattered on the ground, Lachlan and I followed Ishbel and Da. I knew we must have looked as broken and fearful as the Kinnells. Still, I couldn't help glancing back and saying a last word to Rood over my shoulder.

"There's more to justice than what's written on yer papers," I said. "A crime is a crime, even if the law says nae."

"I'll bear that in mind when we are banqueting upon your cows and chickens tonight." Rood laughed. "Though I doubt they'll make much of a feast."

I turned away from him, screwing up my eyes against the tears. *It's just the smoke*, I told myself. *Just the smoke*. But a lie, even to oneself, even for pride's sake, is still a lie.

III. ROGUE'S APPRENTICE

Give to me the life I love,

Let the lave go by me,

Give the jolly heaven above

And the byway nigh me.

Bed in the bush with stars to see,

Bread I dip in the river--

There's the life for a man like me;

There's the life for ever.

—Robert Louis Stevenson, "The Vagabond"

With the smoke from a dozen burning farms and steadings making dark clouds foul enough to hide the sun, turning day into dusk, we trudged westward. It was hard going, over steep hills, through tangled gorse, seeking the quickest route away from Rood and his henchmen. I had no doubt he might take it into his head to chase after us, just for sheer wickedness.

To run from danger is one thing, even natural. But it's a terrible thing to have to flee from your own home, the place that's always meant warmth and safety. For the first time I understood the minister's stories of the prodigal son and the lost sheep. It's awful to have no home to go to.

So where *could* we go? The question hung over us like a black cloud heavy with the threat of thunder.

"Just a wee bit farther," Da said to encourage us each time we hesitated.

To anyone watching, we must have looked like a pack of beggars, stooped and weary, with nothing to our name but what we carried on our backs. Ishbel had only managed to pack up some clothes, a jar of porridge oats, some water skins, bread and cheese, and a bit of bedding. The only thing we had to be thankful for was that there was no wind or rain to add to our misery.

After many hours—going slowly down the sloping path because

of Da's injured leg—we took shelter among some rocks at the foot of a craggy hill. Da was still shaken from the blow Rood had given him, and his ribs ached whenever he was breathing hard. Ishbel supported him part of the way, when he lowered his pride enough to lean on her shoulder.

I was puffing and huffing like a lad unused to walking, though only days earlier I could have run down this path without stopping. And Lachlan, who was always up for a lark, was unusually somber and grey as the day.

Were we off Kindarry land yet? We hardly knew. So tired and defeated, we scarcely cared. My feet felt as if we'd walked the breadth of Scotland already just putting ourselves past danger.

Now Da slumped against a mossy rock. It had an overhang, which was just as well, as a wind had started wuthering through the trees. It was way past midday, the birds were quiet, but it was too soon for hares and deer to be out in force. It was as if the whole countryside had stopped still.

Da winced at the pain in his side while reaching gratefully for some food. Ishbel took out some of the bread and cheese from her bundle and tore it into pieces with her bare hands—for none of us had a knife—and then she shared it around. There was not a lot to eat. For drink, we got water with our cupped hands at a near-by burn.

"This bread and cheese won't last beyond tomorrow," Ishbel said apologetically as we swallowed the last of our meager meal.

"There'll be places where we can work for food," said Da, his voice recovered a bit now that we were stopped and fed. "And maybe we can snare a rabbit or two along the way." By *we*, he must have meant Lachlan and me, for he was surely not in any shape to make a snare or capture a rabbit.

"Along the way to where?" Lachlan asked, his face a dark scowl.

Da and Ishbel looked at each other, as if wondering who should answer, if either of them actually had an answer.

"To our new home," Ishbel replied at last. She forced a smile, but there was no happiness in it.

I knew that was no answer at all. We had no new home any- where, nor the money for one. We had no food, no clothes but those on our backs, no . . .

We started on the path again, avoiding the worst of the stones. Lachlan and I went a bit ahead because Da was so slow. We were barely talking at this point, just intent on getting as far from our old home as possible. But after a while, when we looked back, we realized that Da and Ishbel were no longer in sight.

Turning as one, we raced back to find them around the second bend, sheltering under an overhanging tree.

Da was slumped against a rocky cliff face and drinking from a water skin. Ishbel was pressed close to him for warmth.

We sat down with them and tried to pretend that nothing was different, though *everything* was different. We'd lost our house, Da was weak, and Lachlan and I had to be men now.

"Are we going to a city, then?" Lachlan asked, as if we'd been discussing this all along.

Ishbel nodded.

"To Glasgow?" I tried to say the name softly, but still it felt harsh in my mouth.

"Aye," said Ishbel, putting enthusiasm in her voice. "Glasgow will be fine for us. Work in the factories with regular pay, nae scrap- ing a living off a thankless patch of land."

Da turned and glared at her. "Was that life so bad there?" he challenged. "I never heard you complain of it before!"

"What would have been the point?" Her voice was soft. "There was naught else but make do. But now that we have nothing, we must think again, find a way to make a new life, a better one."

"There's nothing better about being locked up in a factory all day working for another man's profit," said Lachlan, his lips thinned down with anger.

"By the time ye find a roof and a bed, ye'll be glad of whatever ye have to do to earn it," Ishbel told him sharply.

"Is that all ye want for these laddies?" Da objected. "That they should slave and toil inside a factory all their days, too tired even to lift their eyes to what's left of the sun as they crawl home to sleep? I'd rather we died right here under the open sky."

Ishbel folded her arms crossly. "Have you something better in mind, then?"

For a moment, Da was silent, grinding his teeth, though whether against the pain or Ishbel's words, I couldn't say. All this talk was like a knife severing us, one from the other.

Suddenly there was a sound from up the path a ways, and Lachlan and I stood up, to take positions in front of Da, in case Rood and his men were tracking us. But seconds later, a little rabbit hopped down the path. We broke into laughter, and the startled rabbit raced over the far side of the cliff.

I let out a breath and looked around. This was as good a place for our night's sleep as any. The road wound down the glen, but under the overhang we could keep out of the worst of the wind. And if it should rain, the tree and its heavy roots would shelter us from that as well.

I was about to suggest this when Da ran a hand over his beard.

He often did this when thinking. At last he said, "We'll take a ship to America."

"To America? For what?" Ishbel's face was grey as the rock behind Da's back.

"To find land again, land that's all our own this time, not rented from some grasping laird." Da smiled grimly.

Ishbel laughed and tossed her head like a young girl. "They're no giving land away for free, no even in America. Nor do they give away passage there for the asking."

I looked at Lachlan, and he stared at the ground.

"Lachlan," I whispered, "what do you want to do?"

He shrugged. That was so unlike him, I felt defeat for the first time, like a weight upon my back.

Da pulled out a small leather purse and shook it, jingling the coins inside. "I've been saving what money I could," he said, "and I've kept it by me always." It didn't sound like much was there.

"Will it be enough?" Ishbel asked. Her voice was skeptical, but she'd softened. I think the hope in Da's eyes carried her along.

"Martin Murty's cousin Neil left for America four years past," said Da, trying his best to sound confident. "He's written Martin to say there's land aplenty, and none of it dear."

"Nae, Murdo, but we'll need food and furnishings, animals and seed," Ishbel said. "Even without paying for the land, there'll be a drain on that poor purse."

"We'll need tickets for the boat trip too," Lachlan added, his voice low.

"We'll make do," Da insisted, "somehow."

Ishbel's shoulders slumped. "I suppose we'll have to trust in God to provide."

"He's no been generous so far," said Lachlan, a bit of spark back in his voice.

Da clipped him lightly across the ear with the back of his hand. "Blasphemy's no way to win His favor, boy."

"There's something yer all forgetting!" I burst out, unable to keep silent any longer. Since I was standing, I had no shelter, and the wind had started up again. I pulled my shirt closer around me, and Ishbel held out one of the blankets she'd managed to bring out of the burning house. I wrapped it about me, and it smelled of fire and ash.

They all turned to face me. Ishbel crossed her arms and frowned. "And what notion do ye have that's beyond our poor wits?"

"There's the Blessing!" They stared over at me in the fading light. "The Blessing," I said again into their doubt. "It would give us all the help we'd need."

From the looks Da and Ishbel gave me, you'd have thought I'd just let out a curse in church.

"Ye coof!" Lachlan gave a high laugh.

Da stood tall, ignoring any pain, and shook his head at me. "I've told ye before to leave off that nonsense, lad!"

Taking a deep breath, Ishbel uncrossed her arms and tried to speak more kindly. "Look, I know it was a pretty story yer ma told the two of ye, Roddy, and it was just the thing to cheer ye as ye were lying abed at the end of a cold day. But that was when ye were wee bairns, and that's all done now. It's haverings, nonsense." She put a hand out to touch my arm. I drew back. "We need to take a hard look at the road ahead, like grown-up folk, and not flinch from it."

In spite of their doubt, I was certain it was me that was talking sense. Couldn't they see that? "But the Blessing . . . ," I began.

The wind chose that moment to whuffle around the rock again, making a ghostly sound, almost as if taunting me.

"Enough!" Da barked at me. Then he fell back against the embankment with a single moan, clutching his ribs.

"Ye see how it is with yer da," Ishbel said. "And ye want him to go back up the glen after a bit of nonsense? And what do ye think Willie Rood might do to us if we dared return?"

I fell silent, racked with sudden guilt. The wind, however, kept howling. I gave Da the blanket, wrapping it tenderly around him, and he said nothing to thank me for it, but he didn't take it off either.

Lachlan chewed on his lip. Then he gave me a sidelong glance. There was that old glint in his eye again, and I thought: *Ye like my idea, brother.* I nodded at him, and he nodded back.

"We'll get a good night's sleep now," Da said, his voice strained. He gestured around the rocks. "These will serve us for the night. We'll need to be well rested for the journey ahead."

"It's no night yet," I protested. Indeed, with the sky cleared of the smoke, it hardly looked to be time for supper.

But the evening chill drew in, and Ishbel passed out another blanket she'd salvaged from the cottage. One for her and Da, one for Lachlan and me. It was amazing what she'd managed to jam into that bundle before leaving the house. If only she'd been able to bring the Blessing along too. But of course she had never seen it, not believed in it, so wouldn't have gone looking for it. But me, I always knew it was there. I'd always known.

"Never mind there are but two blankets," she said. "Ye boys will be warmer if you huddle together under the one blanket."

Lachlan and I needed no second telling. Many a hard winter we'd done as much back in the cottage on our shared bed.

"Ye and I had best do likewise," Ishbel told Da.

"That would hardly be seemly," Da said uneasily.

"Seemly to who, ye daft man?" said Ishbel. "There's nobody here to gossip. Or do ye not care if I freeze in the night?"

"I care right enough," Da admitted. He let Ishbel squeeze up close to him and wrapped the blanket around them both. "But that's all we're doing, mind. Keeping off the chill."

"Aye, I'll mind that," said Ishbel. But there was a strange softness in her eyes as she looked away from him.

I curled up under my blanket, my body clenching like an angry fist. Twitching about on the rough earth, I did my best to fall asleep.

However, I couldn't sleep at all. I kept having thoughts of Ma looking down on us from heaven, willing me to go back and fetch her treasure. I could almost hear her voice, gentle where Ishbel's was brash. "It's my gift to ye, to all of ye, to see ye happy in the New World."

Why couldn't Da or Ishbel see that if we had the Blessing, it would buy us all we would need to start a new life in America? It was as clear to me as the sun on a summer's morning.

I could feel Lachlan's back pressed against mine, and I knew by his steady breathing that he was asleep. Not far off, Da's low snoring drowned out any sound Ishbel might be making, but I was sure that after this long day's trek, she would be as deeply asleep as he.

Slowly and carefully I wriggled away from Lachlan and slipped out from under the blanket. As I did so, he rolled over in my direction and grunted, somehow aware that something was amiss. His eyes flickered open, searching the darkness. He was about to speak when I clapped my hand over his mouth.

"Shhh!" I hissed in his ear. "Ye'll wake Da and he'll no be pleased."

"What are ye planning, Roddy?" he asked in a groggy whisper.

There was nothing I could do but tell him the truth. It was that or give up.

Before I could speak, an owl on silent wings, a shadow's shadow, flew across the path. Seeking, hunting. I took it for a sign.

"I'm away back to Dunraw," I said. "I'm going to find the Blessing."

I had to press my hand to his lips again to keep him from crying out. He pried my fingers away but kept his voice low.

"We've been through that, Roddy. Ye heard what Da and Ishbel said. It's a story for wee bairns."

"Do ye really think Ma would lie to us?" I asked. "Is there not a sma' piece of yer heart telling ye the story is true?"

He hesitated at that. It was mean of me to mention Ma, knowing how that always affected him, but it did the trick. "Aye, I suppose there is. But that disnae mean ye're going to find it after all this time. We never found it, no once, and no for lack of trying."

That was certainly true. After Ma had died, Da had looked for the Blessing everywhere in a fever of activity—amongst her meager belongings, all about the trees where she liked to walk, under the bedding, in the small byre where the cattle and Rob Roy stayed— and he found nothing.

"I'll find it this time," I insisted in a harsh whisper. "Now is the time she meant us to have it."

"Are ye sure it's the Blessing ye're going back for and not something else?" Lachlan asked, sitting up with the blanket wrapped around him.

"What do ye mean?"

"Only that Bonnie Josie's been on yer mind all these past days, like a moth flitting about the fire."

I bristled. "I dinna think of her that way. She's years older than me. And a laird's daughter as well. I'd *never* think of her that way. Not like you and the Beauty of Glendoun. Only Josie helped us. She saved you and me from Willie Rood and got us our cows back. That's all."

Lachlan leaned close to me, keeping his voice low. "Aye, that's as may be, but her troubles are still her own, and it's no for the likes of us to poke our noses into her business."

Something moved in the hill above us. Deer or rabbit or fox— we couldn't tell. But Lachlan pulled the blanket tighter around himself.

"I'm going for the Blessing," I said stubbornly, "and that's all."

"Promise me that, then," said Lachlan, grasping my arm, "and I'll no wake Da and Ishbel."

"I promise ye, Lachlan, I'm doing this for the good of the family. Ye keep them going on to Glasgow and I'll find ye there."

Slowly he relaxed his grip on me. "And if ye dinna come?"

"Then the family will be better off for having one less mouth to feed." I said it as if I meant it, but my stomach knew better. It had an ache in it that felt as if I'd been dealt a blow.

Lachlan's brow furrowed, then he nodded his agreement. I reached out to give him a quick, clumsy embrace, feeling the warmth of the blanket. Then I started off.

I heard him whisper after me, "Good luck, Roddy."

Looking back, I gave him a final wave. I knew I'd need all the luck he wished me—and more.

15 ❧ THE RETURN

I hoped to be long gone before Da and Ishbel woke, so far away that they couldn't even think to follow me.

At first I wound my way over the hills and through the gullies we had crossed to reach our makeshift campsite. There was a good half-moon, and it made a shining path for me, miles on either side. I spied rabbits leaping about on the hillsides. "Dancing for the moon," Ma used to call it.

Without Da's slowing the pace, I was able to go at a good clip, stopping only to catch my breath every hour or so. One stop, as I stood between two separate stands of trees, I listened to the call of a single owl and then a second owl answering him from the right, like two old friends singing a duet.

Renewed, I went on. Luckily I was on a single path. But then I came to a fork in the road, leading to other villages, other glens. I hadn't been paying attention as we stumbled along. All we'd worried about was putting enough space between us and Rood's men.

"Which turn should I take?" I wondered aloud, my voice strange in the night's stillness.

I hadn't thought before how easy it might be to get lost when the contours of the land are suddenly strange. Even if there were landmarks that could have guided me, how was I going to recognize them in the shadowy hills? Now the moon was straight overhead, so I couldn't even tell east from west. And when I looked up at the stars, glittering coldly above me, I wished that I had a sailor's skill to read them like a map.

Even as I made that wish, clouds began rolling in to cover the stars, turning the moon into a smear of grey light, plunging the landscape into deeper shadows. I felt utterly alone, with no hope of finding my way. I turned round and about trying to decide which way to go.

Ishbel had been right. I was following a wee bairn's story, a tale I desperately wanted to believe in. And like the fairy piper in one of Ma's old stories, it was going to lead me to my death.

I began to shiver. For the first time I thought about turning back. And I would have, if only I could tell which way back was.

As I paused in mid-step, a breeze gusted into my face and I smelled the faint but unmistakable hint of smoke in the air. I sniffed, and there it was again. It could only be coming from the burnt-out homes and fields of Dunraw. It was like a signpost to the road home.

Turning to face the direction of the wind, I began to follow the sooty smell back to its source. I pressed on through the dark, pausing now and then to test the air and make sure of my way.

Now the clouds dropped a light drizzle, which gradually turned into a steady rain. The grass and stones beneath my feet grew slick and treacherous, and the muddy ground sucked at my boots. It was too cold and rainy for owls to call, too cold for rabbits.

My legs ached from all the walking. My calves were sore to the touch. Now the rain made it hard to catch the scent of burning, but it was better to go slowly than to give up.

I'd been awake for hours by that time, with only that scant meal to keep me going. My sodden clothes hung heavy on me, and I began to stumble more and more, tripping on roots, catching my boot tips in holes. I worried that I would end up flat on my face with a twisted ankle, unable to carry on to Dunraw and equally unable to crawl back to my family.

Still I pressed on until finally a wrong step toppled me into a deep bowl-shaped depression in the heather. There I curled up, wrapping my arms around my knees to ward off the cold. The wet, the chill, and my hunger made me forget about the Blessing. All I wanted to do was sleep and wake to a morning's breakfast with my family.

Drifting off, I remembered being four years old with Ma pulling a blanket over Lachlan and me and giving us each a good-night kiss on the brow. It had been a hard winter during which many of our cattle had died. We found it hard to sleep for the nagging of our bellies, but Da said we had to make what food we had last until the spring.

"Dinna ye worry, my bonnie bairns," Ma had crooned to us. "There's a Blessing I've kept for ye that will see us through when we need it most. Ye just keep the hope in yer heart like a wee spark of fire, and when the time is right, the flames will rise again."

As her words came back to me, I forced my eyes open and spotted a glimmer of grey light squeezing over the eastern hills. Had I slept and dreamed of Ma, or had the memory sustained me till sunrise?

Suddenly I knew it didn't matter which. The dawn was here at last, and the sight of it was enough to poke me on. I got to my feet, ignoring the aching of my legs, the dampness of my shirt and breeks. The rain was thinning to a damp haze that cleared as the sun rose.

Looking around, I recognized the outlines of familiar hills. They were like the faces of old friends welcoming me back. There was Caer Ludden with its knobby peak, and there was Maggs Law, where they said a witch had been stoned to death long ago. I grinned and waved at them.

That's when I saw the first of the burnt-out crofts. Nestled on the side of the road, with its byre snugged up close, I recognized it only by the stone chimney with the black cap on top, for there was little else to know it by. It had belonged to the McDiarmids, an aging couple with two scrawny daughters and a son that was soft in the head. I didn't like to think how they'd be faring now that they were homeless.

A fox darted from cover, dashed through the ruins and out of sight. He was as much an intruder as I, and if I was to survive this dangerous adventure, I knew I'd have to be as quick and cunning as he.

I kept to the shadow of the hillside, using trees and rocks for cover. Since I was on Kindarry land now, I had to be wary. The laird's men might still be scouring the glen, searching for stragglers. I would need the fox's guile to reach Dunraw, make my search and get away safe with the Blessing tucked inside my shirt.

Lack of sleep was making me weary, and my temples ached. Suddenly a mist passed before my eyes, a kind of dizziness. I shook with cold as if I'd been plunged into an icy pool. I had to get hold of myself, so I leaned back against a stunted tree and took one, two, three deep breaths to steady myself.

"Just a wee bit farther," I said aloud, my own voice but Da's words. It worked like an old granny's charm. Gradually the haze lifted from my eyes and I stopped shaking. But I was still cold, as if mountain streams ran through my veins instead of blood.

A few more breaths and I was ready to carry on. It couldn't be far now. The McDiarmids lived only about an hour down the glen from us.

As I went along, my head was pounding so hard that all I could do was place one foot in front of the other over and again, squinting to keep my eyes focused on some familiar object up ahead. And all of a sudden, I stumbled into Dunraw and was almost through it before I even realized I'd reached my goal.

Turning around slowly, I surveyed the scene. Naught but blackened ruins and scattered debris. That heap of smoldering ruins had been Hamish Kinnell's cottage and byre. If not for the still fresh smell of burning, I'd have thought no one had lived here for a century. The laird's men had done their dark work well.

A crow landed on a charred stump of wood and cocked its head at me suspiciously, fluttering ragged black feathers. Then it let out a loud caw, as if I were a trespasser in this dead place.

In spite of the crow's warning I carried on to the remains of our own cottage on a different road out of the town. A last turn of that road and I gasped. Even having seen the other ruins, I was not prepared for it.

All that remained of the place where I'd been born and raised for fifteen years was a blackened shell. Those stone walls, once so sturdy they'd kept the deep winter winds from blowing in on us, had been broken to half their normal height. They looked so flimsy now, a stiff breeze could have scattered them.

As in Glendoun, I'd a sense that ghosts haunted the place, only this time me and mine were the ghosts. I could almost hear Ishbel tutting over her darning, smell her freshly baked bannocks, hear Da shouting at Lachlan and me to stop our squabbling. The wind through the trees sounded like Ma when she sang us to sleep. For an instant, I thought I glimpsed myself, leaping over one of the rocks in a nearby burn, splashing in the water with a careless whoop.

There was no sign of any of our animals. I hoped they were running free among the hills, but it seemed more likely the laird had taken them to eat or sell.

I stepped over the broken walls of the cottage and stared about me. It was like looking down on my own skeleton in an open grave. In an instant, I went from being too cold to being too hot. My face burned, and I trembled all over. The whole glen began to spin around me. My stomach lurched, and I toppled forward onto the back wall. The weakened stones gave way beneath my weight, and I crashed down on top of the jagged heap. Pieces of flint dug into my ribs.

Pushing up, with weakened arms, I slid off and lay gasping for breath. For a moment I was struck with the fear that I might die here in this dead place and that it would be sheep that would come upon my corpse. All for the want of a thing in a story that even a bairn would have known was just a magic tale.

"Och, Da," I whispered, "I'm sorry." To die in battle would have been glorious. To die alone on a heap of stones because of a boy's foolishness was too awful to think about. I felt hot tears well up. Not only was I going to die, but I was also going to die weeping. It was the worst possible end I could imagine.

Then a glint of light caught my eye. I twisted about, trying to find it. Stones pinched me, scratched me, but I didn't care.

There, among the pile of stone, was something reflecting the feeble grey light. I was close enough that I could touch it if I stretched out my arm. And so I did, reaching out till my fingers closed around cool metal. I brought the thing close to my face and stared.

It was a jeweled brooch with the figure of a rampant lion on the top.

A brooch.

For a moment I couldn't think what it was. Ishbel had no such thing. Nor had Ma. It was like something out of Bonnie Josie's house, small and precious and beautiful.

I sat up, laughing. Of course, of course. It was the Blessing! How could I have doubted Ma or my dreams?

A surge of excitement made my head spin afresh. Ma's words had been true. Her gift had been waiting here for me, hidden in the walls, needing the factor's bullies to knock down the walls and free it.

In that moment of triumph, with my fingers clutched about my prize, exhaustion overwhelmed me. Dark night closed over me, though it had just turned day, and like some peely-wally girl, I fainted dead away.

16 ⁊ ROBBED

I don't know how long I slept, but I was finally stirred by the sound of voices and a clopping, like hoofbeats. It was already twilight, the shadow-dark hills looming up over me. Not a bit of wind stirred. I had slept away the day.

At first I couldn't tell if the voices I was hearing were real or imagined, if I were awake or still asleep and dreaming. For a moment I even thought the voices were ghosts calling me to stay in this place of death.

Place of death. I sat up, fully remembering where I was: inside the broken-down remains of my own house.

The hoofbeats were close, just outside the walls. I huddled down, trying to make myself small as a mouse.

"Could you salvage nothing from all this?" I recognized the voice, and my heart jumped in panic. It was the laird, his voice like butter spread thin on dry bread. "All the muddle of houses you have shown me, and this the last of them, and not one thing of value?"

"Value, my lord?" Ever faithful, Willie Rood answered him. "Not unless you put a high price on stale bannocks and rags. I tried to tell you. . . ."

The moon was overhead, though night had not yet pressed in. From somewhere close by, the doos were cooing. I inched back, pressing against the broken stones so hard they bruised me. If Rood found me, I was surely done for. We were all to have been off the land by this time, and Rood was never slow to use his cudgel, as I well knew.

"The cattle, then?"

"We've already gotten what was in the byres and in the fields, my lord."

He meant stolen, as when he took our cows and Rob Roy. But how could I complain? I had to remain hidden or die.

Rood's oily voice went on, "But there's plenty still lost in the hills. My men are herding them together for market, though I doubt they'll fetch much. All hide, bones and fleas."

"Aye, well, never mind," the laird told him. "I'd hoped for better, but still, the estate's well rid of those wretched beggars and their half-starved beasts."

Beggars! We'd never begged from anyone, least of all from him. My right hand clenched at the shock, and my fingers closed on a hard edge of metal. Glancing down, I saw the golden brooch, and memory flooded back. The lion, the jewels—the Blessing!

The horses seemed to shift and move off, perhaps down the road. I could hear the hooves clattering away from where I cowered behind the wall. I could wait till they were gone or try and sneak off now, in case they turned back.

Then I heard the hooves come closer again, as if they were circling the cottage. If they came to the side where I'd stepped over the wall, they'd see me for sure. I'd not a moment to lose, and I looked around for a place to hide. There was the fireplace, standing a few yards away. If I could crawl inside, I might just escape their eyes.

I set out slowly. Only then did I realize that my deep sleep had been from more than simple tiredness. I was exhausted, starving, feverish. When I pushed myself to my knees, everything whirled about me. I hadn't the strength to support my own weight. I fell back, rolled over, and ended with my face in the sooty ground, where I choked on the black dust and soot from the fire. The little I'd eaten the past two days came up in a loud, foul rush. I heaved again, then a third time until I was panting for breath and the ground beneath me stank of sick.

"What's that there, among the ruins?" the laird exclaimed.

"A scavenger," said Rood, "looking for pickings?"

"That loud? That large?"

I could hear them ride right up to the ruined cottage. Could hear the horses' huffing breath.

"Look, man—that's no badger, no fox!" cried Daniel McRoy. "It's a damned crofter!"

"I'm sorry, my lord, I thought we'd driven them all off. I suppose this one might have hidden and died in the night."

I was too sick to move and might as well have been dead. I held my breath. Not just from fear. The stink around me was unbearable.

"Died? He was scrabbling around in the dirt a moment ago and making enough noise to wake the dead."

"You're right, sir. He's alive. I can see him breathe."

And I thought I'd stopped breathing, but now I was gasping and afraid I was going to heave again.

"That's Murdo Macallan's boy, the one that gave us such trouble at the Lodge," Rood said.

"So, was he left behind?" They talked about me as if I were a dead lump that couldn't speak for itself.

"Nae, I drove him off with the others after I'd taught his father a dose of respect." I heard the creak of leather as Rood dismounted.

"Then why did he come back?" drawled the laird.

"To make trouble, that's for certain," said Rood. "You don't suppose Mistress Josephine called him, do you? She took a liking to this whelp."

"She's no time to spare from tending her mother," said the laird. "I doubt she's given him a thought."

For a moment I gave thought to Bonnie Josie and not myself. But then Rood advanced on me, warily, as if he were watching a coiled snake. I clutched the Blessing tightly and tried to hide it up my sleeve.

"For heaven's sake, man, show some backbone," the laird chided him. "He's half dead."

"He's sick," Rood answered defensively. "I don't want to be catching anything off him."

At this point I turned over and looked up, staring back at him defiantly. If I were going to be beaten to death, better to see it coming. But I saw Rood as if through a thick sheet of ice. The twilight shimmered around him as he bent over me, and my eyes blurred. As I turned, the brooch slipped down my sleeve and into my hand.

Rood reached out with a suddenness that made me flinch. Grabbing my right arm, he said, "He's got something here."

He pulled my arm straight and I was too weak to resist. Then he ripped the Blessing from my grasp. I tried to cry out in protest, but the words only bubbled in my throat.

The laird stiffened in the saddle. I could see him there, a pale, blurred presence. "Give me that!" he ordered Rood.

Rood handed the brooch over immediately. "It's a pretty bauble and worth a goodly purse, I'll wager." He spoke as if expecting a fee for the finding of it.

At last, I gathered what strength I had and poured it all into my voice. "It's mine!" I gasped. "Mine by right!"

"*By right,* is it?" the laird scoffed. "*Ha!* And how would a wretch like you come by such a thing except by thievery? I've a mind to have you flogged."

"It was a gift to my grandfather from the Bonnie Prince." Just saying the prince's name gave me strength.

This time the laird burst out laughing, and Rood dutifully added his own mocking bray. "A fine fairy story, but who'd believe it?"

"Let . . . let the law decide," I challenged, wondering how I knew to say such a thing, then remembering how Rood himself had used the phrase when talking to Bonnie Josie.

Suddenly the laird was no longer amused. "I'll not see the likes of you call in the law against me," he said. "Whatever is found on my land is mine by right, and you are no more than a trespasser here now."

"Then take me to the magistrate," I said. "I'll tell my story there."

He made a snorting sound through his nose. "I'll not waste his time with your lies nor soil his hands with your punishment." I could see him clearly now, though the light was almost gone. His face was sour and his lips were pursed.

Rood looked away from me for a moment, addressing the laird. "Even weak as he is, he might find his way back to Miss Josephine. . . ."

The laird pondered this. "All the more reason he should be on his way." Then he added grimly, "And you'll oblige me, Mister Rood, by ensuring he never shows his face here again, if you take my meaning."

"I take your meaning, sir," Rood replied slowly. "In his condition, if he was to take a bad fall and break a leg, I doubt he'd make it through the night."

And then I understood. They meant for me to die. I pushed

myself to my feet and turned to run. At least I would not go down easy.

But Rood was too quick for me, grabbing me by the collar and spinning me around. Then before I knew what was happening, he rammed his fist into my nose, making my skull ring. Barely conscious, I felt him hoist me up and fling me over his saddle.

"It must be clear to any that find him that he has died through his own misadventure," said the laird.

"I know a spot that will suit," Rood answered.

He climbed up behind me, and the horse started moving. At that point my thoughts were little more than the flicker of a guttering candle. I hadn't even enough strength left to be afraid.

17 ❧ TAKEN

The laird set off—toward Kindarry House, I supposed—while Rood rode in the other direction, with me slung across his saddle like a sack of oats. I couldn't lift my head high enough to check where we were going. All I could see was the damp turf and heather passing beneath the horse's hooves, the tracks of small animals by the side of the path, and the roots of trees.

All the while we traveled, I refused to think about what was surely going to happen. I didn't *dare* think of it. Instead I worried about my poor family. How they'd never know my fate or how I'd found—and then lost—the Blessing.

My stomach heaved again. This time I'd nothing left to bring up but bitter-tasting bile.

At last we stopped, and Rood grabbed the back of my shirt. With one swift yank, he pitched me to the ground. I landed on my belly with a thud that jarred my bones and made crimson sparks shoot across my eyes. I managed to turn onto my back and stare up at the sky, where the stars were already coming out.

Goodbye, stars, I thought. For a moment I thought they dimmed in answer. Or else it was my eyes playing tricks. Then Rood's flushed face loomed over me, an ugly, disfigured moon.

"Now ye'll get payment in full for all yer trickery," he said. "Come on, get up, ye gowk! I'll not carry ye." He bent over and put an arm under my shoulder, dragging me to my feet.

My knees started to buckle right away, and he had to support me.

"Just a few steps," he said, heaving me forward, one hand locked on my upper arm, the other clutching the front of my shirt.

I hadn't the strength to struggle or the voice to protest. Squinting through the twilight, I saw bare, craggy hills ahead, rising like a row of badly carved tombstones. Before them yawned the rocky edge of a steep precipice.

Fuzzily, I thought: *I know this place. One of our lambs strayed here last year and fell to its death.* Recalling that frail, broken body, some last flash of resistance sparked in me. I wouldn't—I *couldn't*—go down like a lamb.

Twisting away from Rood, I tried to wrench my arm free. He looked surprised, then angry at this last show of resistance.

"Damn you, Highland scum," he cursed, punching me hard in the belly, then chuckling as I doubled over. He gave me a contemptuous shove and I stumbled forward, trembling with pain and fever. "That will teach you to hold out on the laird."

Perhaps, I thought, *perhaps it might not be such a bad thing to die, to meet my mother again.* Perhaps in spite of all the Reverend McGillivray had told us, there was a small chance I might sneak into heaven through some back door kept open for daft boys.

"Nearly there now, lad," Rood said, his voice strangely low, cozening, even sweet, as though he'd heard me musing on heaven. "Don't worry. Ye willna even have to jump. I'll give ye a good push to see ye on your way."

I knew that I should at least have a prayer on my lips, but exhausted and dazed, I couldn't summon one up. I felt the edge of the cliff beneath my feet and did my best not to look down at the rocks below.

Then Rood's fingers pressed against my back, and I said fare-well to my life.

Suddenly a shot banged in my ears, so loud it might have split a mountain in half.

Rood loosed his hold on me and I crumpled at his feet, scrab-bling away from the ledge. At the same time, Rood wheeled about, raising his cowardly hands over his head, all the while edging ner-vously toward his horse.

"Get to yer horse and ride, Willie Rood!" called a mocking voice. "Try to get out of range before I can reload!"

I stopped, turned, raised myself up on one elbow as Rood darted for his horse. He scrambled into the saddle with such desperation that he almost toppled over the far side. I would have laughed if I'd the strength.

A crow laughed for me, from a nearby pine.

Digging his spurs savagely into the horse's flanks, Rood gal-loped off like the very devil was after him.

I sat up slowly and looked around. A figure stood on a nearby crag. Not the devil, just one of his friends—Alan Dunbar, the Rogue o' the Hills. I began to shake and then to weep. Big, blub-bing tears rained down my cheeks and I couldn't stop them.

Dunbar started down toward me, the barrel of his musket rest-ing casually on his shoulder. He hadn't even tried to reload.

Had I just exchanged one captor for another? I tried to scramble to my feet, but my legs wouldn't let me. Dunbar's footfalls quick-ened to a run.

Soon he was kneeling over me. "Roddy Macallan," he said, "what are ye doing here in such bad company?"

I groaned. "Do ye mean Willie Rood or yerself?" I managed, and he laughed.

The next thing I knew, he'd hefted me up onto his shoulder and marched off at a brisk pace, carrying me as easily as a soldier carries his pack. I closed my eyes, letting relief wash over me. I knew in my heart that Dunbar would not kill me. Not now.

I fancied as I drifted off that instead of killing me, he would sell me, just as he sold herds of stolen cattle. Perhaps the army would buy me for a drummer boy, and I would march into battle beating out the rhythm to keep our soldiers in step. I could actually hear the beat of the drum and wondered dreamily who was fighting.

I can hardly say I woke. Rather the fog I was lost in grew thinner. Dimly aware that I was now in a cave, I realized slowly that the drumming was actually rain falling beyond the cave entrance. And so I carried on, slipping in and out of sleep, either ablaze with fever or shivering as if buried in snow. Whenever I roused, I found a damp rag laid over my brow.

"Mother," I cried at least once, for who but she would have taken care of me? "Ishbel," I called another time. And then I remembered a third woman who cared for me. "Bonnie Josie," I whispered.

The fire was lit, and there was water and bread by my bedside. But it was none of them, only Alan Dunbar, who saw me through the worst of my sickness, never leaving my side.

I had no idea how long I'd lain there in Dunbar's cave, but finally the fever burned itself out and I was only weary and weak. At last I was well enough to sit up and drink water out of a silver cup.

"Have I . . . ," I started, and had to clear my throat. "Have I been here awhile?"

"Aye, lad, near five days." Dunbar set the back of his weathered hand against my cheek and nodded. "Ye're through it now, though," he said. "In a couple of days ye'll be dancing a jig and chasing the lassies again."

I took a deep breath and got my first clear, un-fevered look at his hideout. The cave was only a bit snugger than our old cottage and the fire placed so that the smoke went up a crudely fashioned chimney. Animal skins hung on the walls, part decoration and part to warm up the cold stone. Deerskin, mostly, but I saw a badger skin and two fox skins as well, their tails hanging down, the red well faded. Whisky jugs clustered together in a corner. And a cupboard made of rocks piled on rocks held his meager clothes and a cloth-covered cheese and three round breads.

Now that I could think more clearly, I began fitting my jumbled memories back together. The thing that stood out the most was that I owed my life to the Rogue.

"I have to thank ye, Alan Dunbar," I said. "If not for ye, I'd have been broken on the stones below that ledge, and that's sure."

Dunbar took a draw on his pipe and let the smoke slip through his lips in a thin ribbon. "Aye, ye would have been gone, no doubt of it."

I nodded, waiting to hear the rest.

He smiled, and for the first time I realized he was a handsome man. His thick brown hair was pulled back from his face, and his cheeks had a chiseled look as if worry and weariness had filed him down. Yet there were laugh lines in the corners of his eyes.

"I was out about my business," he said, not mentioning what that business might be, but I guessed I knew. "And who should I spy but the factor himself, riding along with somebody slung over his saddle." He leaned forward. "I knew that wasna right."

I nodded. "No right at all."

He continued. "At first I thought ye were already dead and he was just getting rid of the body. Still, I reckoned it worth following, just for the chance to make some trouble. I was surprised to see ye still alive."

"It's still surprising me," I said with a weak grin.

"Where's yer family, lad?" he asked. "I'll not believe they ran off without ye."

I reached for the silver cup again and took a sip before answering. "Gone to Glasgow. They plan to take a ship to the Americas."

Dunbar raised an eyebrow. "Then what brought ye back here?"

My stomach quivered at that question. For all that he had saved my life, this was still the Rogue o' the Hills. If I told him about the Blessing, he'd likely try to steal it for himself.

"I dinna care to go to America," I lied. "I hear it's full of savages and wild beasts."

"Is *that* what ye hear?" He threw back his head and laughed. Then he looked straight at me. "Those stories dinna bother yer father or brother, then?"

He'd known at once it was a lie. I drank a bit more water instead of answering. Then I changed the subject.

"Have Rood and his men come looking for me?"

"It's hard to judge," said Dunbar, rubbing his jaw. "The laird's laddies are scouring the hills, gathering stray animals from the crofts they've burned. Who's to say some of them aren't after a different quarry? Maybe ye. Maybe me."

"Then . . ." I looked around the cave. "Are we safe here?"

"As long as I keep one sharp eye open, lad. It's nae easy to climb to this spot less ye know the path, and I keep that well hid. I only set the fire after dark so the smoke is hid as well. But what makes ye so blessed important that Rood wants ye dead?"

My mouth sagged soundlessly as I tried to think of a way to steer him from the truth. "It's no just Rood. It's the laird too. He's angry with me for . . . for visiting Bonnie Josie."

Dunbar shook his head slowly. "That's a poor enough reason for murder, even for that poison-hearted pair. Unless I miss my mark, there's more to this tale than ye're telling."

When I made no answer, he looked at me closely. "There has to be another reason." He leaned back against the wall and said casually, "Did ye steal some coins from his purse?"

"I'm nae thief!" I answered hotly.

He chuckled and pointed to the silver cup. "Well, I am!" Then he pointed a finger at me. "I knew ye'd nothing of value on ye. I checked. So whatever Willie Rood thought about ye holding out on the laird . . ." His finger went to his lips, and he took a moment before speaking again.

I said hotly, "Ye were eavesdropping."

He laughed loudly. "Of *course* I was eavesdropping. How else to know whether to save yer life at the risk of mine? So what *is* it ye've held out?"

I clamped my lips together.

"All right, lad, we'll do this the hard way. I'll guess, and ye refuse to answer. But I'll figure it out in the end. Now I'm thinking that whatever it is, ye might have hidden it elsewhere. Perhaps ye can tell that." There was a twinkle in his eye. "After all, ye surely owe me something for the service of saving yer life, especially now I've fallen on hard times."

I couldn't stop myself. I sat up straight and asked, "Hard times? How did that happen?"

"Och!" Dunbar exclaimed, as if there was a bad taste in his mouth. "The laird's men were stumbling around the hills, and they came upon one of my stills. It was sheer luck, mind, for it was well hid." He took another puff on his pipe. When he spoke again, his voice had a hard edge to it. "They smashed it to bits, though not before they helped themselves to the last of the whisky. Aye, with only a single still and few customers left in the glen, it promises to be a lean year for me."

With all the suffering I'd seen, it was hard to feel sorry for him. And he certainly didn't sound as if his spirits were down. "I'm sure ye'll get by," I said. "There's always food for foxes, no matter the season."

He laughed at that, a rich laugh I couldn't help but fall in with, even though it pained my belly.

"Ye'll do, lad," he said after a bit. "Ye'll surely do."

That evening, clearheaded at last, I started to think about my situation and what I was going to do. Managing to stand shakily, I headed toward the cave opening. I barely got outside before weakness overcame me, and I sat down heavily on a nearby rock to let the fresh air work its healing magic.

Dunbar wasn't anywhere around.

Probably off stealing something. That didn't bother me as much as it should have. *When good men are pushed off their land by highborn thieves,* I thought, the idea new to me, *what can we do but fight back the same way?*

I looked around carefully. Dunbar's cave was in a hollow on the high side of a hill, as if a giant had pressed his thumb into the hillside, leaving a huge dent. Ahead of me a mossy crag jutted up into the air, keeping the cave's entrance hidden from view. There were high trees, some growing right out of the rock, which further disguised the place.

A thrush was singing in a tree to the right of the cave, the little trills and rills so beautiful I had to smile. But that smile didn't last long because I began to think about my family and where they might be now.

I didn't know how Da and Ishbel had reacted to my running off, but I could surely guess. Swearing at my stupidity, Da probably vowed to follow me. As for Ishbel—well, she cried and said that then she'd lose us both. Still, I hoped Lachlan was keeping them moving on toward Glasgow and the harbors. And I hoped he was promising them I'd show up in plenty of time to go off to the Americas with them.

I would have caught up to them if not for my fever. Had I passed that fever to any of them before I left? I hoped not. They had a long way to go without such a burden.

But with the Blessing now in the laird's slimy hands, what good would my catching up to them have done? What I needed to do was to get it back. *Go to Kindarry House and steal it back,* I told myself. *Ye found the Blessing once, ye can find it again.*

But Kindarry House was no ruined cottage that I could search at the hour of my choosing. There would be servants in and out all the time, more than at Josie's Lodge. And so many rooms, I'd need days to go through them all.

I put my head in my hands. It would take a better thief than me to get the Blessing back.

Then it came to me: *it would take a rogue like Alan Dunbar.*

The gloaming closed in, bringing darkness to the mountain. Still, I remained outside, back against the cave's cold stone, thinking: *How can I gain Dunbar's help without letting him know what's at stake?* I didn't dare tell him about the Blessing, for then he could take it from me as easily as the laird had.

Secrets inside of secrets, I thought. *And me never good with a lie.*

But I had to try. And with that thought in my mind—only the flimsiest of plans—I stood up, steadier than before, for the fresh air had done its work well. Then I made my way back into the cave and immediately fell asleep.

• • •

The next morning I felt stronger. Clambering out from under the woolen cover Dunbar had laid over me, I got stiffly to my feet. Then I stretched the knots out of my back before heading outside once more.

Dunbar sat on a nearby rock, chewing a wad of tobacco and whittling a piece of wood into a stake for one of his rabbit snares. He was dressed in a kilt, a shirt, and a vest of deerskin, with a rabbit's fur bonnet perched upon his head. When he heard me, he looked up and gave an approving nod. "Welcome back to the land of the living, Lazarus."

I knew that story from kirk, and it suddenly crossed my mind that he meant I really *had* been dead for a while and, under his healing hand, risen again. Then I noticed his thin smile and knew he was only joking. I swayed for a moment before finding my balance. Above, the same thrush was caroling away, and blackbirds were calling from the trees far below.

"I've too much to do to stay dead," I said.

"As ye say." Dunbar spat on the shriveled grass. "Rest one more day, then. Tomorrow I'll give ye a pack of food and ye can be on yer way."

But I couldn't let him push me out. I had to get the Blessing first, and to do that, I had to enlist Dunbar's aid. Somehow . . .

"Where to?" I challenged. "There's nae place for me to go."

"Go after yer family," Dunbar told me sternly. "In Glasgow. That's yer only duty."

"They'll have sailed for America before I get there. Let me stay. I'll do fine right here." I hoped I didn't blush at the bald lie. It was my only plan, this begging to stay with the Rogue, and I had to stick to it.

Dunbar paused in his whittling and gave me a hard stare through narrowed eyes. The smile lines disappeared as he spoke. "I've done as much for ye as any decent man should, lad, but ye're no kin of mine and I've no use for ye. Indeed, yer a liability. Makes it harder for me to move about silently, quickly. Makes me have to return here, to this cave, no matter what the signs. Ye get in the way of my . . . business." He looked back down at his whittling as if he'd said everything he was going to say.

"I'm only asking for a few days," I pleaded.

Overhead two crows laughed.

"A few days? For what?" he asked sharply, looking up again. This time his eyes were wide and the brightest blue I'd ever seen, as if he'd stolen a patch of sky. "To eat my food and put me to more trouble? When ye're well enough to march, ye're on yer way, and that's that. I dinna want ye missing yer family."

I pulled myself up straight as I was able, thankful for a sudden breeze that cleared my head. I had to convince Dunbar to let me stay, and I had to get him to help find the Blessing before the family left Glasgow. I figured I had a week, no more. But a week was only seven days.

"I'm not leaving Glendoun," I insisted. "It's my home. My *only* home. I want to be like ye, Alan Dunbar, living free and beholden to no one."

"Then ye've made a poor start, laddie, for ye're already beholden to me. And now you want to vex me further." He brushed the wood shavings off onto the path.

"This is my land, the land of my fathers," I declared defiantly, "and I'll stay on it, whatever it takes." I wondered if I'd overdone it.

"Och, what a gowk." He turned away from me, his back rigid.

Sitting on the stone, he was as tall as I was standing. "It's McRoy's land and always was. Ye and yers were here only on the laird's sufferance." His voice rose impatiently. "Ye trespass on it now at yer peril. If Rood and the laird catch ye up here, ye're done for, and that's sure. And like as not, me with ye."

His words shook me, but I did my best not to let it show. "I can hide or run—or even fight if need be."

Dunbar made a scoffing noise deep in his throat, and that pricked my pride.

"*Ye* do it, Alan Dunbar," I said stubbornly. "Surely I can learn to do the same."

He turned. "Nae, lad, that ye canna. Look what's happened to ye since coming back here." His voice was scathing now, his face in a full scowl. "Ye were already half gone with fever when Rood was readying to pitch ye over that cliff. No a bit of running or hiding or fighting in ye. Ye'd be dead twice over if I hadna happened by." He pointed to the sky. "See those hawks?" There were two, soaring above us. "They miss the meal they might have had of ye."

"But I managed to find my way back to Dunraw and in the dark too," I said. "And I'm alive now. I know my way about. I can take care of myself." I put my fist over my heart. I *had* to convince him.

Dunbar threw the half-whittled stick down. "And how will ye do that, lad? Ye're nae soldier, as I was once, nae thief and smuggler as I am now. Ye've no killed a man in cold blood or in hot. What have ye stolen that was no first given ye?"

I turned my head away as the heat rose to my cheeks. It was as if he could read my very soul.

But he was not done with me yet. "Ye're a crofter's boy, and ye need a family about ye, a roof over yer head, good land to hand, and a hot meal awaiting ye at night."

I said softly, "But I could learn all that running and hiding and fighting from *ye*. I could be yer apprentice."

"*Apprentice?*" Dunbar laughed harshly. "I'm nae smithy or tanner. A man in my line doesna take on an apprentice. That would be as mad as taking on a wife and children." There was a bitterness in those last words that reminded me he'd had a wife and child once.

He stood, towering over me, and shoved the knife into his belt. "Instead of giving me grief, save yer strength for the march. It's a long road to Glasgow and ye go tomorrow, as I told ye."

"And as I told *ye*—I'm no going."

We stood there like men about to battle.

"Aye, ye've been handing me a pretty parcel of nonsense ever since ye woke," he said as he brushed past me. "Ye can find somebody else to try yer havers on."

He stomped into the cave, not looking back at me. I followed after, and watched him stuff his pockets with snares, tobacco, food. Then he picked up his musket and powder horn. Slinging a water skin over his shoulder, he headed outside.

"I've business to attend to," he said gruffly. "Without need of any apprentice. There's neeps I got from the fields outside the ruined cottages. They're in the pot and been stewing all night. There's some bread left to soak up the dregs. Make sure the fire is out until dark. Eat, rest, and make sure ye keep out of sight." He stepped out of the cave, then paused to look back over his shoulder. "If I spot ye wandering around outside, I'll turn ye over to Rood myself."

And then he was gone.

19 ❧ THE CAVE

I thought it safest to stay in the cave until I was sure he was far away. There'd been nothing in his voice to suggest his warning had been a joke. What if there was a reward on my head? Might he not be tempted to give me over to the laird?

I checked around the starkly furnished refuge. There were wooden boxes, some tin pots, like trinkets in a magpie's nest, piled one atop the other along one wall. In the stone wardrobe was a pile of ragged fabrics Dunbar must have used to patch his clothes on the lowest shelf. Small logs for the fire were stacked carefully near the entrance to the cave. Our bedding—just blankets and skins—lay on the floor.

Suddenly I noticed something peeking out from beneath the pile of fabrics. It was a book. I pulled it out and slowly read the title on the cover:

The Life and Strange Surprizing Adventures of
ROBINSON CRUSOE

I'd never come across a name like that before. I opened the book at random and read: *Upon the whole, here was an undoubted testimony, that there was scarce any condition in the world so miserable but there was something negative or something positive to be thankful for in it.*

I tried to read more, but it was too difficult. I'd nae practice at it except for the Bible when Ma—and later Ishbel—had Lachlan and me read a passage out before Sunday meals. Following the long words in this *Robinson Crusoe* was like tracing a row of wobbly stepping-stones. Still, I learned something surprising about Dunbar I'd not known before. He was a reader, though this book seemed to be the only one he had in his cave.

Putting the book back in its place, I ventured outside. Now I was curious to explore this region that had become both my prison and my salvation. I had no idea how far we'd come from the place where Rood had tried to kill me or whether the cave was on McRoy land.

As I walked to the crag's edge, I realized that from below, one would never guess there was anything up here worth the climb. The crag hid everything. In fact, the cave entrance itself was invisible, even from where I now stood.

Yet I knew Dunbar was right to be cautious. Should I be caught, I'd put him in danger as well. Rood had already been made a fool of by Dunbar's actions, and the factor was not a man to take mockery lightly. So, I pressed myself flat against the stone, making myself part of it, while I surveyed the bare country spread below me.

Though I didn't immediately recognize any landmarks, I realized we had to be on the laird's land still. The crag was sitting in a glen, and McRoy owned three entire glens, with my own glen in the middle of the other two. The Rogue could not have dragged me farther away on his back, up and over mountains.

Slowly, stealthily, I circled about the crag, the way a poacher might. Presently I made out what was surely the piney crest of Ben Torr. *So,* I thought, *that stream glinting to the left of it must be the Killieburn.* The morning sun, traveling from the east, gave me the map I needed. From this I worked out that I was on the far side of

Kindarry House. If I were right—and the more I looked, the more I was sure of it—this was a bare stretch of country known as the Barrens, with scarcely a patch of good grazing. I'd heard of it but, before now, had never seen it. Neither man nor animal would be straying this way unless they *meant* to come. No wonder the Rogue made his home here. He was, I supposed, the king of this scrub-and-rock realm. From up here, he could spy out anyone coming for miles before they got here.

As, I suddenly thought, *can I!*

But I also realized that the cave was much farther from where Dunbar had found me than I'd originally thought. Only now did I understand how strong he must be, and I marveled at his stamina. He was right to question mine.

Squatting down on my haunches, I thought: *How can I change his mind?* I needed him, but it was amply clear, he didn't need or want me. I let out a deep sigh. I knew we had to stay together; I hadn't the skills to survive on my own. Not yet. And come to that, I had no musket for shooting or knife for slicing.

Och, Lachlan, I thought, *if only you were here to talk with me.* But of course he wasn't. He was on his way to the city of Glasgow and from there to a boat bound for America.

My nose began to drip and I snuffled it up. Some blackbird heard me and cried out in alarm.

A gowk indeed! I was already showing myself a poor enough rogue without being scolded by a rook.

I sat down on a log and thought gloomily that even being hanged for a thief would be better than taking the westward road alone. If I did find my family, what could I tell them? That I'd found our treasure, only to lose it again? That I put myself—and them—in danger? That I was a boy, a bairn, who wasn't fit to go to Glasgow,

much less the Americas? And yet . . . and yet . . . how I wanted to
see them again. To lark about with Lachlan and listen to Da's stories, to eat Ishbel's good food.

I stood and shook my head. If I kept up like this much longer,
I'd be blubbering like a baby. But now I knew I had no choice. *Since
Dunbar won't help me,* I thought, *I'll have to break into Kindarry
House myself.*

As I walked back toward the cave, I was afire with this idea
again, already planning my route. After all, I'd been to Kindarry
House twice, once as a bairn and not a week ago, when we brought
the sheep to the laird. I knew what it looked like from the outside.
And I'd been inside the Lodge, so how different could Kindarry
House be? Just as our cottages were alike, all small but-and-bens
with a single door, so I imagined were the great houses alike: doz-
ens of rooms opening one after another off a hallway, with many
windows in each room.

Out loud, I said: "I'll climb in a back window, one far from the
front of the house and the paddock. Then I'll race like the wind
through the rooms, looking into cupboards and drawers." I remembered Josie's cupboard and the way Rood had forced it open. I'd
need a tool for that and wondered if the Rogue might have one in
his boxes.

Once I found the Blessing—and I'd take no more than that, otherwise it would be stealing—I'd sneak off to the stables, borrow a
horse, maybe even Rob Roy fattened up on the laird's oats, and
gallop off westward to Glasgow. All my fears of too many servants
and too many rooms I put well behind me. The more I told myself
the tale of my adventure, the more possible it seemed.

But once back inside the cave, the darkness, the damp sapped
my spirits again. I remembered that I was only a boy, still weak

from fever, without weapons or allies. One blow from Rood's cudgel, one shot from the laird's musket would put an end to me.

I sat down on my bedding and picked at the stew Dunbar had left, but it did nothing to allay my fears. He might be a fine rogue, but he was a terrible cook. Ishbel's stews had flavor. This cold mash of old neeps had none. So I lay down on the wool blanket and, presently, began to doze. In my dreams I stole not one but three Blessings and brought Bonnie Josie to America with me.

When I woke, I felt worse than before. Finding the treasure really was only a dream after all.

Knowing I needed to walk about, to get strong again, I got up and went outside, where I took a cautious stroll around the heather-clad hollow and stared out over the empty countryside. Except for a small, thin, silvery burn running alongside the crag's bottom, too small for good fishing, there seemed to be nothing living down there, no rabbits or deer or sheep or . . .

The count of what was *not* there made me sleepy and once more I dozed, this time sitting upright on a stone.

When I woke, the sun was already sinking in a sky ruddy with pink-bottomed clouds. A light breeze sighed across the clearing, and the thrush took up its evensong, curling and curling higher than even I could hear.

As the dark drew in, I started to get anxious about Dunbar. He'd been gone for hours. Suppose the laird's men had hunted him down. Suppose he'd walked into an ambush and was even now lying in chains.

Shouldn't I go to his aid? I needn't be without a weapon. I could fashion a cudgel from a tree limb. Standing, I looked around until I found a branch that would do. I tugged at it and it scarcely moved, which showed me how weak I was still. In this condition, how could I possibly help the Rogue? And hadn't he told me to stay put and keep out of sight?

"Dunbar's work is not like Da's," I told myself, sitting on my rock and watching the path that wandered into the pine forest below. A rogue's business wasn't something left off at dusk so the man could hurry home for supper.

Supper! I supposed I could go back into the cave and make some more stew so he could eat and not just have my leavings of cold neeps. Once it got fully dark, I could start the fire again.

I smiled at my haverings. Usually Lachlan and I just took off and got into trouble without thinking. And here I'd spent an entire afternoon laying plans ahead of time. *Perhaps,* I thought, *perhaps I will make a good rogue after all.*

As I started to turn, a bit of movement below caught my eye. There was a figure coming from the right at a brisk pace across the flat, rocky ground. I froze. Then when I was sure the man wasn't looking up at me, I drew back into the cover of a gorse bush and peered through the twilight.

It was only Dunbar, no mistaking that rabbit fur bonnet, that deerskin jacket, that swagger. I heaved a sigh of relief. He had a bundle slung over his shoulder, and he'd gone away without any such, just his pockets stuffed with what food and tobacco and stuff he needed. Intrigued, I watched him climb the hill, being careful to keep myself hidden.

Halfway up, he stopped and carefully looked about. I leaned out of sight and took a deep breath, confident he hadn't spotted me.

When I looked out again—*carefully, carefully*—he was hunched over a cluster of rocks. He lifted one up and set it aside to expose a small hole. Into that he stuffed his bundle, then covered it over again. Before he could straighten up, I darted back into the cave and lay down by the cold fire, trying to look as if I hadn't shifted all day.

All the while I was thinking: *What can Dunbar have brought back that's so valuable he's keeping it a secret even from me?*

When he came inside, he cleared his throat, and when I looked up sleepily, he bobbed his head at me. Then he cast a suspicious glance around the cave, as if to assure himself I hadn't interfered with any of his belongings. Luckily the boxes and tins were just as he'd left them. Only the bowl of neeps was disturbed.

Unslinging his musket and water skin, he sat down opposite me. "I've been thinking on what ye said," he told me without meeting my eyes. He cleared his throat again, as if something were stuck there. "There's no harm in ye staying a while longer. Provided ye make yerself useful."

I was so surprised I could hardly speak. In fact my jaw dropped open. This was just what I wanted. But what had changed his mind? And did it matter, so long as he changed it?

"I'll do ... I'll do whatever ye ask," I blurted out at last. "Just name the task." I could feel a big, daft smile spread all over my face.

"We'll speak more on it in the morning," Dunbar said gruffly. "If ye're to come with me, ye'd best get a good night's sleep."

"I've been dozing all day," I lied. "Canna we talk now?"

"We canna." His answer was almost a slap.

We ate a cold, meager supper of carrots and barley in silence. It was as unappealing as the bowl of neeps. I cleared the dishes away, and he nodded. That was as close to a conversation as we came.

I wanted to ask Dunbar why he was letting me stay, but he looked so distracted, I didn't dare. Even when he sat back against the stone wall, eyes closed, smoking his pipe, I had the sense to keep quiet. I feared that if I upset him now, I'd lose all the ground I'd so mysteriously gained.

Still, I was pleased with myself. Pleased for all that I'd figured out. And even more pleased I'd convinced Dunbar to keep me on. But I couldn't help wondering what it was he'd hidden in that hole in the ground.

Well, if he had a secret, I had my own secret too. I'd seen him hide his bundle. So, which of us was the greater rogue now?

20 ❧ THE STILL

The next morning Dunbar seemed more relaxed, as if he'd come to terms with me staying on. Though I was still curious about his change of mind, he brushed me off whenever I tried to question him.

"I'll no have ye fashing me the whole time," he said testily. "If that doesna suit ye, ye're free to leave."

I'd no choice then but to keep myself to myself.

"Pack up some food and drink," Dunbar said, gathering up his equipment, "and get ready to march. Since ye're staying, I mean to put ye to work."

"Where are we going?"

"No place we'll get to by sitting here blethering." He turned his back on me and packed up his weapons—musket, knife, and ammunition and some other strange tools I had no name for—into a leather sack.

In a few moments he was off down the back side of the hill, a rocky path covered with grey scree that skittered away from us at each step. I scurried after, carrying a second sack filled with our provisions. The morning was bright, the sky spotted with three layers of clouds. I had to walk briskly, nearly breaking into a run, just to keep up with him. My legs were still wobbly from being ill, but I was not going to let that show.

After a bit he turned and watched me, and then he nodded, as if approving my efforts to match his soldier's stride.

I can do it, I told myself. And indeed, the longer we went, the stronger I felt.

In this unfamiliar stretch of country I could tell only that we were headed east toward the Kindarry glens. We stuck to the trees, a large stand of oak, and wound our way through them, though what path we were on was unclear. I think Dunbar must have made up a different route each time to make it harder to track him. I turned to look behind us. I couldn't see the crag and the cave at all, only a solid wall of trees.

After a while, we left the protection of the forest and entered a stone gully with broken walls of grey flint. Our feet left no track here either.

Dunbar didn't speak to me, and so I kept silent as well. But it was hard. I wanted to know where we were going and why. I wanted to know if we were silent because it made us safer, or if we were silent because he had nothing to say to me, or if we were silent because of our secrets.

Suddenly fear rose up like bile in my throat. Could Dunbar be carrying out his threat to turn me over to the laird? Was I a lamb being led to the butcher? I gnawed on that for a while until I saw that even though he'd threatened, it made no sense. Why would he go to all the trouble of saving my life, carrying me all the way to his lair, nursing me for days, only to betray me? And surely, since he'd saved me by shooting at the factor, he was as much a wanted man as I.

But then, I reminded myself, *he is a rogue. Who knows what rogues think?*

Almost as if he'd heard my thoughts, he said in a gruff whisper, "Ye'll be wondering where we're headed." He nodded at the long gully.

"It's crossed my mind." I tried not to sound too keen.

"Word reached me yesterday that Rood's not taken our run-in well." He smiled, a slow smile that lit up his face. "He's got men scouring the hills."

"Hunting for me? Or for ye?"

Dunbar gave a wry laugh and signaled me to sit on a log that must have washed down the gully in some fierce storm years ago. It was as grey as the stone. Settling himself against a rock, Dunbar crossed his legs, took out his pipe, and stuck it in his mouth unlit. "They've no got the nerve to come after me. They know what a good shot I am, and they're all too scared of catching a musket ball between the eyes. Nae, lad, it's my other whisky still he's got them hunting. He wants to take my purse, not my head."

"Surely if it's stayed hidden this long, it's safe enough."

"Nobody's ever been minded to seek it out before. After all, why should they cut off their one source of cheap whisky? They came upon the other still by chance, but now they are looking for a reason."

I crossed my legs as well and felt a small wind through my hair. A hawk screeched above us. The clouds scudded by. And here we sat, two rogues together, talking and plotting.

Now that I'd thought it through, I no longer feared he was going to turn me over to the laird. But I had to win him to *my* plan. Suddenly I realized that I didn't know how.

"But things are changing now," he said.

I leaned forward. "What do you mean to do?"

"I need to take the still apart and shift it to a new hiding place, somewhere off McRoy land. Ye can stand lookout for me while I'm working. Think of it as yer first lesson in roguery." He grinned.

Not my first, I thought, but I couldn't tell him that. I grinned back. "Is it far?"

"Far for ye, not far for me."

Sharing his plans, Dunbar started to talk to me in a friendlier fashion, giving me advice on how to always have an eye out for cover. He also said that if I heard animals stir—rabbits and grouse were the best indicators, and crows loved to talk about intruders—it meant there was somebody snaking around close by. I nodded and made a great show of taking in his words, for I didn't want him to stop talking. He knew everything I needed to know. And more.

"There must be times," I said, "when ye have to find a way into somebody's house . . . for shelter or food."

Dunbar threw me a long glance, almost measuring me. "Hard times make for hard means," he said at last. "I'll not deny I've taken charity off some as never knew they were giving it, but never from any that couldna afford it. Still, I'd be doing ye no favor to put ye on that track. It's dangerous work. And a hanging matter if ye're caught."

I bit my lip to hold back my protest. I needed him to tell me more. Those were exactly the things I needed to learn about. I had to get the Blessing back—and soon. But he had no more to say.

We got up and carried on for a good two hours more, winding up through craggy hills scattered with shriveled saplings and a lot of prickly gorse. It seemed a good place for hiding a still or a bad place for a murder. There were bushes and boulders that kept a man from seeing more than a few yards ahead at any step.

"This looks like a good . . . ," I began softly.

Suddenly Dunbar raised a hand, signaling me to halt and be silent. He cocked his head to one side and listened intently. I did the same, and then I heard voices up ahead.

Dunbar put a finger to his lips and beckoned me to follow. We stopped by a thorn bush and he listened again.

"Damn, but they've beaten us to it!" He cursed under his breath.

There was a gust of drunken laughter.

"From the sound of it, they're sampling my wares for free." His whisper was fierce. "How many do ye reckon there are?"

I listened hard. At last I ventured a guess, holding up two fingers.

Dunbar nodded. "Good lad. Ye've got keen ears when ye choose to use them. Now, best stay out of sight. There's no sense letting on that ye're with me." Unslinging his musket, he started forward in a poacher's crouch. I kept close behind him.

"They have ye outnumbered," I whispered urgently. "They'll be armed too. A still's not worth dying over, is it?"

Dunbar grinned back at me over his shoulder. "I'm counting on them to see it that way."

He paused at the space between a boulder and a thornberry thicket. The gap was so narrow I could hardly see past Dunbar at all. But what I *could* see made my stomach go cold. As I'd guessed, there were two men, their muskets set down on the ground at their feet. They were enjoying their drams of whisky, a jug nestled between them, and they had that soft, muzzy look that men just slightly drunk often seemed to get. They weren't at the fighting stage yet, just happy and unaware. Beyond them, against the rocks, were the tin drum and pipes of the Rogue's still, an odd contraption I could make no sense of.

Dunbar rose slowly to his feet. A rook cawed a warning; the men didn't look up. They were having too much fun drinking. But at the sound, I held my breath.

Then Dunbar stepped nimbly into the clearing, cocking his musket and laughing out loud.

The laird's men leapt to their feet, and one of them kicked over the jug by accident. It rolled across the ground, the last of the golden liquor dribbling from its neck.

I edged forward for a clearer view. The man on the left was a thin, nervous type, while the bearded man to the right had a flushed and angry face.

"I'd not expected to find customers so thirsty they'd come all this way for a wee dram," said Dunbar. "How are ye two enjoying my drink?"

Both men had their eyes on his gun. They must have known only too well how quickly he could get off a shot. They were hired men, but *he'd* been in the king's army. They moved back against the still, perhaps thinking that Dunbar wouldn't harm them so near it. They didn't know what I knew—that he was already planning to dismantle it.

The thin man cleared his throat. "We're here on the laird's business, Dunbar."

"And what business would that be, McInnes?" The Rogue's musket never wavered. That he knew the man's name surprised me. What surprised me even more was how calm he sounded when he should have been furious with anger.

"He wants ye off his property," answered the one with the beard. He took another step back.

"If that's what he wants, he'll need better men than ye two to do the job."

"Take a telling, Dunbar," the thin man pleaded. "He'll have the militia on ye before long, and how would that serve ye?"

Dunbar laughed again, but this time there was no mirth in it. "The militia, is it? I must be a very dangerous breed of scoundrel."

"Och, man, if ye've any wits at all, ye'll pack up and make a new lair for yerself far away from here," the bearded man warned.

"I'll take that advice as well meant, Sinclair," Dunbar told him. "Ye've been good customers to me before. But surely ye know, I come and go at no man's bidding. If ye're truly concerned for my welfare, I'm sure ye'll be wanting to pay for the whisky ye've drunk."

The laird's men exchanged glances, each expecting the other to answer.

"Come along," Dunbar urged. "If ye've come without money, I'll have to take it out of yer hide." His voice was the more frightening for its calmness. "After all, I canna have ye robbing me like common brigands."

"There's no call for that," said the thin man, McInnes. He fished in his pocket for his purse and lifted it out with shaking fingers. Obviously he didn't think Dunbar was all that calm. As he tried to open the purse, it slipped out of his hands and hit the ground with a dull clink of coins.

"Ye're over-canny with yer pennies, McInnes," Dunbar said, gesturing at the purse. "Pick it up and pay yer due. Dinna worry, I willna take more than is owed."

As the nervous man bent to pick up his money, my eyes flicked to his companion. Taking advantage of the distraction, Sinclair had

slipped a stealthy hand inside his coat. What he was drawing out
had the glint of sharpened steel.

"Dunbar!" I cried, jumping out of hiding.

At my shout the Rogue spotted the danger. He whipped his
musket about, took a long stride forward, and cracked the butt hard
across the bearded man's face, knocking him flat. McInnes aban-
doned his purse and had his hands in the air before Dunbar had
even turned the gun on him.

The thin man blinked warily. "Ye've an accomplice now,
I see."

"An *apprentice,* if ye don't mind," Dunbar corrected. "Before
long, these hills will be full of wee rogues and it's Daniel McRoy
who will be packing his bags."

The bearded man lay groaning on the ground, a bloody bruise
branded across his cheek.

"Help him up, McInnes, for I'll not give him a hand," Dunbar
ordered, his voice now like stone. The thin man helped his dazed
comrade to his feet and they began to edge away.

"Drop yer steel and yer pistols first, then run back to yer master
and tell him about the brave job ye've done. And if ye cross my path
again, I'll not be so kind to ye."

They did as he directed, and I stepped well aside to let them
pass. They hurried away like frightened lambs.

Dunbar rubbed his grizzled jaw. "I can't abide folk trying to kill
me," he said, though there was a hint of laughter in his voice. "The
French came close enough to put me off the notion for good."

I smiled, feeling good about the part I'd just played. But Dunbar
gave me no time for triumph.

"Ye think ye've done me a good deed, lad. But all ye've done
is show our hand. Now they know yer with me, they'll guess it'll

be easier to track me down. And so it will." He looked over at his still. "Come on," he said. "Help me break up this blasted thing and hide it. Sinclair will want to return for vengeance soon. And if those gowks are right about soldiers coming, we'd best be out of here. I'll no be serving drink to the king's men."

IV. THE BLESSING

Farewell to the Highlands, farewell to the North,

The birth-place of Valour, the country of Worth;

Wherever I wander, wherever I rove,

The hills of the Highlands for ever I love.

—Robert Burns, "Farewell to the Highlands"

We hid the still in a rocky fissure miles from where we found it, covering it over with branches. It took us two trips before we were done. The Rogue carried the heavier pieces, and I carried a few of the pipes as well as his tools, though he kept the musket, already primed with its charge, in his hand, the two weapons of the other men stuck down in his belt and his knife in his stocking. Eventually the effort of keeping up with Dunbar's brisk march started to wear me out. I had fallen a good dozen paces behind when the Rogue paused to look back at me.

"Ye're not at yer full strength yet," he said, not unkindly. "It willna hurt us to stop and catch a breath."

We were heading back to the cave: I recognized the stone gully. I thought to protest and make a show of courage, but he silenced me with a wave of his hand.

"It's a bad general that marches his men beyond their endurance. It's nae more than a couple of days ago that ye were pounding at Death's door like a laird's factor come for the rent."

I laughed at that, and Dunbar gave a thin smile. "I'm glad Death didna answer," I said. "Maybe he's as deaf as old Tam Mackay."

We got past the slatey walls of the gully and into the small wood, settling at last in the shade of a scrawny elm, its thin leaves enough to keep the fading sun off our faces. It looked to be mid-afternoon. My stomach told me it was well past time to eat.

I was relieved to see that our brush with danger had given Dunbar a thirst as great as my own. We drank deep from our canteens and shared the bread and cheese I'd packed.

"See that stream over there?" said the Rogue, gesturing toward a spur of rock jutting out of a nearby hillside. Indeed, I had missed it, but once he pointed it out, I could both see and hear the water flooding over stones. "We can get a refill there."

I shook the last few drops of water into my mouth, then followed Dunbar around the hill.

The stream was narrow and rippling over a bed of colored pebbles. On the far side a ewe was lying on her side at the foot of a rocky slope. She was a stunted specimen, clearly not one of the laird's precious English Cheviots, and mewling pathetically to herself. As we approached, she tried to get up, but one of her forelegs gave way beneath her on the stony ground.

"She must have skidded down those rocks there and broken her leg," said Dunbar, his sharp eyes catching the telltale signs of the animal's fall. He pointed to the scrape down the hill, and I looked at it carefully, promising myself to remember how it looked.

We crossed the stream slowly, not wishing to frighten the ewe any more than was necessary.

"She's been trying to crawl the rest of the way to the stream," I said, and was pleased when Dunbar nodded.

"Aye—she must have been separated from the flock when they were driven off by the burning," said Dunbar. "And a ewe makes a poor rogue when left to fend for herself."

"Aye, they're liable to panic at the slightest thing, even at the best of times," I agreed. "It's a shame to let her suffer."

"That's soon taken care of," said Dunbar, pulling his knife from his stocking. Kneeling down beside the miserable creature, he pulled her head back and in a quick, easy motion drew the blade cleanly across her throat. The sheep twitched a few moments as the blood gushed from her wound, then was still.

"No more pain for the sheep and a fine supper for us," Dunbar said, hoisting her onto his shoulder. "This day's taken a better turn than I looked for."

I filled both our canteens, and we were ready to continue on.

The thought of hot, juicy mutton put a fresh spring in my step. Even with Dunbar carrying the heavy sheep, our trek back to the Rogue's lair seemed to take only half the time as our outward journey had. Birds sang overhead with gusto, as if telling us we'd nothing to fear.

We walked through a stream to lose any possible trackers and stayed on the rocks as often as we could—harder going than walking in dirt but better to fool any followers, so Dunbar told me. And that was how we made our roguish way back to camp.

Once at the cave, Dunbar skinned the sheep and cut the meat into strips in half the time it would have taken me, farmer's son though I was. He fixed the joints of mutton to sticks, and we roasted them over a blazing peat fire inside the cave as soon as it was dark so that no one could see the smoke.

Shadows danced around the cave as we ate, but they were comforting shadows. Familiar. And after all the hardships of the last few days, that mutton was the most delicious meal I'd ever tasted, for all that it came from one of our scrawny Highland ewes and had no seasoning other than hunger to recommend it.

"Ye did well today," Dunbar said, using the back of his hand to wipe grease from his chin. "If ye hadna been watching my back, that villain might have pricked me with his wee knife, and then I'd have had to kill them both."

"They would have deserved it," I said. Even in the shadowy cave I could see him smile.

"Aye, but then I'd have had the law down on my head for sure. As things stand, I do little enough harm with my poaching and whisky, but killing a man would make me more than a nuisance. It would take me from rogue to criminal. And the taking of a man's life is a scar that heals hard. I did enough of it in the king's army to know." Now his face was solemn, drawn down, the sharp planes of his cheeks darkened.

He reached for his whisky jug and yanked out the stopper with a sharp pop. Throwing back a hearty swig, he wiped the neck of the jug with his sleeve, then offered it to me. "We'll drink together like comrades after a battle."

I took it from him and raised it to my lips. I was wary of the Rogue's personal brew, and Pa had never let us drink whisky except once to wet our lips at Mother's funeral and again at our celebration of the victory over the laird. But I couldn't show any want of courage, not now, when Dunbar was making a gesture of friendship. I needed that friendship. If he thought himself my friend, he would offer help. I took as big a mouthful as I dared and swallowed.

The liquor blazed down my throat and settled in my stomach like a bonfire. I gulped hard, almost dropping the jug. I prayed silently that the mutton I'd eaten would stay put.

Dunbar chuckled and took the jug out of my hands. "That was a giant's dram you put away there," he said. "Next time just take a sip so there's some left for me."

He took another swallow and sighed contentedly. "This is more whisky than we ever got after a real battle," he said. "And it's got more bite too."

I leaned back against the wall. My head was going slightly

muzzy, even after just one long drink. I heard myself saying, "So, ye fought at Waterloo."

He smiled into the darkening cave. "Aye, that's a fine tale and true. I never got Napoleon in my sights, though," he added with a wink. The firelight flickering over his face made him look more roguish than ever.

"Tell me about it, then." *Was that* my *voice, so soft and yearning?*

"Boys always want to hear about battles," he said with a chuckle, "but if ye've the sense God gave a mouse, ye'll steer clear of them." He gave me the jug and let me have a couple more sips before he took it back. Then he leaned forward and began his story.

"I was with Gordon's Highlanders, as rough and foul-mouthed a pack of fighting men as ye'll ever meet. Drawn up along a ridge in Belgium we were, with Napoleon's army in all their finery lined up on the other side of the valley.

"I remember the French cannon booming all through the morning, iron balls tearing through our ranks and ripping men limb from limb. Our Scots cavalry silenced them for a while, but not for long. Eventually we were ordered to fall back to the far side of the ridge so we'd have some shelter from the guns.

"The French thought we were running away, so Marshall Ney mustered the whole of Boney's cavalry to come after us. Ten thousand strong they were: lancers, hussars, cuirassiers and all. They were hoping to catch us by our breeks and give us a good hiding."

"Never!" I said.

He frowned slightly at the interruption and continued. " 'Form square!' came the order. Aye, the square—that was how we were trained to stand against cavalry. A big jagged square we made, three ranks on each side, our bayonets bristling like thorns on a hedge.

"It was all bustle and shouting till we were in formation, then

. it went deathly quiet. It was in that silence we heard them coming, the drumming of forty thousand hooves, the loudest thunder you ever heard.

"Then they broke over the ridge, like a giant wave bursting the dams of hell. I swear I gripped my musket so tight I came close to snapping it in two. Down the slope they charged, a flood that looked to sweep us away like driftwood. The sun was flashing on their lance points and on the curved blades of their sabers. The horses were snorting like devils in the fury of their charge, kicking up clods of muddy grass as they bore down on us."

I could see it all, even in the dark of the cave, but this time I knew better than to say a word.

He took a wee sip of the jug to wet his mouth, then shouted: " 'Present arms!' "

I must have jumped a foot.

"That's what the captain bellowed. So, I braced the gun against my shoulder and took aim at the oncoming line of horsemen. 'Fire!' came the command.

"Every man of us pulled the trigger at the same moment, and our volley went off with a roar. Fire and smoke billowed out from our lines, bringing down horses and shooting riders right out of their saddles.

"Then they burst upon our red-coated squares like a raging sea, a mad tide of horseflesh and iron. The horses shied away from our wall of bayonets and the riders swirled about, stabbing and slashing for all they were worth.

"All around me was a frenzy of reloading, orders being yelled and curses spat into the dust that was flying about us. A French cuirassier, dreadful to behold, sliced the head clean off one of the lads kneeling in front of me. One stroke of his saber and all I saw was his body toppling to the left."

I gasped and looked to my left as if expecting to see a headless body there.

"Then his horse, a huge, terrible beast, black as midnight, took a bayonet in its flank. It reared up high, kicking its forehooves in the air and whinnying its pain. The cuirassier rider waved his bloody sword above the crest of his helmet and roared his defiance at us.

"Well, I'd reloaded by this time and took careful aim at the beast's head—and fired. The musket ball tore right through its skull, spilling out its brains, and the poor beast dropped dead right in front of us. The rider fell clear and scrambled to his feet in a fury, yelling curses at us in his Froggy tongue.

"Instead of running away, he came at us, blade held high. Whether it was revenge for his horse, I dinna know, but I could see in his eyes that he meant to murder as many of as he could while breath remained. I'd nae time to reload again, so I lunged with my musket, driving the point of my bayonet right through his throat.

"I yanked it free and the blood spurted out over his shiny armor. His eyes were still wide open as he crumpled to the ground. His gloved hand pawed uselessly at his throat, trying to stanch the wound."

Dunbar's eyes had a faraway look to them, and his left hand drifted to his own throat. Then he muttered the same thing he'd said to me earlier: "The taking of a man's life is a scar that heals hard." He went silent for a long moment.

I let out the breath I was holding. I didn't know whether to be afraid of this man or warm to him. He was a strange puzzle. "What happened then?"

"Then?" He shook his head. "I dinna remember much after that. They pulled back and charged again, then again and again till we lost count of how many times they'd come. But we didna break. After the battle was won, I was ordered to walk about the field shooting any wounded horses I found lying on the grass." He lapsed into another silence. "The men we left to die on their own."

"It was a famous victory," I said lamely.

"They were brave men, those Frenchies," Dunbar said, "and I suppose they were dying for something they thought worth the price. I only wish to God I knew what it was." He raised the jug to his lips and took a gulp, then another and another until I began to fear what it might do to him. When he stopped at last, he smacked his lips and spoke with a hard edge to his voice.

"I fought for money, for the king's shilling, lad." He gave a short, hard laugh. "The king—a half-mad German who didna care if I lived or died so long as I kept fighting. There's glory for ye!"

I reached tentatively for the jug, hoping to take it away from him before the drink made his mood worse. He glowered at me.

"Ye've had enough, lad," he said. "Ye're no a man yet, let alone a rogue. And never, never—lad—never go for a soldier."

He pressed the jug to his chest and started singing to himself in a low crooning voice. The song was something about bloody Waterloo. Gradually his chin sank down onto his chest, then softly he began to snore.

My own eyelids were growing heavy as well, and when I lay down on the bedding, an odd dizziness overcame me. *Too much whisky,* I thought. Dunbar was right about that, as he was about everything.

22 ❧ THE BUNDLE

When I woke up, my mouth felt like it had been scoured with sand. Sometime in the night I had rolled off the bedding and must have slept hunched up on the cave's cold stone floor. My back and legs creaked as I straightened out. I got to my feet, rubbing my eyes and swaying dizzily.

Aye, too much whisky. One large swig and a few small ones to follow and I was a roaring drunk.

Dunbar was still slumbering, his face turned away from me, his breathing deep and heavy. One outstretched hand was clenched tight, as if he were clinging fast to something unseen, maybe some memory out of his past.

I picked up the water jug, but there were only a few drops left in it, scarcely enough to moisten my lips. The early morning sun cast a round shadow through the cave entrance, and a small breeze carried in the scent of high grass and bluebells. *Ah—fresh air!* I thought. It would clear my stuffy head better than the cramped confines of the Rogue's lair.

Dangling the jug by its handle, I stepped outside and took a deep breath. I felt immediately refreshed, but my tongue still tasted of peat and ashes. So I decided to walk down the crag and to the stream at its bottom to fill the jug.

I was careful, like a rogue, not striding down but picking my way along so that I couldn't be seen from below. Overhead a hawk soared, and for a brief moment its outstretched wings blotted out the sun. Then it spotted something in the long grass and fell down on its prey. I watched its long stoop and then tried to see where it ate its breakfast, but the grass hid it from view.

When I reached the thin wee stream, I plunged in the jug, then brought it to my lips, gulping the cold water as thirstily as Dunbar had downed his whisky the night before. Once I'd sated my thirst, I filled the jug to the brim and headed back up the crag to the cave.

It occurred to me that I could give Dunbar a rude awakening by dashing the cold water over his face as I used to do with Lachlan on those mornings when he was slow to stir. I laughed at the memory, then felt a pang of loss. What if I never saw my eager, good-hearted brother again? I scrubbed my fist against my right eye. After all, rogues don't cry. And then it suddenly occurred to me that Dunbar wouldn't take the joke half as well. A comrade was not a brother, no matter how many lives are saved—he saving me from Willie Rood and me saving him from the laird's men at the still.

As I walked toward the cave, I suddenly remembered Dunbar's suspicious behavior of the evening before last, how careful he'd been to glance about him before opening the hiding place, how furtively he had stashed away a bundle like a miser burying ill-gained loot. Loot he was determined to keep from my sight. With him sleeping off his drink, I now had a chance to uncover what it was he'd hidden.

The boldness of my decision made me feel strong, stronger than the Rogue himself. Quickly, I headed toward his hiding place, but then felt a prickle at the back of my neck, a kind of warning. I admired Dunbar's courage and skill and didn't want to spoil the comradeship that had grown up between us. And I admired his fighting abilities. But suspicion is a hard thing to kill. Surely, I told myself, it would be wise to learn exactly what he was keeping from me. Once I knew what it was, I could tease him with my knowledge and he would realize what a good rogue I could be.

And then I had another thought. *What if the thing hidden in the rocks is the Blessing?*

That thought made me shiver. After all, Dunbar had readily admitted to being a thief. Might he already have done what I'd only been planning? After all, he'd suspected the laird and Rood had taken something from me. Maybe he'd caught the laird before he'd made it back to Kindarry House and had wrested the Blessing from him, afterward rescuing me from Rood's grasp. Maybe *that* was why the laird had mounted such a campaign against him.

Suddenly I knew I had to learn the truth.

I found the spot easily, then checked around me to make sure I hadn't been deceived by the early morning shadows. Setting the jug on a rock, I looked guiltily up at the cave to make sure Dunbar wasn't up and about.

A sharp cry startled me, but it was only the hawk that, having finished its meal, had taken to the sky again, screaming out its victory.

I bent over and took hold of the thick, flat rock that was set on top of the others and pulled at it. It was surprisingly heavy. Dunbar had lifted it with such ease. Once again I was reminded how strong he was.

Setting the stone aside, I gazed at the rough bundle that lay nestled among the rocks. As I lifted it out, I was as careful as I would have been with a swaddled babe. If this were some honest property of Dunbar's, I didn't want to give myself away by breaking or nicking anything.

Laying it on the ground, I crouched over it, slowly peeling aside the coarse wrappings. I don't know what I expected. Gold bars? Jewels? Silver coins?

To my surprise, what lay inside was a silver plate embossed with flowers, a trio of painted statuettes—a shepherd and two dogs—and a necklace decorated with a single clear stone.

As I examined the treasure, a disturbing suspicion dawned on me: I recognized some of these things. But how? Nothing like them had ever adorned our poor cottage, and I had never been anywhere that would be home to such ornaments.

Except once.

When I'd been taken to the Lodge.

Yes, now recognition hit me with a cold shock. I touched the statues in turn, recalling where I had seen them—on a table at Bonnie Josie's house.

How could he? I went hot and then cold with anger. *Robbing the laird was one thing. But robbing Bonnie Josie . . .*

Then I made myself stop and think things out calmly. It made quite a bit of sense, for wouldn't Dunbar regard Bonnie Josie and her mother as people who had plenty, whose family was stealing from the poor folk all they had? And they were much easier targets than the laird, whose house would be bristling with guards.

But Dunbar knew nothing. *Nothing.* Josie had been using her own money to help the crofters. To steal from her meant the Rogue was stealing from all of us.

Another hot flush rushed across my face; my fingers trembled as they touched the damning evidence. I clenched my fists, my heart pounding with the impulse to hurt Dunbar for this betrayal. And I felt ashamed of myself for admiring him, ashamed that I had ever wanted to be like him. *The Rogue's Apprentice?* Well, no longer.

I wrapped the stolen goods as carefully as my passion would allow, picked up the water jug, and started up the hill at a steady march. A part of me wanted to catch Dunbar still asleep and be revenged on him before he could awake, though I couldn't think how.

Striding boldly into the cave, I was pulled up short when I saw that he was already sitting up and rubbing his palms against the sides of his head. *Good!* I thought. *His head aches.*

Giving me a tired grin, he stood, arching his back to work out the kinks. "Morning, lad!" he greeted me. "Been out to fetch me some water, have ye?"

His friendly air made my anger flare afresh. "It's not water I've fetched." I set the jug down. "It's this!"

Bending down, I unwrapped the bundle and spilled the contents carefully at his feet.

Dunbar's body stiffened and he fixed me with a hard, questioning glare. Straightening, I met his eyes without flinching. "What do ye think ye're doing, lad?" His voice was low and grim.

I swallowed to keep up my courage. "Showing ye up for the damnable thief ye are."

"Those are strong words for such a weak boy," Dunbar said. "Ye've time yet to take them back, if ye're quick about it."

He was leaning toward me, his eyes bright with anger. More anger than he should have had, for hadn't he boasted about being a thief?

I knew I was no match for him if it came to a fight, but it was then I spotted his musket leaning against the cave wall by the stone wardrobe. It was loaded, I knew, and ready to fire. He usually slept with it by his side.

Before Dunbar could make a move, I snatched up the musket and leveled it at his chest. I cocked the weapon and set my finger to the trigger.

The Rogue drew back and eyed me warily. "Do ye mean to murder me then and take the little I have? Is that all the gratitude ye're capable of?"

"I recognize those things," I said, nodding toward the trove on the floor. "They're from the Lodge. They belong to Bonnie Josie and her mother."

"Do they, now . . ." He never took his eyes off my face.

"I've heard some bad talk about ye, Alan Dunbar, and now I see it's all true. Ye'd even steal from a widow and her daughter to line yer own pockets."

Dunbar's face was set hard, his voice as sharp as the edge of a sword. "As much as ye owe me, ye're still keen to think the worst of me, and that is low."

My finger ached on the trigger, and I was wary he'd try something. No—I *hoped* he'd try something, because then I would be justified in shooting him where he stood. "I was a fool ever to believe ye cared for anything but yer own greed," I said. I felt tears spring to my eyes but fought them back. I wouldn't let him see my pain—or my weakness—only my anger. "Tie that bundle back up."

"Ye'd turn my own gun on me" Dunbar sneered. "Why, Judas himself would spit on ye."

"I'll take no Bible lessons from ye, ye villainous creature," I answered. I jabbed the musket barrel at him to show I was serious.

Keeping his eyes fixed on me, Dunbar crouched and re-wrapped his stolen loot. I motioned him to back off, and he retreated, but only a tiny step.

"So what do ye intend?" he challenged me. "To take these to the laird and make him yer friend? Maybe ye can be the new factor when Willie Rood is busy with his sheep."

"I mean to take them back where they came from," I said, struggling to keep my voice and the gun both steady. "To the Lodge. If ye're wise, ye'll flee this place before the law catches up with ye."

"Big words . . . big words," Dunbar said through gritted teeth. "They'd be smaller, I think, if ye weren't holding my own gun on me."

"Not half as small as yer thief's heart." My voice threatened to break. I steadied it as I steeled my hand on the gun.

"It's ye that's the thief, ye two-faced ingrate!" he roared. "Sneaking around behind my back, betraying my trust! If ye were a man, I'd kill ye for it!"

"I'm man enough!" I shouted back, though my voice sounded thin after his, my anger only a torch to his bonfire. "If there's any killing, ye won't be the one to do it."

Suddenly the Rogue took a lightning step forward. In one quick move he grabbed the musket barrel and yanked the gun from my hands. My finger was on the trigger, though, and as it came loose, the gun went off, booming like a cannon in the confines of the cave.

The shock of it startled Dunbar as much as it did me.

"Ye damned fool!" he exclaimed, tossing the musket aside. "Did ye want to see murder done?"

"Tell me ye deserve better!" I answered him. My rage was still red hot, driving me to defiance, but almost at once other feelings settled in: shock, grief, loss—and fear. The heat that had possessed me slowly turned to an icy cold. I started to shake. My eyes grew watery, my chest heaved with an unwanted sob. Snatching the bundle up off the ground, I whirled about and ran out of the cave. I rushed down the front of the hillside, stumbling as I went, hardly able to see for the grief of it. I had but a minute or two before Dunbar could reload and fire.

He strode out of the cave and shouted after me. "Aye, run! Run like a dog that's bitten its master!"

Though I knew him now for the dirty thief he was, his words still stung me with shame. But because of all he'd done to keep me alive, I ran all the faster trying to escape.

23 ❧ BONNIE JOSIE

I stumbled and slid down the rugged slope, my heels cutting troughs in the turf. I cared little that I was leaving a trail even a rogue's apprentice could follow. Clutching the bundle, I tried desperately not to fall. The weight of it made my movements slow and clumsy, but I would not give Dunbar the satisfaction of dropping his loot.

Above me swallows seem to laugh in the air, circling and diving. But I felt no such laughter inside. The Rogue's final words still rang in my ears, their bitter edge cutting as a knife. By now he'd had time to reload, and there was I, exposed on the bare hillside. If Dunbar wanted to stop me, I couldn't outrun a bullet. And he was, by his own admission, a fine shot.

I tried to pray but feared God would never listen to such a sinner as I. And if Dunbar fired, I doubted I would even hear the shot before it killed me. Forcing myself not to look back, I kept on running.

At the bottom of the hill I took a deep breath. Perhaps Dunbar's villainy had already reached its depth in the robbery and he wouldn't sink to cold-blooded murder. After all, he'd let the men at the still go free with no more than a fierce warning.

I had to find Josie and her mother and return their property to them. That and warn them about Dunbar and his thieving ways.

Wading the stream, I felt a pain in my heart. I knew what it was: I'd lost my only ally.

Worse, I told myself, *I let him charm me into thinking him a better man than he is.*

Then I headed off to the right across the flat ground. There was no cover here, so I hunched over to make myself a small target and ran until my chest hurt with each breath. But by then I was in the trees. Safe at last.

Or safe as any trespasser on the laird's land can feel.

I reached Bonnie Josie's Lodge by early evening, proud of how well I'd read the map of sun and sky to get there. Though I was slower than I might have been had I not had to make sure to stay hidden.

I remembered the last time I'd come to the Lodge, with the men and the English sheep. It had been in a spirit of adventure. Now I skulked among the rocks and bushes, as Dunbar must have done when he came to do his dirty work.

When I was sure it was safe to move, I tiptoed through the violets and bluebells in the back garden and glided beneath the branches of a pear tree. I found the back door unlatched and opened it, only enough to squeeze through into the kitchen. I was lucky that no one was about. Or perhaps we were all unlucky, because the Glendoun folk had clearly been moved on.

The memory of my time inside the Lodge made my head ache. I could hear a servant moving jars about in the pantry. By padding along the hallway on the soft carpet, I managed to sneak by unnoticed.

Pressing my ear to the sitting room door, I hoped to hear the voices of Josie and her mother. Bad luck. No one was speaking, but I did hear a rustling that let me know someone was inside. Of course it was always possible the laird might be visiting, so I opened the door cautiously.

I smiled at what I saw, for it was Josie seated alone at her desk. Her head was laid upon her arms, her eyes turned to the window and the grey sky beyond. Before I could speak, her back trembled and I heard her sob.

The theft of her things must have been even worse than I thought. No doubt Dunbar had stolen more than the few pieces I had with me and concealed the rest in another of his hiding places. Hearing Josie's grief made my blood hot against the Rogue all over again. Closing the door silently behind me and stepping closer, I spoke softly, not wanting to startle her.

"There's nae call for tears," I said. "I've brought back what ye've lost."

Josie sat up straight, turned and stared at me with red-rimmed eyes. She rubbed the tears from her cheeks and frowned.

"How could you do that, you daft boy?" she asked in a grave voice. "Have you gone weak in the head?"

I was taken aback to see her so low, with no sparkle in her eye, no laughter on her lips. I held the bundle out in front of me so she could see it plainly. "Look, I have it here. Or at least some of it."

I laid the bundle down carefully on the table and pulled away the wrappings. I stood proudly by as Josie stared at her stolen property, reaching out to finger one of the plates.

She glanced up at me, looking more puzzled than grateful.

"I thought ye'd be happy," I said feebly. "They must be worth a few pennies. Enough, I think, to eat for several months."

Then it struck me what must be wrong. She surely thought I was the one who'd robbed her.

I put up my hands. "*I* didna steal it!" I protested. "I took it off the thief who did and brought it back to ye."

"Of course I don't think you're a thief, Roddy," Josie said.

"It was Dunbar took it!" I declared. "The Rogue. He sneaked in while ye were sleeping and robbed ye. It's him that's brought ye to these tears."

"Oh, Roddy, Alan Dunbar's not the reason for me weeping," said Josie. She took a deep breath to steady herself. "Today I buried my mother, dead these two days past. I'm supposed to go off to my uncle's, where a party will be going on. But they won't be celebrating my mother's life. They'll be cheering her death." She caught her breath. "Och—I canna stand it."

My cheeks burned with the news. "Oh, that's sorry tidings indeed. And I'm a fool for bursting in on ye. I helped bury my own mother two years ago, and the hurt still sits in my chest all this time later."

"No, Roddy, I'm sure you meant well," Josie answered kindly, putting her hand out to me, "and that's a comfort. No one else has offered me as much. The servants are not even my own, but my uncle's spies. Still, what are you doing *here*? You and the folk of Dunraw should all be long gone."

"My family are in Glasgow by now," I said, "ready to take a ship to America. If I dinna get there soon, they'll be forced to leave without me. So ye see, it's just me that's come back."

"Whatever for? There's nothing here for you."

I replied cautiously, "There was . . . something. I came in hopes of finding it—and I did."

She smiled a thin smile. "It sounds like you've a story to tell. Maybe it will lift my spirits to hear it."

"The way it's come out won't lift anybody's spirits but yer uncle's, but I'll tell ye anyway."

Josie sat me down by the fireplace, which had a roaring fire even though it was spring. Then she went and fetched oatcakes, cheese and a bottle of cordial from the kitchen. She closed the door firmly behind her and locked it from the inside. "I told the servants I was not to be disturbed. They think it's more mourning. So no one will know you're here. But we have to speak quietly."

She refused to hear a word till I had eaten and drunk my fill, but when I started my tale, she leaned forward to catch every detail. The words came faster and faster as I spoke, till my story was rushing like a river in spate.

She made me stop at the part where I'd found the Blessing.

"A brooch? From the Bonnie Prince?" she said. "It's like a tale out of olden times."

"I've no made it up, I swear!" I raised my hand as if I was taking an oath. "It was passed down to my mother from her father, who had it from his father, Duncan MacDonald." I put my hand over my heart.

"I believe you, Roddy, and I know that you and your kin have even greater need of such a treasure than I would." She put out a hand again and this time patted my fingers where they lay on my chest.

"Ye speak as if ye have nothing," I said passionately, "but ye've this fine house." I looked around. The Lodge could house a dozen families easily. It had to be worth a fortune.

She took her hand off mine. "This fine house, such as it is, belonged to my mother, and with her death it passes to my uncle. The lawyers are making the transfer even now."

"But surely yer mother's left ye jewels and the like," I said. "She was a laird's wife, after all." I leaned forward, wanting to take her hand to comfort her, but I didn't dare.

"She had little enough, and it's all long sold. How else could we feed the poor folk who took shelter on our doorstep?" Josie's face was so drawn in and grey, for a moment she looked years older.

"Have ye nothing else left?"

"Only the money my father left for me in a bank in Edinburgh, though that's a tidy sum."

"There ye are, then!"

"It's not mine till I wed. And if I wed before my twentieth birthday—that's a year off yet—then it goes to my uncle Daniel to disburse on my behalf." Some color came back into her face, and she was almost bonnie once again.

"If he gets his pasty fingers on it, ye'll see naught but a few coppers in change," I warned her.

"Aye, I know it and you know it. And my uncle knows it best of all." She sighed. "That's why he's been pressing me so hard to wed his tame beastie, Willie Rood, before the year's out. He doesn't guess, though, that I understand his plan. He thinks all women are dumb or daft."

I hardly dared speak my thoughts now, but I took a chance. I whispered fiercely, "It's my aim to get the Blessing back from him."

"I don't doubt you've the courage for it," said Josie, "but where's the means?"

I shrugged. "That I havna thought all the way through yet. I've considered stealing it from his house."

She shook her head. "No, no, Roddy, that's much too dangerous."

I shrugged as if to say danger meant nothing to me.

But Josie suddenly brightened even more. "There *might* be a way, though it sickens me to think of speaking sweetly to that grasping miser."

I almost jumped up at the hope in her voice. "Do ye have a plan?"

"Nearly. As I told you, my uncle is holding a party at his house tonight, to 'honor his dear departed sister-in-law,' he says. In truth it's to celebrate getting his hands on the last of the McRoy land. Still, there *might* be a way I can—"

Josie's thoughts were interrupted by a knocking at the front door. She put her finger up to her lips to silence me. Moments later, a maid tapped on the door of the room we were in.

"Mistress," she called, "it's that Willie Rood to see ye." Her voice was scratchy and ended in a whine.

Josie pondered a moment, then said, "Show him in, Mairi."

As soon as the maid had gone back to the front door to deliver that message, I jumped to my feet like a deer that's just heard a hunter's horn.

"Stay calm," Josie whispered. "This calls for a cool head and a steady hand. Go hide behind that curtain and don't make a sound. There's a peephole about halfway up, so you'll see what's afoot. I put it there myself with my sewing needle when we lived in the big house and I came down here to spy on my uncle for fun."

I did as she told me, and she waited till I was completely concealed before unlocking the door and letting the maid show Rood into the room. I breathed shallowly for fear of making the curtain move. The last time I'd seen Rood, he'd tried to murder me. I doubted he would hesitate finishing now what he'd started then, even in front of Bonnie Josie.

I began to sweat with fear till I found the little peephole. Josie was right. It *was* a good hole. I could see straight ahead and a little on either side.

Rood had his back partway to me. Josie had managed to maneuver him right into my line of sight. He'd taken off his hat and was evidently pressing it against his belly with both hands. His orange hair stuck out like the rays of an ugly sun.

"The laird yer uncle's compliments, Miss Josie," he said in a softer voice than I'd ever heard him use before. "He'd be obliged if ye'd join him tonight at Kindarry House to celebrate yer mother's wake." He took a deep breath, and I did so at the same time. "To dine with him and certain others as wish ye well, and I include myself in that number."

Josie thought a moment, then sighed. "Tell him I'll come, but I'll not look a pauper among those fine folk. I no longer have jewels of my own to wear, so I'll thank him to provide me with some that are worthy of a laird's kin."

Rood fidgeted with his hat. "The laird's not a man for giving things away."

"Oh, tush, Willie Rood!" She looked up at him under fluttering lashes. "I'll not tax my uncle's generosity. Let him find me some bauble to wear for this night only and he'll have my gratitude for all the time to come."

"Yer gratitude, ye say . . ." He shuffled his feet uncomfortably.

"Aye, and you'll have it too if you persuade him to do me this small favor. I'll need—let's see—maybe a set of pearls for around my neck or a tasteful brooch. And I only have these old bobs." She touched her ears. "Or perhaps a small ring. Nothing ostentatious."

His feet were shuffling again. "Ostentatious?"

"Nothing too ornate, Mr. Rood. I am not that kind of lass."

He fidgeted with his hat, turning slightly sideways. "I've never known ye to ask anything of me before, Miss Josie."

"I've been thinking on my position," she said softly, moving to his right so he was forced to turn to look at her, which put his back to me once again. "A funeral prompts such sober reflection, don't you think?"

His head bobbed in agreement. As did the fire, which took that moment to crackle loudly.

Josie let out a huge sigh. "And I see my uncle was not wrong on *every* point. I understand now that a woman might face many a cold, unhappy winter with only herself for company. Now that my dear mother is gone . . ."

I was sure Rood was grinning at her, like a fox at its kill. "It's true what ye say, Miss Josie, truer than ye know."

"Aye, and you'll be the manner of man that understands a woman's needs." She looked down at her clasped hands, which were remarkably still.

"Well enough, Miss Josie. I've land of my own now, and animals, and the laird's favor to further my expectations." He stopped fidgeting and drew his shoulders back.

"It's a comfort to know that, Willie Rood." She looked up and stared right at him. "And all I ask is this one small thing so that I may hold my head high in genteel company."

"Ye can hold yer head high in any company, Miss Josie. But I'll press yer case with the laird. I promise ye that."

"Good. I'll attend him at seven o'clock, then."

"I'll look forward to that, Miss Josie."

He was about to say more, but Josie waved him away. "I need to grieve for my mother alone now."

Nodding, he moved out of my sight, but I waited till I heard the front door close after him before I came out of hiding.

"Oh, Josie!" I gasped.

She put a finger to her mouth and locked the door.

I whispered, "Ye played him like a fiddle!"

She clapped a hand on my shoulder and smiled. "If fortune favors the brave, Roddy, we'll flush out your Blessing and have the best of both Willie Rood and Daniel McRoy this very night."

All of a sudden there came four sharp raps at the window. I started in surprise and dove for cover behind a chair. I was afraid Rood had doubled back and caught a glimpse of me.

However, Josie, wasn't at all concerned and threw the window wide open.

A weathered, unshaven face appeared, one that was all too familiar.

"Alan Dunbar!" I whispered. At the sight of him I jumped out of hiding, amazed that Josie should be so careless of her own safety.

Without so much as asking leave, the Rogue stretched a lanky leg over the windowsill and climbed inside. Immediately, I placed myself between him and Josie, clenching my fists and ready to fight.

"Have ye come to commit more thievery?" I demanded. "If so, ye'll need to fight me first." I couldn't help wishing my voice were deeper and more menacing.

Dunbar's musket was slung over his shoulder, but I was tensed and ready to leap on him should he make a move to use it.

"Ye mind yer tongue!" warned the Rogue, threatening me with an upraised hand. "I've good cause already to give ye a sound cuffing!"

"Hush, Alan, we'll have no talk of fighting here," Josie chided him, then turned to me, a finger against her lips. "And both of you

must be quiet. There are ears outside of every door in this house."
Then she smiled at me. "Roddy, that knock was Alan's signal so I'd
know it was him."

"Don't let the Rogue fool ye," I warned her in a harsh whisper. "He's got a flock of tricks up his sleeves. They'll fly out without warning."

"Tricks is it?" Dunbar exclaimed before Josie shushed him. He
whispered, "Ye're a fine one to talk about tricks, ye treacherous
pup! What's afoot here anyway? I saw Rood running like he'd just
pocketed all the eggs in the henhouse."

"I've sent him to do a favor for me," Josie answered. She crossed
her arms and smirked at him. "Much as I did with you."

With a grunt the Rogue slid the musket off his shoulder and
flung himself, sprawling, into an armchair. He plucked off his bonnet and used it to wipe some sweat from his brow.

"A gentleman wouldn't sit down before a lady invited him to,"
Josie told him. She walked over to the window and eased it closed,
tugging a lace curtain to cover it.

"It's a gentleman that's taking this bonnie house off ye,"
Dunbar retorted. "It's me that's helping ye. Calculate that sum
for yerself."

"It's a queer kind of help to make off with a lady's goods,"
I said.

"Shhhhh!" Josie waved him to be quiet and said to me, "You've
seized the matter by the wrong end, Roddy. I *gave* Alan those things
to sell for me."

My jaw gaped. "Sell? For money?"

She nodded, a lock of her hair coming loose and dangling over
one eye. "I need to raise as much as I can before my uncle takes pos-

session of this house and everything in it. I can't leave the estate myself right now without being spied upon, so I needed an agent."

I was flustered to find I'd so badly misunderstood but too stubborn to back down before Dunbar's insolent gaze. "But *him?*" I
asked. "Of all the people to trust!"

"He's been doing me this favor for several weeks now," said
Josie, raising her finger and shaking it at me, like a mother with a
naughty child. "And he's played me fair so far."

Dunbar glowered. "I've had no chance to do yer business this
time," he said, stabbing an accusing finger in my direction, "on account of being *robbed* myself!"

It goaded me to have him make *me* out to be the villain, especially in front of Bonnie Josie. "I saw ye hide the goods sneaky as a
common brigand," I said hotly. "What else was I to think?"

Dunbar surged to his feet, and it took all my nerve not to back
away from him. "My business is my own and none of yer affair, ye
upstart!" he growled. "Has Miss Josie not told ye it was all to be
done in secret?"

Groaning, Josie held the finger up to her lips. "Will the two of
you cease your bickering for a minute? You'll have the whole house
down around us. I am not alone here, you know. Uncle has spies everywhere. And my plan will not work if both of you are taken." She
lit a taper from the fire, then threw open the door, looking around
carefully. There was not a sound anywhere, and she whispered back
over her shoulder, "Come, now. Off to the cellar with both of you!
I'll not risk somebody coming upon a pair of fugitives squatting in
my parlor."

"I'm not biding here," Dunbar protested.

"You'll stay until I bid you go," Josie told him firmly, as if she were a general and he a soldier. "It's dark and cold enough down there to cool even *your* blood." She smiled at him in a way that was much too fond for my liking. "And afterward I will tell you my plan."

She brought us quickly into the kitchen, which was strangely deserted. "They must all be over at the big house helping get ready for the party this evening," she explained. Opening a door at the back, she pointed down the short flight of dark stairs. Then she lit an oil lamp and showed us the way with her hand.

Dunbar went first and had to duck under the lintel as we entered the windowless, low-raftered cellar. I came second and Josie last. The place was gloomy and seemed to swallow up the yellow light like a hungry beast. The only difference between it and a dungeon were the few dusty wine bottles sideways on a shelf and a pair of empty kegs squatting on the floor, their bungs wide open.

"You keep hidden here," she said, "while I fetch some food. Then you'll not have hunger as an excuse for your rough tempers."

The Rogue and I picked a keg each to sit on and stared at the floor in sullen silence, with only hooded, sideways looks passing between us. I could feel the heat of his anger even in the cool of the cellar, anger that I had accused him of a shameful deed in his own refuge. But I'd no intention of apologizing for that. He could have told me, after all.

The truth was, it galled me that Josie seemed to prefer Dunbar to me. Wasn't it I who'd fought Rood on her behalf? Wasn't I her little terrier?

After a few minutes Josie returned with some bread and cold meat, plus two cups of water to wash it all down.

"There's only one maid about, and I've sent her upstairs to sort through my clothes for tonight's party. But I cannot stay down here long lest someone find me with you," she told us.

"Ye shouldn't be in this place at all," I said. "It's no right."

She laughed. "I used to hide here as a child, Roddy, and tell ghost tales to my dolls. You have such a strange opinion of me."

I was glad it was too dark for her to see how red my face had turned.

Without waiting for any invitation, Dunbar helped himself to a slab of the meat. A shadow chewing a shadow.

"I'm glad you've left off being contentious for a while," Josie said to him as he chewed in silence. "Eating is better than scolding."

If she liked watching a man eat, I could do that. I tore off a chunk of the bread and nibbled at it. Then, emboldened, I made a small dig at Dunbar. "He's used to covering his secrets with silence."

Dunbar rounded on me, his mouth still full of meat. "Ye're the one hiding secrets. Why not tell us why ye came sneaking back to Dunraw, abandoning yer own family to their fate? What were ye up to, laddie, getting the laird so riled up he wanted you dead? Ye've never answered any of *those* questions."

"Leave the boy alone and let him eat, Alan," Josie interceded. "I know he has good reason for all he's done." She held the lantern between us.

Dunbar's lip curled. "I watched over him because ye asked it of me, Josie, but I warn ye now, he'll turn on ye quicker than a mad, slavering fox."

"Mad, slavering fox am I?" I stood, dropped the bread, raised a fist and might have swung at the Rogue, but Josie grabbed me by the shoulder and held me firmly in place.

"No, Roddy, when he came to see me the other day and told me how he'd found you, I made him promise to care for you and keep you safe from my uncle. He's done that much, even if he is being ungracious about it now."

"The lad's healthy enough now to need nobody's care," said Dunbar. "Best send him on his way, but search his pockets before he leaves." He took the lantern from her and started to guide her to the stairs.

"*Enough*, Alan!" Josie said sharply, laying a hand on his wrist. "There's been only one robbery here, and it's Roddy who's the victim."

Dunbar turned and shoved the lantern in my face till I had to move back or be burned. "What have you been telling her?" he demanded.

Josie pushed the hand with the lantern away from me. "Nothing about you," she said. "You're not the sole cause and center of everything, Alan Dunbar, though too often you act like it." She looked at me as if asking permission to tell the tale.

I wasn't happy to be sharing my secret with him, but there seemed no way around it now. Reluctantly I nodded.

"It was my uncle took his prize off him," said Josie.

The Rogue cocked an eyebrow. "Prize? Aye, that'll be what brought ye back to a burned-out ruin, then." He paused, then continued to think aloud. "A secret store of money? But then why would yer father, canny soul that he is, ever leave without it? No, it must be something else, something worth tossing ye over a cliff for."

"It was a keepsake left by his mother," said Josie. "Does that explain it to you?"

Alan held the lamp over me again, though not so close as before. He leaned toward me and said quietly, "A right dear knickknack it must be to risk fire, rain and death for it."

"And no one ye'll be getting *yer* hands on," I told him.

"Oho!" Dunbar exclaimed. "Ye'd sooner Daniel McRoy sold it off to buy himself a new set of hounds and a fine suit of clothes."

"A choice of robbers is no choice at all." I stood up and put my hands on my hips, trying to look bigger and older. He hadn't expected that, pulled back, and the lantern sent shadows dancing around the cellar.

"And what if I took it, lad? Wouldna it be a fit reward for saving yer worthless life?"

"Och," said Josie, "you're like a couple of cats squabbling over a fish in the water. You'll drown each other before you ever catch it."

"We'll go to the magistrate," I said, guessing that any mention of the law would scare Dunbar off. "I'll tell him my story and see Rood and the laird in gaol."

"What dream are ye sleeping through?" Dunbar mocked me. "The magistrate would never arrest the laird. That would be taking gold out of his own pockets."

Josie turned to me. "Alas, Roddy, Alan's right. The magistrate's one of the guests at my uncle's house tonight. He'd never believe a poor crofter could own something that a laird would stoop to steal."

"So all that's left is to break in and steal the bauble back, then," said Dunbar.

"That's what *I'd* thought of. At first," I told him. "But Miss Josie has a better plan."

Dunbar turned toward her and held the lantern high. I could see that he'd raised one eyebrow, waiting for her to speak.

Josie smiled slowly, the yellow lamplight sparkling mischievously in her eyes. "The house is too well guarded by servants to outright *steal* the bauble," she said. "And I'll not have either of you getting caught or harming innocents to make your escape."

Dunbar looked at her shrewdly, then laughed. "Ye're a bonnie lass after my own heart. Ye've charmed Rood into helping ye get the thing back somehow."

Nodding at him, she clapped delightedly. "I'm to be a guest at the house tonight so my uncle can show me off as his latest piece of property." She drew herself up as if doing the showing herself. In the lantern's light it was a right beautiful show too. "I've agreed to go only if Rood persuades Uncle to let me wear some bit of jewelry worthy of a lady. There's none in that house I can think of except what's been stolen from Roddy. He may have some bits and bobs from his mother, my aunt. But the real jewels were my own—and those I've sold off. He'll be forced to give me Roddy's Blessing."

"So once ye have it, what will ye do?" asked Dunbar with a low chuckle. "Swallow it?"

"I'll throw it out the window for Roddy to catch, and when my uncle notices it's gone, I'll say I misplaced it."

"*Misplaced* it?" Dunbar snorted. "Do ye take the man for a dunce? He'll have ye clapped in chains before ye've time to catch a breath."

I was stunned. It had certainly sounded like a good plan to me. But what if Dunbar was right? He had more experience in roguery than either of us. "I'll not have that on my conscience, Miss Josie," I said. "I'd sooner the laird kept the Blessing."

"No need for such an extremity," said Dunbar. He gave us both a wicked grin. "All ye need is a plan with a bit of craft to it. I'll tell ye what, Mistress Josephine McRoy, get yer wee treasure out of the house and I'll steal it off ye. As a favor."

I jumped to my feet and pointed at him angrily. "I *knew* it! I *knew* that was his aim all along! Don't listen to him, Miss Josie."

"Wheesht, Roddy," Josie answered me softly. "It might be the only way."

25 ❧ THE GARDEN

Rood himself came to collect Josie that night, and the maid was sent off to her bed. By then our plans were well laid, and, little as I liked them, I could see no other way forward. While it had been Josie and me plotting, there was something special between us, almost as precious as the Blessing itself. But now Dunbar had taken charge, and I felt reduced to the role of a minor helper.

He and I crouched by the window in the darkened parlor where I had told Bonnie Josie of my plan. We were careful to keep out of sight as we watched Rood escort Josie to the carriage. She nodded at him with mannered politeness as he opened the door for her.

"It's a wonder she can stand to be cooped up with yon lizard," I muttered, twisting the lace curtain between my fingers.

Dunbar growled. "It's a short way, 'tis all." But his body was so tense, he could have been mistaken for stone.

"Long enough," I said.

As he watched the carriage disappear down the drive, Dunbar rubbed his rough chin. "She plays her role as if she's just stepped out onto a stage," he said. "I hope this trinket of yers is worth half the risk we're taking over it. If anything happens to Josie because of it, I'll . . ."

"It's nae ordinary trinket," I said sharply. "It was a gift from Prince Charlie."

Dunbar raised an eyebrow. "The Bonnie Prince, eh?" He gave a short, scornful laugh. "I knew ye were keeping something close to yer chest, lad. Maybe it's worth the taking after all."

Silently I cursed myself for letting that information slip. Even in the dark, there was enough moon out so I could see the faint trace of a smirk on his lips. He'd provoked me deliberately, and I'd fallen for it.

"It wouldna be worth much to a man like ye," I said, "that can make his living on whisky and poaching. But my family needs it to make a new life for ourselves in America."

"A new life?" Dunbar repeated. "Wouldn't we all like a chance at that!" Again there was a brief flash of another man beneath the Rogue's rough exterior. Then his old gruff manner returned as he pulled out his pocket watch and held it up to the fading light. "We've quite some time to pass here. We'd best keep ourselves to ourselves lest we wake that maid."

It had already been agreed that we should wait two hours before leaving so as not to allow any hint of suspicion that Josie might be in league with us. Once the laird and his guests had dulled their wits with too much food, wine and whisky, she would come outside so that we could stage our "robbery."

Dunbar settled himself in a chair, and it was soon too dark for me to see any expression on his face. His breathing was so soft, it was lost in the sound of the breeze whispering down the chimney.

I sat opposite him and wondered if he could see me, his eyes being more used to darkness and danger than my own. Then, weary as I was from the morning's trek, my mind began to drift and I fancied I might transform into a mere shadow, slipping off by myself to retrieve the Blessing without Dunbar's assistance. I saw myself floating down the passages of Kindarry House, sliding under doors and squeezing through keyholes to explore every nook and cranny of the great house. Searching and searching, but not finding until—

Dunbar's hand shook me by the shoulder and startled me out of the dream. I jerked my head up and swallowed a yelp.

He turned away and headed for the door. "No time for sleep now, lad," he said with a hint of mockery. "We need to be about our work."

"I wasna sleeping," I said, then gave up my feeble protest and followed him out into the night, closing the door behind us with deliberate care. By now I was well practiced at keeping up with him and stuck as closely as a shadow.

If I hadn't been so tense with nerves, I would have marveled anew at the expert skill he used in seeking out every scrap of cover, every spot where the faint light of the stars and moon was swallowed in shade. I imitated him as best I could, an apprentice of the night. The moon rode high above us, but slipped in and out of the clouds, and there was little wind. No one saw us leave, and no one watched us on the road.

A mile along, we spotted the lighted windows of Kindarry House.

Moving even more carefully now, we kept our eyes open for anyone wandering the grounds. Some half-dozen carriages were parked outside, their horses asleep standing up within their shafts until their owners were ready to leave. The sound of a fiddle wafted from one of the windows, and voices raised in laughter. Occasionally a horse roused, houghed noisily, then sank back into sleep.

We crept into the cover of the low wall that surrounded the garden on the western side of the house. If all went according to plan, this was where Josie would appear with the Blessing—if the laird

had lent it to her. And this was where she would become an innocent victim of robbery.

"Can ye find the stable?" Dunbar asked.

"Of course," I answered. "I'm nae bairn."

Dunbar merely nodded. "Fine. Pick us out a good horse and
keep it ready."

Frowning, I set off, running in a crouch to keep from sight. Josie
had told us that the stables were on the far eastern side of the house
and that the two lads who usually worked with the horses had been
made into servers for the party, so it would be unguarded. How she
knew this was a puzzle. House gossip, I supposed.

As I ran, I once more considered Dunbar's plan. It seemed
simple enough. Overcome with the heat of dancing, Josie would
come outside in the garden to take some air. And there, in view of
one of the windows, the Rogue would steal the Blessing from her.
Her false screams would attract witnesses to prove that she'd been
waylaid so that no guilt could be attached to her. None here knew
of the connection between her and the Rogue. Meanwhile, I was to
wait behind the stable with a horse saddled and ready to go.

Josie had assured us that all the Kindarry House servants would
be busy dancing attendance on their master and his friends, the
coachmen happily drinking in the great kitchen with the cook and
her scrub maids. But if anyone did come upon me, I was to say I'd
been sent to prepare a mount for one of the guests.

Yes, simple. Yet the scheme worried at me still. There was so
much that could go badly. What if Josie couldn't get away? What
if someone glanced out of the window at the wrong time? Worst of
all, what if the trinket the laird offered Josie was *not* the Blessing?
A dozen different disasters rose up to haunt me, each one worse
than the last. But when I'd raised them with Josie, she'd hushed

me, saying, "I trust Alan is resourceful enough to handle whatever occurs."

Trust him? Yes, everything depended upon our trusting the Rogue. For all that I had learned of him, for all that I owed him, I still couldn't help but fear that the Blessing might prove too great a temptation for him. The idea that I might be robbed a second time was more than I could bear.

I tried to put such thoughts aside as unworthy, but when a seed of doubt is planted, it needs no rain to make it grow.

The stables were unguarded as Josie had said. Any servants who weren't at work about the house were sitting at a long table in the manor kitchen, helping themselves to whatever fine food was left over from the laird's dinner party, or so Josie promised.

I'd never seen such a huge place for animals. Our byre had been small, cozy, crowded, stinking of horse and cow. The laird's stables were fully five times the size of our small holding, a place of shadows, the horses themselves denser shadows, snorting and rustling amongst fresh straw, each in separate stalls. But it still smelled like our byre, that musky combination of dung, feed and leather harness.

There were plenty of horses to choose from. Josie had told us that the laird loved his horses and treated them better than his servants. Every one of them put our poor old Rob Roy to shame. And he was nowhere to be seen. Perhaps he hadn't been good enough for the laird's stable and had been handed over to someone else, a guard or Willie Rood. I pushed that thought away and went slowly down the line of stalls.

The well-groomed, sleek horses all stared at me, snuffling and snorting and stamping their feet. I felt most unwelcome there.

At last, I picked out a shaggy walnut mare, chiefly because she didn't stamp her hooves and snort when I approached her. Fastening on her saddle and bridle, which I found in a small room full of saddles and bridles, I led her out across the grass to a stretch of pine trees. Stroking her muzzle to keep her calm, I tied her up to a sapling, on the windowless side of Kindarry House. Then, with my suspicions of the Rogue like a burr under a saddle, I headed back to the other side to keep an eye on him.

Dunbar was still crouched where I'd left him, so I took up a position among the bushes where I could spy on him without being seen. Once again, I wondered at how easily Bonnie Josie depended on him, as if she had some insight into his heart. It made no sense to me. And how quick he was to do her bidding, which made even less sense.

After a long wait, I saw him check his watch, then stuff it back into his pocket. He slid over the mossy wall and disappeared among the garden greenery, like a blackbird among shadows. I scrambled to the wall and took over his previous hiding place, but when I peered over, I couldn't see any sign of him. It was as if he'd disappeared, a part of the greenery or a part of the wall.

The fiddler took up a fresh tune inside the house, and there was a clatter of some dishes being dropped. The laird's voice rose like the keen of a pipe to berate the luckless servant. I couldn't help but wonder what it must be like in there, to have all the food and drink you could wish for and obedient folk to bring them to you while you sat at your ease.

I was trying again to pick out Dunbar when the terrace door opened and lamplight spilled out, framing a pair of figures, a man

and a woman. They stepped into the garden, closing the door behind them. As soon as I heard their voices, I knew it was Josie and
Willie Rood.

"A spot of fresh air will settle yer dizziness," said Rood in a
voice oily with concern.

"Yes, dear Mr. Rood, I am already feeling better," said Josie,
gathering a linen shawl around her shoulders. With the light framing her, she looked like an angel. Or a queen. "Even a sip of that
French wine has proved too much for my sensitive constitution.
And may I say it was very gallant of you to accompany me. I had
not thought such manners came natural to you."

Rood missed the bite in her remark. "I seek to better myself,"
he said, "not only in my situation, but in yer eyes too, Miss Josie."
I could hear a slurring in his speech and knew he'd taken more than
a few sips of the wine.

"Well, it's too dark out here for my eyes to make much of you,"
she answered as she walked slowly across the garden with Rood
following like a puppy at her side. Her hand drifted to her breast,
where she fingered something.

I peered hard at it, hardly daring to hope. In the dark it was hard
to make out. A brooch for sure. But was it the right one?

My heart skipped a beat as she turned and walked back, closer
to me, Rood trotting at her heels like a lady's dog. The shadows
passed, the clouds uncovered the moon and I saw the brooch clearly.
The shape was the same as mine. I knew it had to be the Blessing!
And she was pointing it out to let Dunbar know she'd achieved
her purpose.

"Bide here a while," said Rood, "by the rose arbor. Ye'll find the
scent very agreeable."

"There's something here that offends my nostrils," said Josie, too sweetly for Rood to take her true meaning. "Besides, I want to walk off that heavy meal."

What Rood did not know was that she was making her way to the far side of the garden, where the Rogue was waiting among the bushes. As she moved off, Rood laid a hand on her arm to detain her.

Bonnie Josie stiffened at once. "I don't believe I gave you permission to make so bold with me, sir," she said.

"Surely ye'll not deny me a wee kiss after all I've done for ye," said Rood, the wine in his belly making him lose what sense he had.

Josie pushed his hand away. "You are too forward too quickly, Mr. Rood. Such presumption ill becomes a gentleman."

"It's money and property as makes a gentleman," Rood countered, "and I'll soon have plenty of both. That should make ye friendly enough, if nothing else will."

He made a clumsy move to block her path, and even from where I crouched, concealed, I could feel the steeliness of the look she gave him. At any other time she would have hurried back into the house, but tonight that would ruin our plan.

"You mistake me," Josie said, every word as cold and pointed as an icicle off the roof of a house. "I'm not one of your tavern wenches who will sell a kiss for a shot of gin. I am a laird's daughter."

Rood moved closer so that his drunken breath must surely have been gusting in her face. "A *dead* laird's daughter, with none but me to protect ye from yer uncle. Do ye no understand how fast he'll rid himself of ye for good as soon as the chance presents itself?"

My muscles tensed. I wanted to rush at Rood and punch his

piggy face. But that would be the end of all our hopes. Besides, if Rood even guessed she was helping me, it would put her in terrible danger.

"I can protect myself," Josie said calmly. "Don't ever think me defenseless."

"I'll test yer defenses right now," said Rood in a joking manner, as if he were a young lover. Then with an impulsive lunge, he grabbed her by the shoulders and tried to press his lips to hers.

Josie twisted free and gave him a slap across the cheek as loud as the crack of a whip.

I gasped but Rood never heard it, for his ears must have been ringing with the sound of the blow. There was no sign of Dunbar, and I wondered if he'd fled, fearing to be exposed. In that case, I was Josie's only protection. I clambered over the wall and scrambled across the garden.

Rood rubbed his cheek ruefully, his voice an angry rumble. "I'll not be led to the trough without taking a drink!" he declared. He stretched out his beefy hands to grab Josie, but before he could seize her, the butt of a musket cracked against his skull.

He dropped like a sack of neeps.

As if from nowhere, Alan Dunbar had risen out of the shadows like an avenging spirit. He stood over the factor, his eyes ablaze with righteous anger. In the moonlight I could see that his knuckles stood out white where he gripped the barrel of his gun.

For a moment Josie stared at Rood, who lay groaning on the ground. Then she gathered her wits and faced Dunbar squarely.

"Who are you to be so bold?" she asked, sounding affronted. "I asked for none of your help!"

Dunbar hesitated before realizing he still had his part to play.

"Ye've had it anyway," he answered harshly. "And since yer so ungracious about it, I'll take some payment for my trouble." He reached toward her. "That wee brooch should cover it nicely."

"This is my uncle's property," Josie said, placing a hand over the Blessing, "and I'll not let some vagabond have it."

"I'm a vagabond with a gun," said Dunbar, brandishing the musket. Brushing Josie's hand aside, he tore the brooch from her dress and cast an appraising eye over it.

Rood started to push himself up, but Dunbar placed his boot on the factor's back and pushed him down again. "I've heard tell of a bauble such as this," he said to Rood. "The tale is that ye and yer master stole it from a sick boy, then tried to murder him to cover yer tracks."

"What do you mean?" cried Bonnie Josie, as if she'd never heard the story from my own lips.

"Nobody will believe yer lies, Dunbar," Rood grunted, making a grab for Dunbar's leg, but he came short by a hand's length and Dunbar kicked him in the rump, driving his face into a prickery rosebush.

"Well, now that this trinket is out of yer hands, Rood," said the Rogue, "I reckon there's means by which its true owners might be identified, should the need ever arise. And if the story came out, it would do little for yer prospects or those of that weasel ye serve."

More playacting, I guessed, since Dunbar had already told me that the magistrate was in the laird's pocket.

From the safety of the ground, Rood cried out, "Fool! It'll take more than stories to keep ye safe, ye worthless lout." Then he moaned. "Did ye no hear the garrison's already on the march from Fort William? The laird's summoned them to round up ye and any others that are living off his land without his leave. Ye're all to be transported to a prison colony."

Dunbar's hand clenched around the brooch.

"Aye, that's given ye pause," said Rood, speaking still into the bush. "By morning the whole country will be crawling with redcoats." Slowly he turned over to glare at Dunbar.

Dunbar slid the Blessing into his pocket and loomed menacingly over Rood, pointing the barrel of the musket straight into his face. "If ye'd like to be alive to hear tidings of my fate, ye'll lie right there and not stir till I'm long gone."

"Oh, please, Mr. Rood," Josie simpered, "do lie still. He has a murderous look about him."

Rood lay still, though his eyes remained fixed on Dunbar's gun.

The Rogue tipped his hat to Josie as if he'd been making a social call, and she gave him a quick nod. With that, he turned and strode off into the darkness.

Suddenly Rood leapt to his feet, knocking Josie rudely aside as he did so. The instant he reached inside his coat, I knew what he had hidden there. I burst out of hiding and ran to stop him, but there was no time.

"Alan!" Josie screamed as Rood drew a pistol and cocked it.

"This time I'm ready for ye, ye brigand!" the factor barked.

At Josie's cry, Dunbar wheeled about on his heel and brought the musket to his shoulder. With only a split second to aim, he pulled the trigger and both shots went off like echoes of each other.

26 ❧ THE FLIGHT

Rood crumpled to the ground and lay on his back unmoving, his eyes staring up vacantly. Blood gushed from a hole in his chest, staining his waistcoat, trailing down his sides. Meanwhile Alan was staggering as if he'd been punched.

Pressing her hand hard against her mouth, Josie trembled, looking like someone seized by a sudden chill. "Alan!" she said. "Are you hurt?"

Dunbar touched a finger to his left shoulder and dabbed at the blood trickling there. "He's made a hole in my jerkin and tore some skin from my arm, but nothing worse than that." Narrowing his eyes at me, he asked, "Well, why are ye standing about? Ye're meant to have got us a horse."

"There's a horse waiting," I told him. "Dinna ye doubt it."

We both bent over Rood. There was no question but that he was dead. I'd thought I'd be glad of such a sight, but instead it made me feel sick, like we'd done a shameful thing. My stomach turned over, and I feared I might throw up.

"I never looked for this," said Dunbar grimly. "The devil take him for drawing on my back!"

"It's my fault," said Josie. "It was me dragged you into this."

"What's done is done," Dunbar told her, "and there's none to be blamed but the fool himself. He'd have killed me over a bauble."

Over more than a bauble, I wanted to say. But whether I meant the Blessing or Bonnie Josie, I didn't really know.

As Dunbar spoke, his eyes flicked nervously about, but so far there was no sign that an alarm had been raised. That the two shots had sounded as one bought us a small amount of time. That and the fact that the whole household was more concerned with drinking and dancing than anything happening outside.

Josie gave Dunbar a push. "Run!" she said. "Run quickly and I'll cover for you as best I can."

"But what's to happen to ye?" I asked, shocked at the turn of events. "We never meant to leave ye with a dead body."

"There's nothing can be proved against me," Josie answered calmly. "As soon as I can, I'll go to my mother's kin in Ardmussen. They'll give me shelter till I move on."

"Ardmussen," Dunbar repeated. He leaned close to Josie. "Wait for me there. Promise ye will."

"I'll promise you anything if you'll just go," Josie urged desperately.

Lamplight flared close to one of the upper windows. It had been flung wide open, and I saw the face of a maid gaping down at us. Josie saw her too and whispered, "Annie Dayton! Always where she shouldn't be." She gave Dunbar another push, this one rough and almost angry.

The window flew open and Annie Dayton screamed loud enough to stir the graveyard.

"Hit me!" Josie said to Dunbar. "Go on! You're meant to be robbing me!"

He hesitated only a second, then gave her a shove back that knocked her into a black currant bush.

"Come on!" he ordered me, setting off at a lanky run.

Mounting the wall in one bound, he leapt off the other side. I scrambled after him and we raced for the stables. A figure appeared by the stable door and wandered into our way.

"That's Old Dougal," Dunbar said to me, his voice low. "One of the laird's servants and a good customer of mine. He's harmless."

Dunbar ran straight to him, and I saw him pull something out of his coat. For a moment it shone in the moonlight.

"No!" I yelled, thinking he had drawn his dirk. Then I saw it was only a whisky flask.

"Alan Dunbar!" Dougal exclaimed in a drawl. I guessed he'd already helped himself to some of the laird's store. "What's afoot here, man?"

Dunbar pressed the flask into the old man's hands. "Here's a helping of my best liquor," he said, "if ye'll just play dead like I knocked ye out."

Dougal grinned as he stuffed the flask into his jerkin. Then he slid to the ground and curled up with his eyes tight shut and lay still as a dead man.

Dunbar and I ran on, and I was relieved to find the horse still where I'd left her. Dougal might have already come upon her and taken her back to her stall.

Now there were shouts from the direction of the house. The servants, having made free with whatever drink they could lay hands on, were reeling about in all directions, tripping over one another. The guests were just as drunk, some of them even laughing at the uproar. Above them all, I could hear Bonnie Josie, crying out and, I hoped, pointing in the other direction.

Dunbar untethered the horse and swung himself into the saddle. Offering me his hand, he pulled me up behind him.

"They'll chase killers harder than thieves," I said as I wrapped my arms tight about his waist.

"Aye, but Josie will set them on the wrong track if she can," said Dunbar. "So let's make the best of the lead we have."

With that he set his heels to the horse and we shot off into the night. I had never ridden so fast and had to cling around his waist desperately as we galloped for the westbound road.

At first I was reeling from all that had happened and too intent on keeping hold of Dunbar to give any thought to where we might be going. Overhead the clouds flitted across the quarter moon like fluttering curtains, now hiding us, now letting the moon pick us out along the road.

We rode a good ways, both intent on the road and staying on the horse. There was neither time nor energy for talk.

Once we'd put a good distance between us and the house, we slowed so as not to exhaust our mount.

Dunbar threw back his head and let out a peal of relieved laughter. "That's as narrow an escape as ever I made!" he declared.

"I didn't know a horse could run so fast," I gasped, then echoed his laugh. *What a man,* I thought. *What a rogue!* He'd never hesitated, and here we were with the Blessing in hand.

"Ye picked a fine beast, lad," Dunbar said, patting the mare's neck. "She'll last the course, sure enough."

I glowed under his praise. "So are we headed for Glasgow now?" I had no idea which way that was, for the moon was behind the clouds and we were on a road I'd never seen before.

"That's where ye're bound eventually," Dunbar replied, "but first I've a wee stop of my own in mind. After that we'll go our separate ways."

Now I was confused. "What are ye talking about?"

Dunbar gave the horse a prod with his heel to keep her trotting. "I've no time for traipsing about the country seeking yer family. I know where we can turn this brooch into coin. We'll split the money, then ye can go where ye please. That way, the brooch canna be lost again and ye'll be on yer way."

"No!" I said vehemently. "It'll not be sold to swell *yer* purse. I'll take it to my da and let him decide."

Dunbar swiveled around and stared at me. "Think, laddie, think. Yer da could already be on a boat to America or even dead for all ye know." He looked disgusted. "Ye're letting sentiment blind ye, and that's a bad weakness for men on the run."

My anger brought a surge of bile into my throat. I remembered the pocket Dunbar had slipped the Blessing into, and before he could stop me, I plunged my hand in and grabbed it up.

"Let go of that, ye dog!" Dunbar exclaimed. He reached back for my arm and we struggled, still sitting on the horse.

Though he was bigger and stronger than me, he had to twist around in the saddle and could not get a good hold. Instead he just pushed me off balance and I fell to the ground. The wind was knocked out of me as I rolled across the turf, but I jumped up, gasping. As I rose, a startled rabbit bolted away from me.

Gripping the Blessing tightly, I started for the cover of some trees, running as swiftly as the rabbit had. When I looked back over my shoulder, I saw Dunbar had turned the horse around and was bearing down on me like a hawk on a sparrow.

I worked my legs hard, but he caught up and swerved around in front of me so suddenly, I fell backward dodging the animal's hooves. Before I could get up again, Dunbar had jumped from the saddle and pinned me down under his foot. I tried to struggle free, but he drew his dirk and fixed me with a ruthless stare.

"Leave off yer stubbornness now," he warned, "while I've yet a drop of mercy left in me."

With his boot planted firmly on my chest, I could only watch helplessly as he tugged the Blessing from my fingers and returned it to his pocket. Sheathing his dirk, he let me free and watched while I got slowly to my feet. I kept my distance from him, rubbing the spot where his boot had bruised my ribs.

Dunbar climbed back into the saddle and looked down darkly.

"Ye'll be running off now to save yer skin," I said.

"I'd as soon leave ye here, troublesome whelp that ye are," he said, "but I doubt Josie would forgive me that."

"I thought nobody's forgiveness counted with ye."

"Then ye've judged me wrong again. Have we not been partners these past days? Should we not be saving our anger for the laird?"

I didn't want to admit it and just hung my head.

"Here's my offer, then," said Dunbar, stretching his arms down toward me. "Ye can hold to your stiff-necked pride and stay here to be hanged, or ye can promise me no more tricks and I'll do my best to get us both away safe."

I had half a mind to try to drag him down, but I knew it would be foolish. I had to forget our quarrel for the present or I'd be undoing all we'd achieved. The horse stamped the grass impatiently and gave me a warning look. Hesitantly I reached out to take the Rogue's hand.

"Give me yer promise," he said.

"Aye, I promise," I answered, not meeting his gaze.

Dunbar gave a nod and pulled me up behind him. "I hope this faffing about hasn't cost us," he muttered as we rode off.

• • •

We soon hit the main road, one the English had built after Bonnie Prince Charlie's rebellion. They reckoned if their troops had good roads to march on, they could move swiftly to crush any fresh trouble in the Highlands. *If all the Highlands were going the way of Glendoun and Dunraw,* I thought, *there will soon be no one left here to trouble the English at all.*

The horse's hooves made a dull clopping sound as we trotted along the road. It would soon start to grow light, and we needed to get as far away as possible. At daylight people could start tracking us.

Dunbar pointed to the right, to the north of us. A loch flanked the road. "Loch Dearg," he said.

It went on for miles, a long stretch of dark, silent water. To the south rose a line of bare, rocky hills, steep as a rampart. If they had a name, he didn't tell me, and I didn't ask.

Neither of us spoke more, but I held on tight to the Rogue's waist. I guessed if I fell off again, he wouldn't stop for me but thank his good fortune and ride on.

Our mutual silence was broken only when Dunbar let out a sudden stream of foul oaths under his breath. I leaned to one side to see what had irked him. There were fires burning in the night up ahead and a tang of smoke was on the breeze.

"I havena seen any houses along this road," I said.

"Army campfires," Dunbar grumbled. "I know that smell well enough."

"So Rood was telling the truth about the garrison soldiers." I peered through the gloom, for the clouds were once more obscuring the moon, which had been hanging low before us for some time. I could just make out the shapes of tents and the murmur of distant voices.

"We must chance it anyhow," said Dunbar. "There's no other road, and the countryside will be slow going, and we dinna know it."

He urged the horse on with a kick of his heel, but already a voice up ahead was shouting out orders. They must have heard our hoofbeats. Sure enough, as we closed on the camp, a line of redcoats spread out across the road, loading their muskets as they took up position.

"Hold up there!" called an officer's voice. "Halt and be recognized!"

"Ye're taking us straight onto their guns," I said anxiously.

"Och, I never thought they'd be so quick!" snarled the Rogue. He reined in the horse so sharply, she bucked and kicked and I almost fell off.

"Stop, I say!" barked the officer.

"Should we stop?" I asked. "Do ye have whisky for them? They canna know who we are."

Dunbar paid him no mind but wheeled the horse about.

Then came the command I'd been dreading.

"Take aim! Fire!"

The line of muskets all went off in a single volley, like the cracking of giant branches. A bullet whistled past my ear and another struck our horse in the flank. The animal reared up, whinnying in shock.

"Steady, girl!" said Dunbar. "Ye're only nicked. On now!" And we headed back at a gallop down the road the way we'd just come— east toward Kildarry House.

V. ROGUE'S BLESSING

Breathes there the man, with soul so dead,
Who never to himself hath said,
This is my own, my native land!
Whose heart hath ne'er within him burn'd,
As home his footsteps he hath turn'd,
From wandering on a foreign strand!
If such there breathe, go, mark him well;
For him no Minstrel raptures swell;
High though his titles, proud his name,
Boundless his wealth as wish can claim;
Despite those titles, power, and pelf,
The wretch, concentred all in self,
Living, shall forfeit fair renown,
And, doubly dying, shall go down
To the vile dust, from whence he sprung,
Unwept, unhonour'd, and unsung.

—Sir Walter Scott, "The Lay of the Last Minstrel"

27 HIGHLAND CHASE

Glancing back through the gloom, I saw soldiers leading horses out of the trees and throwing on their saddles.

"Could we not have passed ourselves off as innocent men?" I shouted into his ear over the beating of the hooves. "They might have let us go."

"They've come to clear the country of the likes of us," said Dunbar, turning his head to shout at me. "And that brooch would mark us as thieves for sure." He threw the horse into a mad gallop down the road toward Kindarry.

"The laird's men will be after us as well," I cried. "What will we do? We're caught between the hammer and the anvil."

"We do what hunted men have always done," Dunbar shouted back. "We take to the hills." He yanked on the reins and the horse swerved to the right, hard away from Loch Dearg and up the rising ground to the south. Before us a rampart of mountains rose up against the night sky, and we began climbing toward them. "We can lose ourselves in the dark if the moon stays clouded."

Of course the moment he said that, the clouds passed and the crescent moon and thousands of stars lit the hillside. Dunbar looked up and cursed again.

"It'll take more than cursing the moon and stars to get us clear of the redcoats," I told him.

He said over his shoulder, "We'd not outrun them for long on the open road." Then he took a deep breath before continuing. "Our horse has been ridden too hard already, and she's been carrying two."

I nodded.

"So, lad, we're heading into the hills, where it's a soldier's instinct to go slow, watching for an ambush behind every turn. That's our chance to steal a march on them." His voice was as raw as the breeze that beat on our faces. "If only the moon hides itself."

This time I was the one who cursed the moon and stars and let Dunbar get on with the business of urging the horse forward across the broken ground, the few hundred feet till the start of the hills.

Soon we were weaving our uphill way through a maze of rocks and hillocks, twisting through the flowering gorse, all in search of a route. Walls of rock reared up, steeper and steeper on both sides, funneling us into a V-shaped defile. Steep slopes loomed on all sides, strewn with loose stone and pebbles, a dangerous scree.

"We've got to go on foot from here," said Dunbar.

Once we'd dismounted, Dunbar led our horse by the reins, but the poor mare plowed through the shale like a boat struggling against a mounting tide. Her chest heaved, and her legs were trembling.

"Och, she's finished for now," said Dunbar. "Even if she could go on, she'd only slow us down and make us easier to spot."

"She's done us good service," I said, giving the mare a grateful pat on the neck. But even then I craned my neck to see where we were going: up and up and up a seemingly impassable slope.

Dunbar turned the mare around and started her back down the slope. "Aye, that she has." He let the reins slip from his hand. "Awa' home with ye, lass," he said. "I hope there's a trough of water and a bag full of feed for ye below."

As the mare made her tentative way down the hillside, she glanced back at us and shook her shaggy head, as if to say we were mad to go on. And maybe we were. The footing was treacherous, the loose stones on the mountainside sliding away at each step, a wind came down the tunnel of stone, while the moonlight made us easy targets for any with eyes to see.

After an agony of clawing and sliding, the ground finally became solid beneath us again as we rounded the shoulder of the hill. We heard no soldiers behind us, and no shots had been fired.

I whispered, "Yer a lucky rogue, Alan Dunbar."

He turned back and smiled at me, a thin smile with not a bit of mirth in it. "We've only just begun, lad. Save yer praise for later and use yer prayers now."

"Then I'll pray for clouds to darken the sky."

"That's a good one," he said, and kept climbing.

More hills and mountains rose beyond the hills where we stood, rearing up ahead of us, a great mass of blackness. Dunbar was careful to keep us below the hilltop so we could not be seen against the moonlit sky. "An old poacher's trick," he called it.

Forsaking talk, we saved our breath for the climb until at last Dunbar called a halt. He'd found a hollow in the hillside and immediately made himself comfortable among the sparse patches of heather. Unslinging his musket, he began charging it with powder and shot.

"We canna go on without rest," he said. "We'll have some food and water, then catch what sleep we can."

"What about the soldiers?" I asked.

"The going's as hard for them as us," Dunbar replied, "and they dinna want to be stumbling about in the dark. We're a small priority for them and no danger. They know nothing about us yet. They have no reason to push too hard. When they find the mare, they'll know we're on foot and relax, thinking that we're easy prey. So they'll find a spot to settle down and try to pick up our trail at sunrise."

"How do ye know . . ."

This time he grinned. "A soldier knows a soldier's tricks."

We took our supper in silence from the supplies in Dunbar's pack, snugged in under a rock in the hollow and out of the wind. However, something besides food and wind was on my mind. We were in a dangerous spot, and I worried what was to become of the Blessing.

"I think it best if I carry the brooch from now on," I said.

"Oh, ye do, do ye?" said Dunbar, barely glancing up from his cheese and bread. "Now, if I was going to run off with it, wouldna I have done that long ago and left ye to the redcoats?"

I chewed on that as I chewed on the cheese, gone a bit moldy from its time in his pack. "Aye, I suppose. But now that we're companions again, why shouldna I carry it for a while?"

Dunbar took a swallow of water before answering. "Are ye better fitted to guard it than I? No, ye're not. And of the two of us, who is more likely to take a fall and wind up dead at the foot of a cliff, lad? And the brooch with him?" He tipped the mouth of his water flask in my direction. "And where would that leave me? All this work, all this danger, a price on my head, and not a penny of profit to show for any of it."

"So if I don't make it through the mountains, what then?" I asked. "What of my family? That treasure is theirs by right. It was given to my great-grandfather by the Bonnie Prince himself, for services in the war and . . ." I tried to remember Ma's stories. "My great-grandfather led the prince across the Highlands to the boat that took him back across the water. The prince gave him the Blessing for his help."

Dunbar pondered this for a moment, then faced me squarely. "Ye've my word that I'll do right by them, lad. I'll see they receive their fair share."

He watched me, waiting for my reaction. At last I nodded. "Aye, I believe ye will."

"Then that's all that need be said." With that Dunbar finished his supper and settled himself down for the night, placing his bonnet under his head as a pillow.

"Should we no set a watch?" I asked uneasily.

"Ye can watch all ye like if ye're afraid of bogles coming in the night," Dunbar said, still settling. "I'll not be fashed. Remember, I've been a soldier. I know a soldier's ways. There'll be nae creeping about in the night. Especially one as dark as this."

The sky was black with clouds now, the moon and stars completely hidden, and from the east came a rumble of thunder. It would most likely rain before the night was through. The very weather I'd prayed for. Good news and bad.

"But what if ye're wrong about the soldiers . . . ," I began, but he didn't answer. His back was to me, and within a few seconds, though he was lying on rock, he was fast asleep.

How could he take his rest so easily after all that had happened and with a troop of the king's men at our heels? But as he said, he'd been a soldier, and a soldier couldn't afford to let fear rob him of his sleep. However, I was not like him. I wriggled about, trying to get comfortable, thinking that I could never sleep in the face of such danger. Every stone seemed to find a tender spot—in my back, on my arms, in my bum. But in the end sheer weariness overtook me, and I slept without dreams.

When I woke, a shaft of sunlight was flickering through a cleft in the mountains like a stick poking through a keyhole. Morning, and a bright one too. That hadn't been part of my prayers.

Rubbing my eyes and yawning, I looked around and saw to my shock that Dunbar was gone.

I jumped up, my heart racing, and cursed his name under my breath. "Dunbar!" I cried. "Dunbar, where are ye?"

I heard a noise from behind me and turned in time to see the Rogue diving down at me from the upper slopes like an eagle swooping on a sparrow. He landed hard on top of me, slamming me backward to the ground. Before I could catch my breath, he clamped a hand over my mouth. I tried to break free, but he pressed me down all the harder.

"Wheesht! Have ye lost yer mind?" he snapped. "There's red-coats all over the hills, lad. Keep yer silly mouth shut. Now blink if you understand me."

I blinked twice up into his grim face and he removed his hand, rolling off me and getting to his feet with his musket at the ready.

"If we're no to die up here, ye must trust me," he said angrily. "If that's beyond yer power, say so now."

I was too embarrassed to look him in the face. "Where were ye?" I asked sheepishly.

"Surveying the land," Dunbar answered. "And a good thing too. Now that ye've given us away, we need to move quickly. Come on, lad, make brisk!"

I bit off the apology that was trembling on my lips and scrambled after him, my heart pounding in my chest. I doubt I'd been so frightened since Willie Rood had tried to drop me over the cliff, and then I'd been too exhausted and sick to care.

As we made the rough ascent, I heard voices echoing not far away.

"Have you sighted them yet?" called one.

"Not yet! They must be over that way!" came the answer.

I cursed myself for a daftie. Maybe the Rogue *should* have left me behind.

Dunbar was a few yards ahead of me, hauling himself up a sheer wall of rock onto a broad shelf. I tried to climb after him, but my feet could gain no purchase on the stone. Reaching down, he seized me by the arm and dragged me up after him.

"Word may have reached their officer by now of the happenings at Kindarry," he said. "Else I doubt they'd still be so keen on our trail."

"Maybe there's a reward out on us."

Dunbar nodded. "Aye, that would put a burr in their breeks right enough."

"Shouldn't we find a better place to hide?" I asked. The shelf was barely disguised with shrubs and vines.

"Speed will serve us better than stealth now," Dunbar answered. "We have to keep on the move going up and over."

This was a countryside even harsher than the place where the Rogue had made his lair. Patches of thorn jabbed into my bare hands and face, and rocks cut and chafed us at every step. "Is there no track through here?" I whispered.

"This is nature's own backyard," Dunbar answered. "A perfect place for a Rogue to disappear."

I was beginning to understand. From here we could swerve off in any direction, and it would take a long time searching for the soldiers to pick up our trail on rock.

Again and again we heard the redcoats calling out to each other.

"Fools," I heard Dunbar whisper once under his breath. "If I were your captain . . ." For each time the soldiers cried out, the Rogue could adjust our route. And I, of course, followed silently.

We mounted higher and higher until the drop below was so sheer it made me giddy to look at it.

"Keep yer eyes straight ahead, lad," warned Dunbar quietly. "And yer head way down. Give them yer back, with no skin showing. Think of yerself as mere heather or gorse."

I thought of our scrawny sheep and cows grazing on the hillside. The whiter their coats, the easier they were to find. Dunbar and I had to blend in with the land. Our dark clothing would do it; our pale skin would give us away. I looked straight ahead and bent over. If the soldiers were going to find me, they would not have an easy time of it.

Now I heard a new sound, a great roaring. When we rounded a section of the mountain, I saw a glittering waterfall leaping off the heights above our heads.

I started up in awe, but Dunbar caught my sleeve and pulled me down low. So I lay on my stomach and craned up at the waterfall. It plunged a hundred feet down past us to rage and froth in a whirling pool. Turning my head slightly, I could see that from there it launched itself down a steep-sided ravine in a series of racing, foam-topped rapids. A shimmering spray kicked up by the waters hung in the air about us.

We began to move downward now, but the edge of the ravine and the rushing current below blocked us off.

"The redcoats have been circling around to get to the top," said Dunbar. "I could hear it in their voices. They do that so we will make easy pickings even for a poor marksman."

"Then what are we to do?" I wondered. "The path is getting too narrow."

"We have to cross to the other side," said Dunbar. For the first time he seemed distracted.

"The other side of what?" I asked, though of course I knew. No need to keep my voice down now. The water's raw shout drowned out everything.

He didn't answer but started toward the edge of the ravine, his boot heels skidding on the loose stones. I wriggled down after him on my belly, clutching the ground with my fingers to slow my descent. We reached a lip of rock that jutted out over the spuming river. When I gazed down, I saw the water raging like a beast over jagged rocks. It looked as if it wanted to snatch the legs out from under us and drag us off to our doom.

Dunbar laid down his musket and unslung his pack. "It's a fair jump," he said, "but there's no help for it."

On the other side, the slope was gentler, with scrub and pines to give cover, but the size of the gap—it looked as wide as a river—made me tremble. I hoped the dampness in my eyes came from the spray and not from tears.

"It's too far," I said. "We'll never make it."

Dunbar narrowed his gaze at me, then suddenly adopted a casual, nearly jaunty air. "Of course we can," he said, as if the feat were as simple as stepping over a rabbit hole. Holding his pack by its strap, he whirled it once, twice, then hurled it across the gap to thump down on the far side, where it rolled over three times before stopping.

He turned to me with a grin. "We're next, then."

"Nae, man, ye're mad," I said, backing away from the edge. The crash of the waterfall was dinning in my ears.

Dunbar took stock of me and cast a wary eye at the slopes above. Any sound of the redcoats approaching would surely be drowned out by the water's thunder.

"I'll go first, then, to show ye the way," he said.

He picked up his musket, took a backward step, then dashed forward, launching himself into the air. His coat flapped about him, and he landed in a crouch on the far side. Drawing himself up, he turned and stretched an encouraging hand toward me.

"Come on, lad! Any more dawdling will kill us!"

I shook my head. My face was beaded with spray, but my mouth was as dry as tanned leather. I couldn't do it. I couldn't jump.

"Ye can do it!" Dunbar said sharply. "Do it for love of yer kin or to spite the thieving laird, but—God's mercy, Roddy!—make the bloody jump!"

The Rogue's words stung me like a lash, and it was more shame than courage that drove me on. In two strides I reached the edge, then jumped. Beneath my feet I could feel the huge empty depth of the ravine. It felt like there was a giant serpent below, its mouth wide open, waiting to swallow me.

For an instant my heart surged with hope, then just as quickly I knew I was falling short. Desperately I stretched out for the other side. As my feet dropped beneath me, I dug my fingers into the far ground, clawing frantically, my face pressed against earth and rock. My feet scrabbled on the sheer slope, searching for some purchase, but I was losing hold.

"Oh, God!" I cried. "Oh, God!" Sheer terror turned me cold as ice.

I was slipping, my fingernails breaking on the hard surface, my shoes tearing. I looked up and saw Dunbar's face above me. He was leaning far over the edge, stretching down with both hands. At the last instant he managed to grab my wrists. I dangled for a breathless moment, then he gave a grunt and heaved me up beside him.

I lay there panting until Dunbar hauled me to my feet. I was shaking badly, but the Rogue supported me with one arm and pressed his flask to my lips.

"Drink!" he ordered. "It'll steady ye."

I took a swallow and the fiery whisky burned down my gullet, easing the icy shock.

"Come now, laddie, we've a ways to go yet," said Dunbar, giving me an encouraging clap on the shoulder.

As we scrambled up the barren slope, I thought: *I did it! Alan Dunbar said I could—and I did!* A warm feeling spread through me, warmer than the whisky, and I grinned.

An open deer track led toward a stand of pine. Beside the track grew tiny knots of heather, still brown and barely budded. It would be months before the hillside would glow with purple flowers. It was as if we were the only living beings on earth. But we were alive!

Finally we reached the shelter of the pines, and at the same time a crack of a musket sounded, louder than the now-muffled thunder of the falls. Quickly, Dunbar crouched behind a large rock and pulled me down beside him. He nodded to the far side of the ravine where the redcoats were working their way down the slope, testing their footing on the treacherous ground. "Here they come, lad."

He braced the musket against his shoulder, resting the barrel on the rock as he took aim. I saw a muscle twitch in his jaw as he pulled the trigger. The shot echoed across the ravine, and the bullet kicked up a plume of dirt right at the feet of one of the soldiers.

The redcoat jerked back, and his companions froze in their tracks, looking around to see where the shot had come from. While they hesitated, Dunbar rapidly reloaded and loosed off another round, which whacked off a rock only inches from another man. Our pursuers blazed off a couple of random shots, then scrambled frantically for cover.

Dunbar gave a satisfied grin as he loaded his gun again. "That should hold them a while. They'll be scared to cross in case I pick them off as they jump." He stood slowly, bent over, and I did the same. "Now we have to stay low so they can't see us above the rising fog from the water and the damp grass."

He turned then, heading up the slope, keeping low in the shade of the pines. I scurried along beside him, wondering what was in his mind.

"Did ye mean to miss them?" I asked.

He shrugged. "I've no stomach for shooting soldiers. I wore that same uniform myself for far too long. But I'm a good enough shot to miss them as I will. Still, if I have to kill to dodge the gallows, I do it, but for now I'll just keep running as long as there's a way forward."

His words gave me fresh respect for the man. Determined as he was to be free, he still abided by a code of honor. And then I thought: *What a puzzle he is. One moment a rogue and the next a man worthy of the Highland chiefs of old.*

Overhead a solitary eagle, in ever-widening circles, surveyed the ground below. I shivered, thinking: *Aren't we lucky that redcoats canna fly.*

A hard day's journey we had of it, clambering over more rocks and shale, chancing the narrow tracks, and sometimes clinging by our fingernails to avoid tumbling from the heights. We were always on a slope and often a slippery one at that. I wondered if I'd ever be able to straighten up and walk right again.

Midway through the morning there was a shot in the distance and then another. I looked around to see where they were coming from, but Dunbar wasn't concerned.

"They're too far off to be shooting at us," he said. "They'll be bagging game for their meal."

"I'm glad of anything that slows them up," I said, wondering at the same time what we were going to do for a meal. My own stomach was so empty, it thought my throat had been slit hours ago. All we'd eaten this day had been river water and a handful of dark berries. The moldy cheese and bread in our pack was long gone.

To make things more difficult, dark clouds rolled in and unleashed a heavy, relentless rain. The ground grew soggy beneath us. Walking became nearly impossible, and we slogged along. I encouraged myself with the thought that the soldiers were not as used to trekking through the hills after cattle and sheep as I. But then I remembered how they were used to going after human prey, and any encouragement I'd felt left me.

By afternoon's end, the rain was beating down in a ceaseless torrent. The steep slopes both above and below us were slick and muddy.

"We must press on," Dunbar told me. "We canna be caught out here in the open."

I answered with a nod, hoping I looked braver than I felt. I promised myself not to fall behind. However, as I toiled up the mountainside, the muddy footing slipped away under me and I started to slide uncontrollably.

Dunbar made a grab for me but only set himself slithering downward at my side. Both of us were clawing at the wet ground with hooked fingers already scraped raw by the climb. But neither our hands nor our feet could find any purchase to slow our sickening-quick descent.

"Cursed fates," Dunbar cried as he dug at the slimy earth and kicked at it with the toes of his boots.

"Double curse!" I shouted.

Then suddenly I spotted a rock jutting out of the ground to my left. I managed to catch it with one hand, then swung the other over to secure my grip.

The Rogue was sliding past me, trailing more curses in his wake. I thrust out my right leg and managed to hook my foot through the strap of his musket. The other end of it caught under his shoulder like a sling, pulling him up short. He immediately took the chance to dig his feet into the earth, then gradually worked his way up beside me.

I groaned in pain, for it felt as if my knee would burst apart under the strain of Dunbar's weight.

Blinking at me through the rain, he laughed. "This is no the way I thought this old gun of mine would save me. Good work, lad."

I grinned under his compliment but wouldn't let him see how much it mattered. "Well, we're even now."

Tilting his head to the left, he said, "Aye—we are. Now listen, lad, there's some wee trees clinging on over there. If we slide ourselves over that way careful like, the going will get easier."

He crawled sideways on his hands and knees and I went after, careful to secure a good hold before making any move. Looking up, I could see the grooves we'd left in the mud.

We took shelter from the rain under a moss-covered overhang. As we sat knee to knee, Dunbar brought out a crust of bread and some overripe cheese from his pack.

"I thought it was all gone," I said.

"I always like to surprise my apprentices." He chuckled and handed me half. "Keeps them on their toes."

I was so grateful I began to laugh, and he joined me. We laughed until our stomachs were sore, and then we ate our meager rations slowly, happy for each small bite.

Soaked through and aching with weariness, I was still buoyed by the fact that our long slide down the hill might have gained us time on the redcoats. And they would be hard-pressed to chase us in this downpour. I said as much to Dunbar.

"Whether we've gained or lost," he said, "we canna yet know. But I can tell you this, lad. There's no sense in dwelling on what's lost." He leaned toward me and said with a kind of forced eagerness, like a father to his flagging son, "We're alive and free yet. That's the good side of things."

I sighed and rubbed my eyes with the back of my hand. "I'm starting to think there's nothing left in the world but us and this wet mountain."

Dunbar gazed out at lashing rain and the grey peaks beyond. " 'I looked now upon the world as a thing remote,' " he said in a strange, faraway voice, " 'which I had nothing to do with, no expectation from, and, indeed, no desires about.' " He smiled at the puzzled look on my face. "It's a line from a book," he said.

"That book I saw in yer cave?"

He quirked an eyebrow at me. "Found that, did ye? Aye, *Robinson Crusoe,* by a man named Defoe. I wish I had it with me now. A book like that's a wondrous thing for settling a man's mind."

"I've never read a book," I confessed. "All I know is the bits of the Bible the minister tells us, and Ma and Ishbel have read out to us. That and stories about fairies and giants. Aye—and the Bonnie Prince."

"This book's a bit different from those tales," said Dunbar gently. He closed his eyes, then opened them again. They were as washed out as the grey skies. "Then again, maybe not so much so. It's about a man named Crusoe, shipwrecked on an island where he lives alone for many a long year with only God for company. The

two of them have some rare conversations that set Crusoe to thinking. Then one day he finds a companion, a savage running from his
enemies, and Crusoe's wee world grows bigger."

"An island, eh?" I said. "Is that what ye're looking for?"

Dunbar shook his head. "Nay, lad. No more. Like Crusoe, I've
had enough of tending to my own wants and hurts and nothing
else. If we get clear of all this—of the redcoats who are as mired
down right now as we—I'm minded to make something more of
my life. Something bigger. Something real. And I'll not live it alone
any longer."

29 ☙ AT A RUN

We slept cold and wet and weary, but we slept nonetheless. By early morning the sky had cleared, and the sun set about its work of drying out the rain-soaked ground. There were three light layers of clouds, white streamers across the blue. The streams were swollen from the rain, and we filled our flasks, drinking thirstily, careful not to be seen.

Dunbar smacked his lips and surveyed the wild landscape. "This is how the world must have looked to Noah when he landed his boat on the mountain," he said. "Fresh scrubbed and new."

"I was thinking we might have need of a boat ourselves." It was as if we'd all but forgotten the redcoats, the night terrors, the dead man behind us.

"A pair of stout legs will serve us just fine," said Dunbar. "By day's end we'll have made it to lower ground, where the forests will keep us hid."

"Hiding will be good," I said, suddenly aware of how open the ground was around us.

All at once Dunbar stiffened, his sharp ears picking up some sound too soft for my hearing. I turned as he raised his musket and took aim. On the slope above us a redcoat was descending, carefully picking out his footing on the rocks.

How had he found us? Why had we not noticed him before? My heart leapt in my chest like a frightened hare.

When the redcoat saw that he'd been spotted, he tried to level his gun, but Dunbar fired first. His bullet smacked into the stock of the soldier's musket, knocking it clear out of his hands. The shock of it made the man lose his footing and he fell onto his back, sliding down the wet slope toward us.

"Here!" he yelled to his comrades. "I have them!"

He dug in his heels and struggled to his feet, pulling a bayonet from his belt. Then he lunged at me with the long, sharp blade. Only a desperate instinct made me grab his knife arm, twisting it and using his own momentum to throw him over my shoulder.

"Well done, lad!" Dunbar cried as the redcoat went tumbling head over heels down into the thick undergrowth far below us.

"How did he know where we were?" I asked.

But Dunbar hardly listened to my question. "Damn yon mud slide!" he cursed. "They must have found firmer ground than we to have gained on us so fast."

For a moment I stood there frozen until the Rogue yanked at my sleeve. "Come on!" he said. "The hounds are on our trail for sure now!"

I managed to keep pace with him, even though my feet slithered wildly in the damp earth. We circled away from the place where the redcoat had fallen and crouched low.

"There!" cried a voice from above us. "There's the two of them!"

A musket rang out. I flinched at the noise, but the shot missed us both by nearly twenty yards.

"Dinna mind that," said Dunbar, as if he could read my fears. "They're trained to shoot into enemy ranks, not pick off a running target. Keep moving. Zigzag. Dinna stay in one place." He ran, and I followed.

Another shot came and then another. Each time I tensed for the thump of a bullet into my body but nothing even came close. Dunbar was right. As long as we kept moving, we were safe.

Still, by the time we reached some sparse cover among a scattering of firs, I was soaked in a cold, nervous sweat. A sharp pain stabbed at my side. "Ye'd best go on without me," I gasped. "I'll just slow ye down."

Dunbar grabbed me by the arm. "Ye're doing fine, lad," he said.

"No, really, leave me."

"Hold yer nerve. I dinna desert my comrades." His voice was as hard and sure as the very mountain we were standing on, and I felt my own spirit take strength from him.

Comrade, I thought.

He looked down at me. "I promise I'll get ye out of this, lad."

The answer sprang to my lips by his will rather than mine. "I know ye will."

"Ahead there!" barked a redcoat. "We'll have them this time, my boys!" It was a deep, harsh voice, and suddenly I was once more deathly afraid.

The words spurred us to dash even faster until we came to a hollow in the ground. Dunbar dived in, dragging me down beside him. He reloaded his musket faster than I could tie a knot, and then he set his eye to sight down the barrel. "If we're to get clear, we must give them pause," he said calmly.

A soldier appeared through the trees at a run, looking more intent on clinging to his gun than anything else. "This is going to sting," whispered Dunbar. He squeezed the trigger and shot the redcoat in the shoulder. The man fell with a grunt of pain, clutching at the wound as he rolled over.

"That should fix up easy once the sawbones gets to work on it," Dunbar said under his breath as he reloaded.

We could see more soldiers now, slowing as they came under the shadows of the trees. Dunbar shot off a branch right over one of their heads. At this, they all dropped to the ground, cursing.

"Unlike the king's soldiers," he said, patting his musket, "I've spent these past years learning to shoot rabbits and wild birds. Needs a steadier hand and a surer eye than hitting a man."

We rolled out the far side of the hollow and wriggled off through the undergrowth, keeping low and out of sight. Beneath me the ground smelled musky and damp and full of life. We heard muskets bang behind us as the redcoats fired at random, but the shots were far off, as if the soldiers hadn't yet worked up the nerve to follow. Dunbar's pinpoint shooting had indeed given them pause.

Once we'd put a good distance between us and them, we got to our feet and began running again. For nearly fifteen minutes, we ran without slowing until we reached a tall, grey rock. Sheltering behind it, I watched Dunbar cast an appraising eye over the nearby crags, grey and slatey.

"If I reckon this right," he said, "I've a trick up my sleeve yet."

"Have ye an army lying in wait, then?" I was panting. "If we had even a small one, we could ambush the redcoats."

"Nae army." He laughed. "But I know this spot because I'd reason to hide out here once." He was still looking around. "An old man showed me an escape route. The Devil's Reach, it's called. Up there." He pointed to a horseshoe-shaped peak, its curved side tilted up toward the sky.

I squinted up. "Devil's Reach? Doesna sound all that inviting. And . . ." I paused, gauging the height of the slope. "It's very far away." Not only far away, but bare rock rising out of thickly wooded slopes, with no hiding place for fugitives like us.

Dunbar clapped me on the shoulder and we started climbing again. "Some folks say it's the very rock where Satan took Jesus Christ to offer him all the kingdoms of the world. Others that anyone going up there is snatched away by the devil and never seen again."

"And that's supposed to make me feel better?" I asked, clambering over a fallen tree trunk. "It looks more like a trap than an escape."

"That's the beauty of it." Dunbar chuckled. "After Culloden many a fleeing Jacobite clansman slipped through the fingers of the Duke of Cumberland's men by this very path."

"Maybe they're all just lying dead on the other side."

"Show a little faith, lad," urged the Rogue. "Show a little faith."

I paused to catch a breath and to pull away some gorse that had tangled around my leg. "Faith? You're leading us into the devil's grasp!"

Dunbar gave me a sly wink over his shoulder. "Did ye not learn from the Bible that salvation lies in taking the hard road?" Then he kept going on down the mountainside.

To get to the Devil's Reach, we had to make our way along a sparsely wooded ridge, darting in and out of the trees. It took a full day. Whenever we broke from hiding, the redcoats tried to pick us off. I counted at least a dozen of them.

"Pay them no mind," Dunbar told me. "They're not taking the time to get their range. It makes me think they dinna know who they're chasing. Or care."

I tried to treat our escape as casually as he did, but I still twitched at every shot, as if a swarm of bees were trying to sting the back of my neck. And even though not a single shot came near us, that didn't make me feel any less frightened.

By late afternoon, we'd gained the lower slopes. There we had better cover—larch and fir, mostly—but our pursuers were hurrying over the ridge after us. The Rogue took up a position between two pines and loosed off a pair of well-aimed shots that quickly had the redcoats taking shelter among the trees.

"Have ye the strength left to make that climb without me kicking ye all the way?" he asked, pointing his gun barrel at the horseshoe-shaped mass of the Devil's Reach that loomed above us.

I was puzzled. "Why are ye asking such a thing?"

"That summit is too exposed for us to climb it without taking a bullet in the back. The far side is even worse. They could stand right above us and pick their shots at their leisure."

"Then why did we come here?"

Dunbar reached into his pocket and brought out the Blessing. "So ye can take this to yer family where it belongs," he said.

When I hesitated, he pressed it into my hand. "This is what the whole adventure has been about, lad," he said. "And if ye dinna get it safe away, it's all been for naught. And then Josie will really have my hide."

I realized then that his mind was bent on Bonnie Josie and had been all along. Why I'd not understood before is still unclear to me, except that I was only a boy with little understanding of a man's heart. But suddenly I remembered the looks he'd given her, how quickly he'd listened to her and fallen in with her plans. I remembered how angry he'd been when Rood had accosted her. And I knew that if we managed to escape, he would seek Bonnie Josie out as surely as I would be seeking out my family.

"I'm truly sorry, Alan," I said, slipping the Blessing into my pocket. "If no for me, ye'd no be in this trouble. Ye said as much, and ye were right."

"Dinna heed words that are spoken in anger, lad." He waved my apology away as if it were just some pesky insect. "I'd have fallen foul of the laird in my own good time and most likely gotten in a worse pother than this."

But I couldn't stop apologizing. It was suddenly important that he hear it all. "I've said some harsh words to ye, Alan Dunbar, and about ye too, and they were undeserved." I held out my hand. "I hope ye forgive me." For a moment I stood there, hand outstretched, feeling more than a little foolish and more than a little shamed.

"We've been a pair of stiff-necked gowks, and that's for sure," said Dunbar, reaching over to shake my hand. "But we'll be friends now, as Josie would have us, and that's how we'll part." Then he returned to loading his musket.

I felt cold all over, as if I'd fallen into a bank of new snow. "What do ye mean: *part?*"

"I told ye, there's no way we can both make it up to the peak with those guns at our backs," he answered dourly. "So I'm leaving ye to make that climb alone."

"But what are ye going to do?"

He didn't answer directly. "Keep yerself hid here among the pines."

I saw where this was going. "No, Alan . . ."

"Listen, lad, this will work if ye listen." He hefted the gun, pointing it toward the ridge where the rest of the soldiers seemed to be biding their time. "I'll sneak over that way, making sure the redcoats keep their heads down. Then I'll lead them into the glen below. Ye've to choose yer moment, then race for the summit as fast as yer legs will shift ye."

"But there's nothing up there except bare rock," I objected.

"I already told ye, that's just appearances," said the Rogue, turning suddenly to take aim at three soldiers who were now advancing along the ridge, their captain's voice goading them on. He put a bullet right into the pack of the foremost man and sent him and his comrades cowering behind the nearest rock.

As Dunbar quickly reloaded, he gave me further instruction. "Once ye reach the top, move to yer left, where ye'll find the split stump of a dead pine. Directly below it, under a flinty overhang, there's a fissure in the rock. It's the only way down, and it's as good as invisible to them that don't know it. Follow it down and ye'll come to thick woodland on a gentle lower slope."

He fired another shot, keeping the redcoats hugging cover. But for all their caution, they were still closing in on us.

"But what of yerself, Alan?"

"Och, I'll lead them a merry chase through the glens. With only my own skin to care for I've a better chance of giving them the slip."

"Alan, I think ye want to stay behind to make sure Josie doesna come to any harm," I said.

The Rogue scowled at me. "That sort of talk's going to spoil my reputation as a ruffian."

"Ye're reading me the wrong way," I assured him. "I think the better of ye for it. She's a grand lass."

A brief smile flickered over his dark features, then he was all business again, speaking quickly, all the while keeping an eye out for the redcoats. "Listen carefully, Roddy. Once ye're over the mountain, follow the shore of the loch all the way to Rannoch Moor and the village of Oichan. Got that?"

I nodded. "Rannoch Moor. Oichan."

"Once there, ask for a man named Angus Durie."

"Angus Durie," I repeated.

"He was a comrade of mine in the wars. He'll see ye safe to Glasgow. Ye can count on him not to play ye false." He was done loading the musket and turned to fire off another shot.

"Alan," I said, "if not for the Blessing and my family, I'd stay with ye to the end."

"Nae apologies, lad." He squeezed my arm. "Just do me the one favor. Should things go awry for me, send word to Josie that I turned out to be a better man than she might have thought."

"I will," I said, "but I'm sure she already knows that, just as I'm sure we'll meet again." I thought briefly about Josie and how she'd looked at Dunbar and was glad that the two of them had found each other.

Dunbar swallowed hard and turned away. He said over his shoulder, "Dig yerself in under that gorse and dinna come out till I've pulled the bloody hounds off yer scent." He pointed to the spreading bush of prickly stems and yellow flowers. "I'm awa' now."

I did as I was told, and he slipped off through the trees to a fresh position on top of a mossy boulder. From there he fired off yet another shot, then moved again. Each time he let the redcoats catch a glimpse of him, luring them on.

As I watched, screened by the yellow gorse, Dunbar became smaller and smaller, moving away from me, from my life, leaving me all alone. I kept as still as a stone, too tired now even to be afraid.

I waited till the redcoats were well away, intent on chasing the Rogue, then I crept out from under the gorse.

Overhead a buzzard soared lazily over Devil's Reach as if showing me the way. I set out for the peak at a mad scramble. Not once did I dare look back. Nor did I need to. The crack of muskets was farther and farther behind me now, fading like the last echoes of a bad dream.

It was a long climb, over loose scree and then shaky shale and finally a scramble through a tiny ravine before I gained the heights. There I found the spot exactly as the Rogue had described it—the broken tree and the rock.

I was out of breath but certainly not out of hope. I said a blessing on Dunbar's head. Then, taking one last look back, I realized that all I could see now were distant plumes of musket smoke. Dunbar and the soldiers were not even smudges on the landscape. As they were to me, so I'd be to them.

I sat for a moment on the fallen tree to catch my breath. Taking the Blessing from my pocket, I stared down at it. Such a wee thing to provoke so much trouble. To offer so much hope. Then I made a silent farewell to Dunraw, the old familiar hills of home, the whole of the life I'd known there, and tucked the Blessing back into my pocket.

"Good luck, Alan Dunbar," I whispered into the wind. Then I started down the far side of Devil's Reach. "May the Lord lend ye wings."

I squeezed my way into the fissure and wriggled through. When I stood on the other side, I could see the gentler country that Dunbar had promised me, a green road to a new world.

31 ❧ NEW SCOTLAND

Just as Dunbar had said, the silver finger of the loch led me to Rannoch Moor. I'd never been at such a place before—miles and miles of little grey-colored lochans, dangerous peat bogs and hidden, twisty streams. Tussocks of grass humped up before me, and I lost a boot in one mucky place, where the bog seemed to reach up and strip it from my foot. I was lucky not to have lost more than that. I had to pick my way across with care. But since no one was chasing me now, I had all the time in the world to cross the moor.

Slowly I found my way—one boot on and one boot off—to the village of Oichan, and there was a small tanner's shop belonging to Angus Durie. Angus fed me and gave me a pallet to sleep on, the softest bed I'd had in weeks.

"A comrade of Alan's," he said, "is a comrade of mine." He asked no questions of my age or why the redcoats might be hunting Alan and me. His doughy face had sharp black eyes like dried currants. They just took me in and seemed to approve of what they saw.

Durie gave me a pair of his son's old boots, which were just my size, and a shirt that was miles too big to replace mine, which was worn through. Then we went by wagon to Glasgow. The horse pulling us—a faded roan named Charlie—was old and settled into his bones. He never hurried, but we got there all the same.

No one questioned us along the way and—surprisingly—Angus

himself never asked why I needed his help. I guess folks fleeing the Highlands had become such a commonplace, all our answers would have been the same: we'd been forced out by the lairds and had nowhere else to go.

It would be pleasant to report that I found my father and Lachlan and Ishbel by hanging around the harbor and calling on the port office day after day. However, I did not.

What I did do was to make a nuisance of myself at one of the shipping offices and then offer my help. I ran errands for a clerk who'd taken pity on me. His name was Master Ochen Lewis.

Master Lewis was scrawny and long-legged, more like a heron than a man. His nose was beaklike as well, and when he spoke, his nose moved awkwardly. He perched on his office stool as if in a heronry. His fingers were stained with ink.

At last he was able to find out from some Highland folk who had settled in Glasgow that my family had sailed three weeks earlier, on a ship called *Valiant,* to America's Cape Fear.

"Cape Fear? I dinna like the sound of that," I said.

"Dinna ye worry, lad," he said, "that's the best place for a farmer, though the fisher folk are none too pleased with it."

"Cape Fear?"

"They say seagoing vessels can go up the river at the neck of the cape for over twenty miles." His nose waggled at me. "Twenty miles, lad, and a lot of farmland in between. Why, we Scots have been settling there for a hundred years. It's a lot of land—but few people. Ye'll find yer family soon enough. Ships leave for that every month or so." He sounded remarkably sure as he turned from me and made a series of hen scratchings on the paper before him.

• • •

I had to work for five months for Master Lewis before I had money enough for my passage. I ran errands, carried maps to the ships for him, made his tea the way he liked it best, "as dark as the grave." He was a dour man but a fair one. I think he liked me because I never complained. Why would I? I was buying my ticket to America to find my family. I wouldn't sell the Blessing to do it, for that belonged to all of us, not just me alone.

At last I had enough for a ticket that guaranteed me a hammock deep in the bowels of a filthy, heaving ship and one meal a day. "If," as a sailor remarked to me, "you can keep it down."

I said goodbye to Master Lewis, and he gave me an extra coin. "Buy something in America and think of me," he said. His pale eyes got watery and his beaky nose dripped. He touched a greying handkerchief to them. "Write sometime."

I nodded, though we both knew I couldn't write.

There were nearly fifty of us crammed onto the ship, and half of them were made sick by the choppy seas. Men, women and some children as well. I was the oldest of the lads there.

At first we were all secretive about our stories, and belongings were never shared. But by the second week, we'd begun talking and discovered how similar we were. We'd all been burned out or bought out or thrown out of our homes.

"Damned sheep," said one man bitterly, and by the end of the day, *damnedsheep* was a single word.

After two months on the ship, we came in sight of America, and the ship's hull shook with the cheering. I kissed a pretty girl, the both of us made bold by the air of the New World, and disembarked at Wilmington.

There I got into a canoe with a half dozen of the big ship's folk. We'd begun as strangers from different glens all over the Highlands, but were now like cousins, each story different, each the same.

At our first landing, I asked the men who helped us off if they'd heard news of Bonnie Josie McRoy, the old laird's daughter, or of the Rogue, Alan Dunbar. One man, a sour Angus farmer with a nose like a neep or, as they say in this new country, "a turnip," said he'd heard that the redcoats were hanging rogues wherever they found them, without taking time for trials.

Turning away, I fought back my grief. I was nearly a man now, and I knew men didn't cry. Dunbar might have been a rogue by any man's definition, but he was a good man nonetheless.

We went upriver slowly, and people disembarked if they had kinfolk at the landings. Over and over, I was invited to stay. I was young and strong. Of course they wanted me.

But I was looking for my own people, and so I kept on going.

Ninety miles upriver, I disembarked and started asking around for anyone from the Kindarry lands, especially Macallans. I found many Campbells there, already rich and powerful, who'd been tacksmen back in Scotland and who could hen-scratch as well as Master Lewis. They had come to the Carolinas to earn the right to be American lairds.

But there were plenty more poor folk too, from Argyll as well as the islands of Arran and Jura.

Of the Dunraw folk, I found no trace.

Ninety miles and still no word of them. So I did what I had to in order to stay alive. I got off the boat and worked at odd jobs, enough to keep me in food and a straw bed, sharing a one-room house with other Scots in what one man called "slave quarters," though we were not black slaves. And I asked every new shipload of folk and every old settler I could find about my family. And about Bonnie Josie and the Rogue. But no one knew a thing.

The land itself was strange and forbidding, yet fascinating too and the animals new to me. Dangerous vipers and large cats big enough to harm a man, as well as terrible bears that could crush you in their embrace. I wished with all my heart that Alan Dunbar could see them. But I supposed he was dead, hanged along with all the other rogues. He could have saved himself, but instead he'd saved me.

I do not desert comrades, he said. I wondered if I had deserted him.

Then, one day a year later, on a trip farther upriver than I'd ever been before, we came to a small landing—really just a pier jutting into the water. I was helping a French trader named Lareaux buy skins to sell back in Cape Fear.

"Go over there, Roodee," he told me, pointing at a man bent over a pile of fox skins. "See what he wants for them. Don't offer much." I'd been with Lareaux a month now, and he still couldn't get his French tongue around my name. He was a homely man with a cast in one eye, but he had a gift for haggling, and he knew his way around the backwaters of the land.

I went over to speak with the man. With a start, I recognized him. His black beard was bushier than it had been in Scotland, his face ruddier and his shoulders more stooped, but still I knew him.

"Tam," I cried. "Mister MacBride."

He looked up, didn't recognize me.

"I'm Roddy Macallan," I said. "From Dunraw."

He looked again, cocked his head to one side, ran his fingers through his beard. Then he houghed through his nose like some kind of half-tame farm animal. "Roddy—yes. Yes, now I see. Ye've grown, lad. Put on muscle and sinew. A bit of a beard."

I laughed and ran my hand over the rough scrub that was growing on my cheeks.

"And here we all thought ye dead. We sang psalms for ye last year."

I was silent for a long moment, then whispered, "*We?*"

"Yer da and his wife and yer brother and the rest of the Dunraw folk who've settled here."

Again I was silent. This time I looked around, beyond the pier. Through a stand of trees, I could see a path beside a smaller winding river and wondered where it led.

And then I thought about what Tam had just said: "My father's *wife?*"

He scratched under his beard. "Ishbel of the sharp tongue."

I threw back my head and howled, half sob and half laughter.

MacBride put a meaty hand on my shoulder. "Welcome home, lad."

Lareaux paid me only half of what he'd promised because I refused to finish the trip. And when MacBride took me up the small rilling river in his flat-bottomed canoe to a little wooden homestead, built with interlocking logs, and I saw the careful garden laid out in the rich dark soil, I knew it had been worth the long, empty days to come to this place at last.

"Mistress of the house," boomed MacBride when we'd walked up to the house, and he hammered on the jamb of the open door.

Ishbel walked out, shaking flour from her apron, blinking into the light of the green clearing.

Wordlessly, MacBride shoved me toward her. She looked up and glared. Then her eyes grew wide. Her mouth opened, then closed again. For once she had nothing to say.

I took the Blessing from my pocket, for I never went anywhere without it. The sun flashed off its jeweled surface. "My mother spoke the truth," I said. "It's just taken me longer than I thought to bring it to ye."

Unaccountably, she began screaming, a sound like a dog howling, crying out, "Oh . . . oh . . . oh!"

Two men came running in from the furrowed fields, the younger one with a scythe in his hand.

They stared at me as if seeing a ghost.

I held out the lovely little jeweled brooch with the rampant lion on the top. "Father, Lachlan, I have the Blessing."

Lachlan laughed, dropped the scythe and clapped. "Roddy! Roddy!"

But Father stepped up to me and put his arms around me. I almost wept to see him fit and strong again.

"Roddy, lad," he said, "ye are all the blessing this family needs."

EPILOGUE

We had a clerk write a letter to Bonnie Josie, telling her of Alan's bravery and of the fine home we had made in the backwoods where the soil was rich and the game plentiful. We didn't know where to send it except to her uncle's house, and so we had to be careful what was said.

One can live like a laird here, I had the man write, *or a laird's daughter.*

A half year went by, and then a letter came in return. It was short. *Coming to Cape Fear,* it said. *Sailing in August.* I suppose if she still lived at her uncle's elbow, she had to be as cautious as we.

But it was already October when the letter arrived!

Lachlan and I took our canoe down the river, not knowing what we'd find. We combed through all the boardinghouses asking for her. Finally in one poor place near the port, we found her. To my surprise, she was nursing a three-month-old child. She'd filled out, her skin rosy and burnished by the sun. Before I could wonder at the change or worry who the child's father was, I heard a laugh behind me.

"Where's that Blessing, lad?"

I turned, stared, then laughed. There was the Rogue himself, big as life, hands on his hips, a broad grin on his face. His eyes, so grey the last I saw of him, were once again that cloudless blue. He walked over to Josie and took the baby from her with practiced ease, setting the child against his left shoulder and giving it little taps on the back. So I hadn't been wrong about his feelings for Josie, nor hers for him. We clasped right hands, like old comrades, and my hands were now as large as his.

"Not hanged, then, Alan Dunbar?" I asked.

"They couldna find a rope strong enough nor a gallows pole long enough."

Josie added, "The soldiers were too slow to catch him."

"And yer uncle?"

She shrugged. "Stewing in his own evil juices. He is not my care."

"Nor mine," Alan added, giving the child back to her and putting his arm around her waist.

We brought them safely back up the river to our farm.

With the family's approval, Da sold the Blessing to one of the richest men in Carolina, of a strong Jacobite family. With the money, he bought land, rich farmland, easy to plow. He gave a great share of it to Dunbar and Josie. "Ye saved my lad's life," he said. "The Macallans do not forget."

"Nor do the Dunbars," said Josie, and Alan nodded at her response.

So we became neighbors and lasting friends, and many was the night we'd sit round the fire drinking and telling tales of the old country. We recalled our daring exploits and narrow escapes: how Alan carried me up the crag and how I saved him from the soldiers at the still, how I caught him out burying Josie's statues and he nursed me through the fever, though the exploits grew with each telling. And then we all sang songs that had been passed down since the days of Bonnie Prince Charlie, the prince whose gift had made our life in America possible. We'd found a new world, sure enough, but we still carried the Highlands in our hearts.

We are clansmen still, with only the tales and songs and kilts to show for it. And the memories of the brave times. Ah, yes— the memories.

Nothing is ever forgotten.

WHAT IS TRUE ABOUT THIS STORY

The Kindarry estate is fictional, but the McRoys who rule it are based on a real family. Bonnie Josie was Mary Chisholm, the spirited daughter of the laird of Strathglass, and when her father died, the lands passed to his half brother, William. Mary and her mother retained part of the estate for themselves and were the champions of the poor folk, resisting the new laird's efforts to drive them off the land. The sufferings of people like Roddy and his family during the Highland Clearances were all too real.

The seeds of the Clearances began after the disastrous battle of Culloden, when the English defeated the Scots and took away their tartans, their bagpipes, their powers to raise armies, and their Scottish language. When the lairds lost their powers, it led inexorably to losing any parental interest in their clansmen. No longer allowed to raise individual armies, the lairds no longer needed to let their poor relatives farm their lands in exchange for service in battle.

The lairds became more and more like the English who had conquered them. They bought English estates, sent their sons to English schools and tried to fit into English society.

Then they discovered that they could lease their glens and braes to sheep farmers from the Lowlands and England, which was much more profitable than keeping crofters on subsistence farms. So the lairds began to clear the land of men, women and children, using soldiers and the local constabulary when necessary.

Were the Clearances brutal? In some cases even more so than we have portrayed here. For example, John Prebbles reports in his book *The Highland Clearances,* that five constables from Dingwall and Fort William "broke the skulls and kicked the breasts of the women of Strathcarron."

Were the Clearances thorough? In one season, two thousand people were cleared off the land of the islands of Barra, Benbecula, and Uist. They were cleared by bayonet, truncheon and fire, driven from the only homes they'd ever known and replaced by sheep.

In the earlier Clearances, before the 1720s, many people were simply removed to other parts of Scotland. For example, the Countess of Sutherland and her husband, Lord Stafford, removed six thousand to ten thousand people from their inland homes to settlements on the coast, where they were supposed to find work in kelp farming or fishing. On paper, this seemed a remarkable experiment in social engineering. In practice, it was a brutal and inhuman move. Later, well into the 1780s, the people removed from their homes were put on board ships and sent to Canada, Australia and America—particularly the Carolinas.

As a writer of the time, Donald Ross wrote of the eviction of widower Allan Macdonnell and his four children. It tells brilliantly all one really needs to know about the Clearances. "Allan Macdonnell now has no value at all. Had he been a roe, a deer, a sheep, or a bullock, a Highland laird in speculating could estimate his 'real worth' to within a few shillings, but Allan is only a man. Then his children—they are of no value, nor taken into account in the calculation of the sportsmen. They cannot be shot like hares,

blackcocks, or grouse, nor yet can they be sent to the south as game
to feed the London markets."

   But the Highland poor, cast off the land in one place, became
the backbone of their adopted countries. Frugal, hardworking, in-
ventive, they were stunning additions to the New World. Consider
some of these statistics:

• Thirty-five U.S. Supreme Court justices have been Scots.
• Nearly half of the secretaries of the U.S. Treasury and one-third
of the secretaries of state have been of Scots origin.
• Of the fifty-six signatories of the Declaration of Independence,
nine were directly or indirectly descended from Scots.
• Nine out of thirteen governors of the newly created United
States were Scots or of Scottish descent.

I will make it ANY BETTER!!!!